Fate of a Highlander

Katy Baker

Published by Katy Baker, 2019.

While every precaution has been taken in the preparation of this book, the publisher assumes no responsibility for errors or omissions, or for damages resulting from the use of the information contained herein.

FATE OF A HIGHLANDER

First edition. May 3, 2019.

Copyright © 2019 Katy Baker.

Written by Katy Baker.

Chapter 1

"Honestly, Doc," Mr Roberts said with a wide-eyed look of innocence. "I dunno why it's got worse. I did everything you told me."

Eleanor Stevenson glanced at the red, swollen foot and sighed. Straightening from where she knelt by Mr Roberts, she pulled off her latex gloves and took a seat behind the desk, resting her palms flat on the smooth wooden surface.

"How many drinks have you had today, Mr Roberts?"

"None!" he cried indignantly. "Well, maybe a tiny dram this morning, just to keep out the cold."

He blinked bleary eyes at her and scratched at his scraggly beard. Eleanor could smell the rum from here. A tiny dram? More like a whole bottle!

"And have you been keeping to the diet we talked about? Cutting out fried food?"

Mr Roberts nodded enthusiastically. "Of course! Nothing but greens and roughage for me, Doc."

Mr Roberts was a long-term patient and seemed determined to do all in his power to thwart Eleanor's attempts to help him. What did they say about a horse and water?

"Mr Roberts," she said, keeping her voice neutral. "Your gout won't improve whilst you're still drinking heavily and eating the wrong things. We've talked about this. I'm going to make a referral to the dietician who will talk to you about your alcohol and calorie intake."

Mr Roberts looked horrified. His bushy eyebrows all but disappeared into his hairline. "There's no need for that, Doc! Just give me a couple of pills!"

"I'll prescribe some anti-inflammatories but you'll be receiving a call from the dietician later this week." She fixed him with a determined stare.

Mr Roberts swallowed. "Oh. Okay. Right you are, Doc. Can I go now?" He sounded like a naughty child desperate to escape the headmistress's office.

Eleanor nodded. "Yes, Mr Roberts. That will be all for now."

He scrambled up with a sprightliness that belied his advancing age, put his shoe back on, and hurried out the door before Eleanor could utter another word.

She leaned back in her chair and blew out a breath. The clock on the wall read 5.30. Home time. Her eyes strayed to the window. It was raining again. Through the rivulets running down the panes Eleanor saw the glare of headlights as the traffic outside began to form its usual rush hour traffic jam. Her eyes slid closed and she took the time to enjoy a moment's rest.

"My, ye look like ye need yer bed, my dear," said a voice suddenly.

Eleanor bolted upright with a small cry of surprise. An old woman was sitting in the chair on the other side of the desk, smiling at her brightly. Damn! This must be a last minute appointment the reception staff hadn't had the chance to tell her about.

"Sorry," Eleanor muttered. "I was just...you know...um..."

Oh, hell! Talk about appearing unprofessional!

"I know, dearie," the woman said. "Gets me like that sometimes too."

Eleanor cleared her throat and clasped her hands on the table in front of her. "What can I do for you, Mrs....?"

"MacAskill," the woman supplied. "Irene MacAskill."

She beamed at Eleanor, her cheeks rosy and her eyes sparkling. She reminded Eleanor of an elderly cherub. She was so short her feet dangled from the chair and her iron-gray hair was pulled back into a bun. Black eyes peered out from a nest of wrinkles and she looked like she laughed a lot. Despite her age, she had a sprightly, vigorous air about her.

"Very nice to meet you, Mrs MacAskill—"

"Pah!" the old woman said, waving a hand, "Call me Irene. All my friends do."

"Okay, Irene. What's the problem?"

"With me? Naught at all, dear. I'm fit as a fiddle."

Eleanor frowned. "You're not ill?"

"Ill? Why ever would ye think such a thing? I've never felt better in all my life!" The woman spoke with a thick Scottish accent that Eleanor found difficult to keep up with.

"So what is it you want?" she asked, puzzled. "A certificate?"

"A certywhat?"

Eleanor pressed her lips into a flat line and schooled herself to patience. "Mrs MacAskill, why don't you tell me how I can help you?"

Irene MacAskill leaned forward and tapped her nose conspiratorially. "Ah, now we're getting somewhere, lass. Ye are starting to ask the right questions. What can ye help me with? Naught much, only restoring the balance of the universe, is all."

The woman fixed her with an unblinking gaze and Eleanor was suddenly struck by how dark her eyes were, like chips of obsidian.

"Do ye believe in fate, Doctor Stevenson?"

Thrown off guard by the sudden change in topic, Eleanor blinked. "Fate? You mean the kind of stuff fairground fortune tellers tout? Hardly. If that was real I'd be married to a tall, dark handsome man who'd swept me off my feet. Isn't that the destiny every girl is supposed to dream of?" She laughed, trying to lighten the mood but Irene stared right at her, a serious expression on her face.

"Nay, lass. That isnae destiny at all, that's a cheap trick. True destiny means finding the right path, the one ye were meant to walk and the person who was meant to walk it by yer side. Sometimes we are born many miles and many years away from those souls who are meant to share our path. When that happens the balance is thrown out of kilter. My job is to preserve that balance. So. Will ye help me do that?"

Oh great. As if Mr Roberts hadn't been trying enough, now she had the ramblings of an eccentric old woman to deal with! Eleanor rubbed her temples where a headache was starting to form. Oh, what she wouldn't give for a large glass of wine right now!

"I'm sorry, Mrs MacAskill, but I don't know what you're talking about. Now if you would just—"

"Dinna ye?" Irene interrupted. "Are ye sure about that?" She cocked her head and the gaze she fixed on Eleanor seemed to pin her to the spot.

Jeez, the woman had a stare like Eleanor's old gym instructor! She tried to think of something to say but found that all her words had flown right out of her head. Under that stern, penetrating gaze she suddenly felt uneasy.

"Ye seem tired," Irene said gently, her smile returning.

"Do I?" Eleanor muttered. "I guess I do. Night shifts will do that to you."

Irene nodded. "Aye, they will. But have ye asked yerself why ye push yerself to the limits of yer endurance, always busy, always exhausted?"

Because I'm trying to make amends. The thought flared in Eleanor's head before she could stop it. *I'm trying to make up for my failure.*

She shifted uneasily in her chair. She didn't like the turn this conversation was taking. Why was the old woman asking these questions? "Because I'm needed," she replied, hearing the defensiveness in her tone. "There are always so many patients to see."

"A noble reason," Irene replied, clasping her hands together and leaning on the table. "But only partly true. Ye do it because ye are trying to prove that ye are good enough. To yer colleagues, yer patients. But mostly to yerself. I see the restlessness in yer soul, lass. I see ye striving for something and never finding it." Her gaze softened, full of something Eleanor couldn't quite place. "Ye willnae find what ye are looking for, my dear. Do ye know why?"

Despite herself, Eleanor found herself shrinking back from the old woman's impenetrable gaze. Who was this woman? And why did she stare at Eleanor as though she saw right into her soul?

"Why?" she whispered.

"Because the answers canna be found where ye are searching. Yer true path lies somewhere else entirely. I know ye have been considering leaving medicine, unable to reconcile yer one mistake, nay matter how hard ye work. But that isnae the answer either. Listen to yer heart—and ignore that voice of self-doubt that forever whispers in yer ear. Only by listening to yer heart, and blocking out all else, will ye find yer true path. Can ye do that Doctor Stevenson?"

"I...um...I," Eleanor murmured.

Irene reached across the desk and patted Eleanor's hand fondly. "Think on my words, lass. Yer destiny is calling and ye have a choice. Make that decision ye have been wrestling with. I hope ye make the right one."

With that Irene hopped down from the chair and crossed to the door. She paused as she opened it, looked back at Eleanor, gave her a wink and a grin, then exited the room and pulled the door closed behind her. For a moment Eleanor sat staring at the closed door, too stunned and too unsettled to move.

What the hell had just happened? Who was that woman to come wandering into Eleanor's office talking like she knew her? She'd never met the dratted woman before!

And yet she seemed to know so much about me, Eleanor thought. *How could she have known about the decision I've been trying to make? How could she have known how I feel so torn between duty and what my heart is telling me?*

She leaned forward and pressed the intercom on her desk.

"Hi, Eleanor," came the cheerful voice of Angela on reception. "Everything okay?"

"Who was that patient I've just seen?" Eleanor asked. "And when was the appointment made?"

"You mean Mr Roberts?" Angela said incredulously. "I reckon you know him better than any of us!"

"No, not him. The one after him, an old lady by the name of Irene MacAskill."

"Hmm, don't recognize the name. Hang on, I'll check the records." There was a pause and Eleanor heard the tapping of a keyboard. "No, there's no record of an Irene MacAskill booked in today. In fact, we don't have any records of an Irene MacAskill registered here at all. Are you sure that's the name?"

"Positive," Eleanor murmured. "I don't think I'll ever forget it."

"Are you okay? You sound a little...strange."

"I'm fine. I don't have any more patients today do I?"

"No, you're good," Angela replied. "Listen, I can do some more digging on this Irene if you like, see if we can turn something up. There must be a record of her somewhere."

"No, that's okay," Eleanor said. Without understanding why, she was suddenly sure that no amount of digging would turn up information on Irene MacAskill.

She cut off the intercom and leaned back in her chair. Outside her window it was getting dark and through the rivulets of rain the tail lights of the traffic jam gleamed like coals.

She sighed then opened her laptop, looking at the job application open on the screen. Irene had been right. She *did* have a decision to make, had been wrestling with it for weeks. Did she leave medicine altogether and cease striving to correct a mistake that could never, ever, be corrected? Did she learn to live with what she'd done? Or did she try somewhere else? Find another place where she might make a difference? Another place where she might finally find some peace?

She scanned the application. The post was for a locum doctor in a remote area of the Scottish Highlands, on the far side of the Atlantic and a million miles away from this busy city.

True destiny means finding the right path, the one ye were meant to walk and the person who was meant to walk it by yer side.

Outside, the rain was getting heavier and people were hurrying along the busy street clutching umbrellas, hunched against the harsh weather. The blaring of car horns sounded loud, even inside the room. Eleanor sighed. What was she waiting for? What was she afraid of?

Everything, she answered herself. *Of failing. Of never making things right.*

Irene's words suddenly came back to her. *Listen to yer heart.*

Her eyes slid to the application on the screen. All she had to do was click 'send' and that would be that. *Listen to yer heart.* Almost involuntarily her hand moved to the mouse, the cursor hovering over the 'send' button.

Find the path ye were meant to tread.

With a deep breath, Eleanor pressed the button.

FINLAY MACAULEY COULDN't remember a day as splendid as this one. Spring had finally come to the Highlands of Scotland. The birds were nesting, the insects were waking up, and the leaves were the bright, fresh green of new life. He stopped walking for a moment and paused to take it all in. Around him spread the undulating foothills that bordered the mountains. They were carpeted in lush spring grass with yellow flowers poking through. Aye, it was a grand day. A day of color and light and hope.

It was only a pity his mission was such a dark one.

Shaking himself, he focussed his attention on what he was here to do. Directly ahead of him two roads met. One led east towards the sea, the other north into the mountains. The two roads formed the border of his lord's land and were the cause of much strife. Right now, the area appeared peaceful, with not a soul in sight. There was only Finlay and the glorious Highland morning. For now. But soon there would be chaos, the clash of weapons, the stink of fear, the senseless slaughter of good men.

Dropping to one knee, he scanned the ground and his tracker's eyes soon found what he was looking for. Hoof prints marked the soft grass, two sets of them, spaced far apart which indicated the riders had been galloping in a hurry. He frowned. The tracks came from the north and then veered onto the eastern road, heading into the territory of his lord's enemies.

Finlay straightened, glancing around. The gentle breeze stirred his dark hair. There was no sign of the riders now and from the look of the tracks they'd been made some time yesterday.

Scouts at a guess, sent to spy on his lord's preparations for war and they'd galloped back to their masters with their news. He squinted into the distance but all he saw was the line of the hills. Were enemies gathering in those hills right now? Were they preparing to march? To bring war and destruction?

He hesitated, battling with indecision. His orders were to scout this area and bring news of any tracks he found. He was not ordered to cross the border and scout any further. But he longed to know what his lord's enemies were up to. He longed to know if the rumors were true.

He took a step down the eastern road and then another. It would be so easy to keep walking, to retrace the steps he'd once walked when he'd left his old life for this new one. But he could not. He'd made a bargain and there was no way out of it. He halted.

Slinging his pack over one shoulder, his bow over the other, he turned his back on the eastern road and cut across country. He travelled on foot rather than by horse, the better to slip close to enemy lines, and left the roads altogether, striking out into the wilderness to the northwest.

He soon found himself passing into a wooded valley with a river meandering along its bottom. Kingfishers darted in and out of the stream like brightly colored arrows and a family of otters looked up in alarm as he passed and then went back to their play when they realized he was no threat. Finlay picked his way carefully down to the river's edge and crouched to splash water on his face. He paused as he caught sight of his reflection.

His dark hair, so like that of his father and eldest brother, framed a face he barely recognized. Finlay had been little more than a boy when he and his two brothers had made their fateful bargain but the face staring back at him was that of a man, a careworn man whose eyes had seen too much.

What have I become? he thought suddenly. *Why am I doing this?*

In a flash of annoyance he slapped the water, shattering his reflection. He was about to continue his journey when he noticed a set of footprints in the soft ground at the water's edge. The footprints were small, either those of a child or a woman. There was only one set and they led along the river bank towards a stand of willows.

Finlay's frown deepened. What would a woman or a child be doing out here alone? It was many miles to the nearest road or settlement and Finlay had believed he was the only one who knew of this valley. He usually came out here to be alone. Now, it seemed, he wasn't.

He began edging along the river bank, following the tracks. They led unerringly towards where the branches of two huge weeping willows hung down over the river, creating a curtain through which he couldn't see. He paused, going still, and listened, all his senses straining for any clue as to who might be about.

He heard nothing but the gurgle of the river and the calls of birds. Even so, the back of his neck prickled and he felt sure he was being watched. It wasn't a feeling he liked. As an expert tracker, Finlay was usually the one doing the watching.

Ye are being daft, he told himself. *It's probably some shepherd boy who's gotten himself lost.*

Steeling himself, he ducked under the curtain of willow branches and found himself stepping into a small glade carpeted with grass. In the centre of the glade sat a tree stump but other than that, it lay empty. Finlay turned around slowly, examining every inch. There was nothing.

"Ye look like yer brother, do ye know that?" said a voice.

Finlay spun. In a heartbeat he'd grabbed his bow, nocked an arrow, and had it aimed right at the speaker's heart. His eyes widened slightly when he saw who the speaker was. Not a child or a lost shepherd boy.

It was an old woman.

She was sitting on the tree stump and was so short that her legs dangled off the ground. Her hands were folded in her lap and she was smiling at Finlay warmly, completely untroubled by the fact that she had an arrow aimed right at her heart.

"Who are ye?" Finlay demanded. "What are ye doing here?"

"Which question would you like me to answer first?" the old woman said jovially.

Her face was a sea of creases and Finlay doubted he'd ever met anyone so old. Her hair, gray like the storm clouds that sometimes gathered over the sea, was pulled back in a bun and she wore a plaid in colors that Finlay didn't recognize. But her eyes...her eyes were dark and deep and sparkled like chips of polished flint.

"My apologies," Finlay said as shame washed through him. Had he been reduced to threatening defenceless old women? He lowered his bow. "I didnae mean to threaten ye. Ye startled me, is all. Forgive me."

"My, but ye are a well-mannered boy," the woman said with a smile. "Nay doubt yer father taught ye well. Laird David MacAuley was always a stickler for such things."

Finlay glanced at her sharply. How did this woman know who his father was? And then the words she'd first spoken suddenly registered. *Ye look like yer brother, do ye know that?*

He fixed her with a hard stare and said in a stout voice, "Ye are mistaken, my lady. I dinna know of this Laird David of whom ye speak."

"Dinna ye?" she replied pleasantly. "Have ye also never heard of yer brother, Logan, either? He's the one ye look like by the way, not yer other brother, Camdan. He got his looks from yer mother's side I daresay."

Finlay fought to remain calm, although his heart was suddenly thumping. He'd been so cautious. For years, ever since he'd left his ancestral home at Dun Ringill, he'd been careful to hide who he really was. Stories of the cursed MacAuley brothers had begun to circulate soon after they'd disappeared, becoming something of a local myth. Only his lord knew the truth but now a strange old woman who appeared out of nowhere had seemingly deduced who he was.

He gritted his teeth. "As I said," he grated. "Ye are mistaken, my lady. Ye obviously have me confused with somebody else."

"Oh? My apologies then. There must be another exiled brother to the MacAuley laird around here somewhere." The look she fixed on him was deep and penetrating.

Despite himself, Finlay took a step backwards. "Who are ye?"

"My name is Irene MacAskill," she replied, smiling up at him like a kindly old grandmother.

"MacAskill? The MacAskill clan live far to the north. Ye are a long way from home, my lady."

"Aye," she replied. "As are ye. But it isnae too late to find yer way back, should ye wish it."

Finlay pressed his lips into a tight, flat line. Find his way home? Not too late? Oh, how little she knew!

"My lady," he said, forcing his voice to patience. "I must be on my way. If ye wish, I will escort ye to the nearest road. Mayhap ye can find yer way home from there."

"There ye go again," she replied. "So polite. Definitely the most polite of the three of ye. Nay, thank ye, my lad, but I can find my own way home. I dinna need yer aid, in fact, I think it's the other way around."

"What do ye mean by that?"

She hopped down from the tree stump. She was so small she barely reached his chest but even so her presence seemed to fill the glade like a thunderstorm. She walked towards him and it was all Finlay could do to hold his ground as she approached. Lord, what was wrong with him? He'd faced down enemies in battle. He'd faced opponents who thirsted for his blood without flinching. So why did one small old woman fill him with such uneasiness?

Fae, a voice whispered in the back of his mind. *Ye have encountered her kind before and look what came of it.*

Irene came to stand in front of him, her head tilted back so she could stare up into his eyes. She smiled warmly. "I know the wariness and distrust that fills yer heart. I know the despair that ye are forever trying to keep at bay. I know ye think this is yer life, doomed to serve a man ye hate, doomed to bring death and destruction to those ye hold dear. But it doesnae have to be that way. Bargains can be unmade, new ones can be made in their place. There is always a way back, lad. Destiny has a way of leading us safely home if we go astray—as long as we have the courage to listen when it calls."

Finlay swallowed thickly. Her words awoke a longing within him. They awoke that terrible ache that was there every time he opened his eyes in the morning. They awoke that yearning for the life he might have led. A simple life full of love and family and laughter. A life that could never be his.

"I wish what ye say were true," he replied, his voice barely above a whisper. "But this is my life, such as it is. I can lead no other."

She took his hand, her skin warm and dry like autumn leaves. "We shall see, my dear. We shall see." She lifted her face to the sunlight and sniffed a great breath through her nostrils. "I smell change on the air. Great upheaval is coming to the Highlands. It will come upon us all like a tide and the only question is will we swim with that tide and allow it to sweep us to new horizons? Or will we fight it and allow it to drown us? That is the choice ye will soon have to make, my dear. Yer destiny will soon be calling. Make sure ye are listening when it does." She patted his hand and then turned and walked across the glade, disappearing through the curtain of willow branches.

For a moment Finlay was too stunned to do anything. Then he came to his senses and ran after her. "Wait! At least allow me to escort ye to—"

His words trailed off as he ducked through the willow branches. The riverbank was empty, with no sign of Irene MacAskill. He knelt, scanning the ground for any sign of her passage. There were none. No footprints other than the original set that had led him here.

Fae, that voice whispered in the back of his mind again. He'd dared to hope the Fae were done with him. Seemed he was wrong.

Hefting his bow, he retraced his steps, picking up the animal trail that would lead him out of the valley. He suddenly wanted to be far away from this place. Breaking into a jog, he turned his steps towards the north and hurried on his way.

Chapter 2

Eleanor put her bags down on the kitchen table, took off her coat and hung it on a peg by the door.

"Now, ye are sure ye'll be all right?" Alice asked for about the hundredth time.

Somewhere in her fifties, Alice was the practice nurse at Eleanor's new surgery and she was taking her duties of settling in the new doctor very seriously indeed. She'd picked Eleanor up from the airport, driven her to the tiny, one-bedroom cottage that she'd be living in, and deluged her with information about the local community until Eleanor's head was spinning. She already knew far more about Mr Croker's bunions than was absolutely necessary and thought she could probably recite in detail all the ups and downs of Mrs MacTavish's latest pregnancy.

"I'll be fine, honestly," Eleanor replied. "I think I'm just going to have a bath and then get some sleep. I'm pretty tired." In truth, she was jet-lagged to hell and feeling more than a little queasy. The journey had been long and uncomfortable.

Alice's face softened. "Of course, my dear." She patted Eleanor's arm. "Well, if ye need me, I live at number two, just down the road. I'll see ye tomorrow."

"Okay. Thanks for all your help, Alice."

Alice smiled and then let herself out, leaving Eleanor alone in the kitchen. She looked around. The cottage was small but homely, with everything she needed. There was a living room with an open fire and a bedroom and bathroom up the rickety stairs. Crossing to the kitchen window, Eleanor looked out. The endless vista of the Highlands, a patchwork of hills and valleys, stretched into the distance, looking resplendent in its spring finery. There wasn't a traffic jam in sight.

Eleanor smiled to herself. Already some of her tension was beginning to lift, to be replaced by a little tingle of excitement. For the first time in a long time she'd followed her heart, followed it to this place, this tiny village in the Highlands that was so different to anything she knew. And yet, it felt right. In a way she couldn't quite explain, she felt like she'd taken the first step along the right path.

Lugging her case upstairs, she put her clothes away neatly in the little wardrobe then pulled on her coat and locked the cottage up behind her. Sure, she was tired, but she was also eager to begin exploring.

The tiny village of Achfarn tumbled down the hill ahead of her, a collection of small, stone-built houses with a single road winding up the middle. She passed the post-office, the pub, and finally the doctor's surgery where she'd begin work tomorrow. It didn't take long to walk around the entire settlement and Eleanor couldn't help but wonder if there would be enough work here to keep her busy.

Reaching the end of the village, she found herself at a small wooden gate that led into a farmer's field. A small way-post marked a footpath that crossed the field and disappeared into a stand of trees on the far side. This place must be a walker's paradise, Eleanor mused.

She pulled the little gate open and took the footpath. She followed the path through the field where shaggy Highland cattle lifted their heads to watch her pass and made her way into the stand of trees opposite. Here a shallow stream wound its way between the trees, gurgling as it passed over rocks.

Meandering along the riverbank, Eleanor found herself enjoying the spring day. It was unseasonably warm for this early in the year and she ought to make the most of it. She'd been warned that the Highland weather could be somewhat fierce.

Eleanor halted. Ahead of her, a huge oak tree grew by the side of the stream, its trunk as big around as a decent sized car and its hoary branches swaying gently in the breeze. The tree's trunk had been split some time in the past, perhaps by lightning, and was now hollow, forming an archway through which she saw the stream glimmering in the sunlight.

Eleanor laid her palm against the trunk and gazed up at the branches. "I bet you've seen a thing or two in your lifetime. I wonder what stories you could tell."

"Ah, ye wouldnae believe half of them," said a voice.

Heart leaping into her mouth, Eleanor spun. A tiny old woman was standing behind her, watching her with a broad smile on her face. Eleanor's mouth dropped open as she realized it was Irene MacAskill.

"You!" Eleanor gasped. "You made me jump out of my skin!"

"My apologies, lass," Irene replied, not looking apologetic at all. "I thought I would answer yer question seeing as the tree wasnae being very talkative."

Eleanor looked around, wondering where the old woman had come from. She hadn't heard her approach. "What's going on?" she asked suspiciously. "What are you doing here?"

"I would have thought that was obvious," Irene replied. "I've come to talk to ye, dearie."

"But...but...how did you know I'd be here?"

Irene tapped the side of her nose. "Didnae I tell ye? Destiny, lass. It pulls us whether we will it or nay and yers has pulled ye here. As I knew it would."

Eleanor stared at her, unease coiling in her stomach. What the hell was going on? The last time she'd seen this woman was in her office back in the US. Now she'd turned up at a remote Highland village the very day Eleanor arrived! Coincidence? Hardly. A shiver walked down Eleanor's spine. She looked around, suddenly wary.

"I don't appreciate being followed," she said. "And how did you know I was coming here for a job? Have you been spying on me?"

Irene didn't answer her question. With a small smile she said, "Oh? Is that why ye are here? For a job? I thought ye'd come for another reason entirely."

"What other reason could there be?" Eleanor snapped. She was feeling off balance. Irene MacAskill's sudden appearance was extremely unsettling.

Irene rolled her eyes. "Dinna I keep saying it? There is only one reason, lass: destiny. Yer true path. Didnae I tell ye that sometimes fate goes awry and we are separated from the place and the people with whom we are meant to walk our path through life? But ye are here now and, if ye wish it, ye can set yer feet on that right road."

Eleanor backed up a step. The old woman's words were creeping her out. What the hell was she talking about? Eleanor had come here for a fresh start. New job. New life. Simple as that. All this talk of destiny was just ridiculous!

"Okay," Eleanor said. "I'm going to leave now. I've no idea how you figured out where to find me but from now on if you want to talk to me I suggest you make an appointment at the surgery like everyone else."

She began to walk off but Irene's hand shot out and caught her arm. Despite her advancing age, Irene had a grip as strong as tree roots.

"Wait, lass," Irene said, her dark eyes flashing. "Dinna ye wish to see what I mean?"

She stepped aside, giving Eleanor a perfect view of the hollow tree trunk and the stream on the other side. Except, when Eleanor looked she couldn't see the stream anymore. Instead, images began to coalesce in the archway formed by the hollow trunk. She saw a ring of standing stones on a lonely shore. Three men stood inside, their hands joined. Suddenly one of the men turned to look at her and although she couldn't see his face clearly, she was pierced by an intense green gaze that seemed to sear her to her very soul. With a gasp, Eleanor felt something shift inside her. She *knew* that man. She knew him intimately, even though she was sure she'd never met him before in her life. Then the image shifted and she saw a castle standing on a windswept hillside with two armies facing each other on the plain outside.

Eleanor's heart was beating so hard she could feel it hammering against her ribs. "What is this?" she whispered. "What am I looking at?"

"Oh, I think ye know, my dear," Irene replied in a soft voice. "The balance is out of kilter. A life has been stolen that shouldnae have, a bargain made that should never have been. As a result war and strife is coming to the Highlands. But ye can stop it, lass. What say ye?"

Eleanor tore her eyes away from the images and looked at Irene. "Me? What can I do?"

"Everything, my dear. All ye need to do is step through the arch. But I warn ye, if ye do yer path will be hard. It will be dangerous and heart-breaking and at times ye will be sure ye made the wrong decision. But if ye have the courage, if ye can find a way to truly follow yer heart, ye have a chance to find what it is ye've always been searching for and to heal that ache in yer soul. What is yer choice, lass?"

Eleanor opened her mouth and closed it again. Irene's stare was intense, her gaze unblinking. She looked from the old woman to the archway and back again. Anyone with an ounce of sense would turn around, walk away from this crazy old woman and return to the village. But it seemed, after all, that Eleanor didn't have any sense, because she felt herself taking a step towards the archway.

Follow yer heart, Irene had told her, and right now her heart was tugging her towards that archway even as her head was screaming at her to stop.

Eleanor took another step. Now she was inside the hollow trunk and above her head was the heart of the living tree, green with life. She glanced back at Irene and the old woman smiled at her encouragingly.

Taking a deep breath, Eleanor stepped through to the other side.

FINLAY CLIMBED OUT of the valley and entered the next, moving swiftly, barely leaving a trace of his presence behind. He slipped through the landscape like a ghost, only the wild beasts taking any notice of his passage. Yet any pleasure he'd taken in the spring day had evaporated following his encounter with Irene MacAskill. Her appearance had stirred up old feelings, ones he'd believed long buried. Now his thoughts churned, whispering one thing over and over.

Traitor. Turncoat.

Gritting his teeth, he strode onwards, pushing his way through thick undergrowth, barely noticing the brambles that snagged his plaid or the branches that whipped his face. He tried to drown out the voice but it would not be silent.

What would yer father think? How would he feel if he knew what ye'd become? Stewart's Hound.

"They wasnae a choice!" he growled aloud.

He wasn't sure who he was talking to. His father? His brothers? Or maybe his own conscience?

There is always a way back, Irene MacAskill had told him. Finlay knew that wasn't true. Not for him. Such hope had died long ago, along with the last vestiges of the man he'd been.

He heard a sound and froze. Cocking his head, he listened intently. Aye, there it was. The rhythmic drumming of hoof beats. They were heading this way. In a flash Finlay ducked behind a hazel thicket. Crouching, he slid his bronze dagger from its sheath and held it lightly as he peered through gaps between the leaves.

The hoof beats grew louder and three riders burst into view, galloping headlong down the trail, lather covering their horses' flanks, mud flying from beneath their hooves. Finlay tensed. The men, warriors with swords strapped to their backs, wore the MacAuley colors and Finlay saw that at least two of them were injured, one favoring his side, the other with a crude bandage wrapped around his upper arm. The riders thundered past Finlay's hiding place without stopping and disappeared into the distance.

Finlay stared after them. What were MacAuley scouts doing in this area? When he was sure there were no other riders following, he straightened and stepped cautiously from his hiding place. He re-sheathed his dagger and squinted down the trail. Those MacAuley warriors had clearly been in a skirmish. That meant they'd encountered a Stewart patrol somewhere nearby.

Finlay scowled. Damn it all. Lord Stewart had sent out a patrol without informing him. Again. How was he supposed to track the enemies' movements if he didn't know where his own forces were? He glanced at the hoof prints. They led to the mouth of the valley, towards the uplands. What had happened up there? He had to find out. With a growl of annoyance, he set out, following the trail.

Chapter 3

Eleanor hadn't known what to expect as she stepped through the archway but this sudden sensation of falling as though she was on a fairground ride wasn't high on the list. Her stomach rose into her chest and for a moment she was certain she would faint. Then the sensation faded as quickly as it had come and she found herself stumbling out into bright sunlight.

She blinked rapidly and looked around. Behind her rose the oak tree with its hollow trunk but it was smaller and appeared, much, much younger. The stream still meandered by, gurgling happily, but everything else had changed. Gone was the woodland she'd passed through. Instead, she was standing on an expanse of open ground covered in hummocky tufts of rye grass that felt slightly spongy under her boots. A few other oak trees were dotted around, widely spaced, and beyond them Eleanor could see an open expanse of green and purple moorland stretching to the horizon.

Her eyes widened in shock. Where was Achfarn? Where were the farmer's fields and the Highland cattle? She spun around to face Irene MacAskill.

"Irene, what the hell just happened? You better have a damn good explanation—"

Her words trailed off as she realized there was no sign of the old woman. Panic flared. Her stomach knotted, sending her pulse racing. Eleanor turned back to the tree trunk and walked around it quickly, certain the old woman must be hiding and this was some sort of joke on the new girl in town.

But she found nothing. No footprints in the boggy ground, nothing to indicate the old woman had ever been there. Eleanor turned around, scanning the landscape, sure Irene must be around here somewhere. But there was not another soul in sight. There was only Eleanor, the oak trees, and the empty expanse of the Highlands.

Cupping her hands to her mouth she shouted, "Irene! Where are you? Come out, this is not funny! Irene!"

Her shout echoed off the hills before fading into silence.

Okay, Eleanor said to herself, trying to think rationally. *You've had some kind of episode. Maybe you hit your head and you blacked out or you've fallen asleep and gone sleepwalking and dreamt the whole episode with Irene. There are a hundred rational explanations for this, you just have to figure out where you've wandered to and then find your way back.*

Calmed a little by her logic, Eleanor took a deep breath. She'd followed the stream on the way out here so, logically, if she followed it back, it would lead her to Achfarn.

Right, she thought. *When I get back, I'll go straight to the surgery and ask Alice to check me over. Maybe I'm more tired than I realized and I hallucinated the whole thing.*

She began walking, keeping the stream on her left, striding purposefully across the boggy, uneven ground. Any minute she would spot a house in the distance or a stone wall that marked the boundary of the village or hear the sound of a car engine. But she didn't. She walked for around thirty minutes, seeing nothing and nobody. Gradually the landscape began to change into a series of craggy hills. Realizing she'd somehow missed Achfarn, Eleanor stopped.

Damn it! This was most annoying! Getting lost on her first day? What an idiot this would make her look! She could just imagine the conversations down the pub tonight when the locals discovered that the foreign doctor had to be rescued on her first day in town!

She pursed her lips. There was nothing for it. She'd have to look stupid and put up with the gossip. She dug her cell out of her pocket and dialed 999 for the emergency services. After a moment's silence the phone let out a shrill beep. Glancing at the display, Eleanor realized there was no signal. Oh, wonderful. Just absolutely perfect! Wasn't that just her rotten luck?

She growled in annoyance, let out a string of curses, and resisted the urge to hurl the phone away in frustration. She dropped it back into her pocket and forced herself to take a calming breath. She checked her watch, wondering how much time might have passed. But as she raised her wrist, she realized her watch wasn't there anymore. She must have lost it when she stumbled through the arch. Great! Could this day get any worse? She was lost, had no cell signal and now she'd lost her damned watch!

Schooling herself to calmness, she took in her surroundings. Ahead, the ground began to slope down into a wooded valley. A dark column rose into the air above the trees.

Smoke! That meant a campfire and people!

She sagged in relief. Hopefully they'd be able to tell her the way to Achfarn and, if she was really lucky, maybe she'd be able to beg a lift. At worst she'd be able to use their cell phone and call a cab to come pick her up. Maybe nobody back at the village had to know about this little episode after all!

Feeling infinitely more optimistic, Eleanor started down the hill. The trail down into the valley was muddy and Eleanor slipped more than once, cursing loud enough to startle a flock of grouse into the air. But finally she reached the spot where she'd seen the smoke and saw the flames of a campfire glimmering through the trees.

She breathed out, relieved. Finally! Surely anyone camping out here would know the route back to Achfarn?

As she wove her way through the trees, approaching the campfire, she got her first look at the people around the fire and realized her first assumption might have been wrong. This didn't look like some family camping expedition after all.

Four grizzled men were sitting on logs around the fire. They wore traditional Scottish dress of a tartan plaid over linen shirts and four horses were tethered nearby.

Eleanor paused, suddenly uneasy.

One of the men glanced up and spotted her. He surged to his feet.

"Who's there? Come out where we can see ye!"

Well, no helping it now. Eleanor walked forward. "Sorry to disturb you," she said. "But I'm a little lost and I was hoping you could tell me how to get back to Achfarn. Could you direct me to the road? Or do you have a cell phone I could borrow so I can call a cab?"

The men looked at each other. The one who'd stood moved forward cautiously, peering behind Eleanor as if expecting others.

"Who are ye?" he demanded.

"I'm the new doctor in Achfarn," she replied, a little startled by his unfriendly tone. "I went out walking and got lost. Look, if you could just point me in the direction of the nearest road, I'll find my way from there."

"Ye are alone?" the man asked.

Eleanor hesitated. Now that she was closer she noticed the men were all unkempt, with dirty clothes and ragged beards. They were staring at her with hard eyes and she saw that they sported cuts and bruises, as though they'd been fighting.

Her unease intensified.

"You know what?" she said, backing away. "It's fine. I'll be on my way."

She turned and hurried back the way she'd come, fighting the urge to run.

"Nay so fast!" the man cried. He ran after her and grabbed her elbow. "Ye think we'll let a spy just go wandering off?"

"Let go!" Eleanor cried in outrage. "You're hurting me!"

His grip was hard and unyielding. "Come with me quietly and ye willnae get hurt," he growled.

He yanked her unceremoniously back to the clearing. The other men had risen to their feet and were holding swords in their hands. Swords! Where the hell had they gotten those?

"Is she alone, Angus?" one of them asked anxiously.

"I reckon so," Angus replied. "I didnae see any other tracks."

One of the men spat on the ground. "Those damned MacAuleys. They must be desperate if they're sending women to do their dirty work for them."

Eleanor glanced from one man to the other. She had no idea what they were talking about.

"Let me go!" she cried. "I don't know what the hell is going on here but you'll take your hands off me, right now!"

Angus, who she assumed was the leader, narrowed his eyes at her. He was a big man with a large, bushy beard. "Ye are in nay position to be giving orders, my lady. Answer my questions. Are ye alone? Are there others following behind ye? Have ye been leading them onto us?"

Eleanor stared at him, bewildered. "I've no idea what you're talking about. Like I told you, I'm just trying to get back to Achfarn. If you let me go, I'll get out of your hair and we can forget this ever happened."

"Trying to get back to MacAuley's camp more like," one of the other men said. "So she can report back on Lord Stewart's deployment or else lead that bastard patrol back so they can finish us off!"

"Nah," a third man said. "She doesnae look like a spy to me. I reckon she's a runaway. Probably a whore after better pay. Mayhap she's come to the right place, eh, lads?" He grinned around at his fellows.

"Shut yer mouth, Balloch!" Angus snarled. "Spies come in all guises, ye fool."

Eleanor blinked. They thought she was a spy? What the hell?

"Look," she said, trying to keep her voice calm. "There's been some sort of misunderstanding. I don't know who you think I am but you're mistaken. I'm a doctor for god's sake, that's all. Let me go before I have the police down on you!"

Angus stared at her. "Ye aren't going anywhere, lass, other than back to Lord Stewart." He pushed her towards Balloch, a broad-shouldered man with red hair falling onto his shoulders. "Tie her up and get her on one of the horses. It's time we were out of here. If she was leading that patrol back here, I suggest we make ourselves scarce."

Balloch winked at her and then gave a cocky grin. "Aye, sir. It will be a pleasure." He grabbed Eleanor's hands and quickly tied her wrists with a piece of rope.

"Get your hands off me!" Eleanor cried, twisting and trying to yank herself from his grip.

Balloch merely pulled her tighter. Eleanor aimed some savage kicks in his direction but he barely seemed to feel the blows. In fact, he seemed to enjoy them.

"My," he said, grinning at her. "Are all MacAuley women as feisty as ye?"

"I'm not a MacAuley woman, you asshole!" Eleanor growled. "My name is Eleanor Stevenson, and boy, are you going to pay for this!"

The threat only made Balloch grin wider.

"Balloch! Stop arsing around and get her mounted up," Angus snapped. He and the other men sat astride their horses, scanning the woods nervously. Somebody had doused the campfire.

Balloch dragged Eleanor to his horse and unceremoniously grabbed her around the waist, ignored her kicking, and tossed her into the saddle. Then he climbed up behind her.

"Keep fighting me," he growled. "Just keep fighting me. Then ye will see just how much of an 'asshole' I can be."

His tone was full of menace and the look in his eyes sent a chill down Eleanor's spine.

"Where are you taking me?"

"Are ye deaf? To Lord Stewart of course. Where else would we take a MacAuley spy? Ye just better hope that the lord is in a good mood otherwise it willnae go well for ye."

Then the men kicked their horses into motion and Eleanor was forced to cling to the saddle horn to keep from being tossed to the ground. Fear fluttered in her belly. Who were these men? There were ragged and travel-stained and the fact that they carried swords—swords! —obviously meant they were not averse to violence. From the looks of them they'd been involved in some recently. Had she somehow stumbled on a criminal gang hiding out in the Highlands? And why the hell did they think she was some sort of spy?

Her heart thundered in her ears and the fear coursing through her veins made it difficult to think. Her cell phone was in her pocket. If she could reach it, maybe there would be signal enough to call the police, but with her hands tied there was little hope of that.

They thundered along a muddy trail through the woods, Angus in the lead, the two other men bringing up the rear.

All were tense, wary, their eyes continually scanning the terrain. They'd put their swords away but even so Eleanor could see they were ready for trouble.

She sucked in a deep breath, trying unsuccessfully to calm her thumping heart. Oh god. What in God's name had she stumbled into?

She tried to keep a track of their journey as they rode but in the unchanging green expanse of trees, it was difficult to know in which direction they were travelling. They followed a narrow trail through the woods and she saw signs of other traffic: more hoof prints and the tracks of some sort of wheeled vehicle, too narrow to be a car. A cart perhaps?

The men didn't speak. Their faces were grim, their shoulders tense. What did they expect to happen? That they would all suddenly get jumped by a band of muggers? All the way out here in the middle of nowhere?

They rode for what felt an age before Angus called a halt next to a stream.

"Water the horses quickly," he instructed.

Balloch dismounted and reached up to drag Eleanor from the saddle.

"Dinna try anything, woman," he said, setting her on her feet. "I'll be watching ye."

He took his horse's reins and led the animal over to the stream to drink.

"Aren't you going to untie my hands?" she called after him.

He glanced over his shoulder. "Why would I do that?"

"I...I...need to use the bathroom."

"The what?"

"I need to pee."

"Ah!" Balloch said, his leering grin returning. "Why didnae ye say so? Yer wish is my command, my lady."

He pulled a dagger from his belt and strode over. Setting the sharp blade against the bonds, he sliced through them.

"This way," he said, taking her arm.

"What are you doing?"

"Escorting ye. Ye didnae think we would let ye go wandering off alone now did ye?"

Balloch dragged Eleanor into a clump of bushes a few metres from the camp. The men had not taken off their horse's saddles and so could be ready to ride in an instant. Her only option was to flee deeper into the woods where the horses would find it difficult to manoeuvre through the thick undergrowth. If she could get free of Balloch, that is.

She yanked her arm from his grip angrily. "Do you have no manners at all?" she demanded. "You could at least turn your back and give a lady some privacy!"

Balloch's grin was so infuriating she wanted to slap him. But after a moment he crossed his arms and turned his back. "Be quick."

Eleanor waited until his back was completely turned then grabbed a branch that lay in the dirt by her feet and swung it with all her strength. It connected with the back of his knee with a loud 'thwack' and Balloch yowled in pain, crashing onto his knees.

Eleanor seized her chance. She took off into the trees, sprinting for all she was worth. Shouts of alarm rang out behind but she didn't dare look back. She pelted between the trees, flinging up mud, doing her best to keep to where the undergrowth was thickest.

As she ran, she dug into her pocket and pulled out her cell phone – or tried to. With a flare of panic she realized it was no longer in her pocket. Oh hell! She must have dropped it when Balloch grabbed her by the campfire! She couldn't call for help.

She was on her own.

Chapter 4

Finlay knelt and examined the ground. He'd found the trail of Stewart's patrol around an hour ago, following it steadily east before it became confused and muddy. Four sets of hoof prints were clearly visible in the thick leaf-litter. It was not unusual for a patrol to consist of four riders but what made Finlay pause was that one set of hoof prints was deeper than the others as though carrying something heavy, perhaps more than one passenger. Had Stewart's patrol captured a MacAuley scout? But if so, surely the man would have his own horse rather than having to ride double?

Finlay frowned. What was going on here? Eyes scanning the ground, he followed the tracks and soon came upon a stream. Here there were footprints as well as hoof prints which showed the riders had dismounted, probably to water the horses. There were five sets of footprints. Hmm. Five people to four horses which meant he'd been right – one of the horses was carrying two riders.

He followed as two of the sets of footprints led away from the clearing to a spot where the leaf-litter had been disturbed by some sort of scuffle. One set led off into the woods, spaced far enough apart to indicate that whoever made them had been running. The footprints were small, although not small enough to indicate a child. A woman?

Finlay pulled his dagger from its sheath and set off, following the footprints. They meandered everywhere; sometimes re-crossing their path and then circling back round to where they started. Whoever had made them was clearly in a panic. The prints were fresh and he could not be more than a few minutes behind.

Finlay paused in a clearing and went very still, listening. At first he heard nothing but the sounds of the woods: the call of birds, the rustle of squirrels in the leaf-litter. But then he detected something else: movement in the trees and the distant sound of men's voices.

Then, as he cocked his head to listen, a woman came hurtling through the trees. She was looking over her shoulder and didn't see him standing there. She slammed straight into him, her momentum strong enough to send them both crashing to the ground.

He gasped, all the wind knocked out of him as her elbow landed firmly in his stomach. She let out a shrill scream and scrambled up, her feet slipping on the slick grass. Finlay scrambled up and, as she was about to run, managed to get his hand around her wrist.

"Wait!"

Her other hand came swinging at him and he only just managed to turn his head in time to avoid getting a fist in the face for his troubles. He caught her arms before she could swing for him again and the woman shrieked, struggling and kicking like a wildcat.

"Easy!" Finlay cried. "Easy, woman! I willnae hurt ye!"

"Let me go!" she shouted. "They're coming!"

"Who's coming?"

Instead of answering, she aimed a kick squarely at his nether regions. Finlay didn't have time for this. Deftly avoiding her kick, he yanked her towards him, spun her around and grabbed her tight, holding her against him and pinning her own arms at her sides. She struggled, desperately trying to break free but Finlay held her fast.

"Calm down, lass," he said by her ear. "I willnae harm ye. Nor will I let anyone else harm ye. Stop struggling!"

The fight went out of her and she sagged in his grip. Her eyes were wide, her nostrils flaring, and from her gasping breaths he guessed she'd been running for her life.

"I'm going to release ye now," he said in a soothing voice, the same one he'd used when trying to calm frightened colts back in Dun Ringill. "All right?"

She nodded and he released her. She scrambled away, spinning to face him. Only then did he realize that the woman was dressed strangely. She wore a long coat with tight trews that clung to her calves and boots that reached her ankles. Thick red hair fell in waves past her shoulders and she fixed him with hazel eyes that glinted with defiance despite her obvious fear.

He held up a hand, palm outwards. "It's all right," he said soothingly. "Ye are in no danger."

"No danger?" she rasped. "Are you kidding me? Listen! They're coming!" She looked around wildly, as if seeking a place to hide.

The sounds of pursuit were getting closer. He could hear twigs snapping and the pounding of hooves.

"Get behind me," he commanded.

He moved to stand in front of her just as four riders burst into the clearing, yanking their horses up short when they saw Finlay standing in their path.

Their leader shouldered his way to the front of the group. "Finlay!" he snapped, glaring down from his saddle. "What are ye doing here?"

Finlay met the man's glare with one of his own. He crossed his arms over his chest.

"I might ask ye the same thing," he replied. "Ye are a long way from the border, Angus. And ye will address me as 'sir'. Last time I looked, I outranked ye. Or has that changed?"

Angus's face turned red behind his beard. He glared down at Finlay with the same scorn with which all of Stewart's men viewed him but the man wasn't brave enough to argue.

"Aye, sir," he replied tightly. "We were patrolling the border when we were ambushed by MacAuley scouts. Then this lass turned up. We were taking her to Lord Stewart but she escaped. She's given us the right run-around, I can tell ye."

Finlay glanced over his shoulder at the woman. She was staring at the four riders with wide eyes.

"Aye, she looks mighty dangerous," he said, his voice low and laced with anger. "I wonder what crime she's committed to warrant being chased through the woods like a beast?"

Angus's face turned even redder. "She's a MacAuley spy and we were taking her in for questioning."

"A spy is she?" Finlay said softly. "In that case, I will take her into custody. Ye may return to yer patrol now."

"Like hell we will!" shouted one of the other men.

Finlay's eyes narrowed as he recognized Balloch Stewart, the spoiled nephew of Lord Stewart. The man was a thug and, if rumors were to be believed, a rapist. It was all Finlay could do to keep the snarl off his face as the man dismounted and took a few steps towards him.

"I owe the bitch," Balloch said, pointing a finger at the woman. "She whacked me when she ran off and no wench gets away with that."

"Balloch," Angus said behind him, in a low, warning voice. "Ye've been given an order. Get back on yer horse."

"Are ye serious?" Balloch cried. "Ye'll take orders from him? From the Hound?" He sneered at Finlay. "Out of my way, dog!"

Finlay didn't move. "Ye would do well to listen to Angus, Balloch."

Balloch's face darkened. "And ye would do well to remember yer place, Hound. Now, move."

Finlay said nothing. He just waited.

With a snarl, Balloch drew a knife and swung it. Finlay had known the blow was coming even before Balloch moved so he swayed neatly out of the way but not before the blade scored a line of red fire across his bicep. The touch of iron sent agony flaring along Finlay's nerves and for a second his vision turned white. But he recovered in a heartbeat. As Balloch staggered past, Finlay grabbed the man's shoulder and used his own momentum to send him crashing to his knees in the dirt.

Balloch climbed to his feet. With a howl of rage he ran at Finlay. In a quick movement earned through years of practice under his father's watchful tutelage, Finlay drew his bronze dagger and threw. The blade flashed through the air, neatly scoring the back of Balloch's hand.

The big man howled, the dagger falling from suddenly nerveless fingers. "I'll kill ye, ye bastard!" Balloch howled. "My uncle will hear of this!"

Finlay strode over, pressed the end of his bow under Balloch's chin, forcing the man to look up at him.

"Oh, I hope so," Finlay said in a quiet voice. "Do ye know what the penalty is for drawing a weapon on a superior officer? Hanging."

Balloch paled. He licked his lips. "Now, wait, I didnae mean—"

"Angus!" Finlay shouted, cutting him off. "Get this sack of meat mounted up and out of my sight. Oh, and I suggest ye take him straight to the infirmary when ye get back. It would be a shame if he lost his hand."

Balloch glared at Finlay with eyes full of hatred but said not a word. He strode to his horse and climbed into the saddle, shrugging off Angus's help with an annoyed snarl. Gripping his reins one-handed, he kicked his horse into motion and rode off without waiting for the others.

Angus looked at Finlay for a moment as though he wanted to say something but seemed to think better of it. Without another word the three men whirled their mounts and went speeding off after Balloch.

Finlay watched until the riders had disappeared before turning to the woman. She was standing a few paces away, her eyes following the retreating riders.

"Ye are safe now," he said. "They willnae come back."

Her eyes snapped to his. They were the color of early autumn leaves. "I...um...I..." she stammered. She blew out a shaky breath and ran her hands over her face. "Okay. Thanks for your help. I need to call the police. Do you a have a cell phone I could borrow? I seem to have lost mine."

Finlay stared at her. She had an odd, rolling accent and that, coupled with the strange words she used, meant Finlay had difficulty keeping up with her speech.

"I didnae understand half of what ye just said, lass. Police? Cell phone? What are these words?"

The woman blinked. "You aren't serious, surely? You've never heard of the police? Or a cell phone?"

"Nay, lass." He looked her up and down, taking in the odd clothing and her unbound hair. "Ye are an outlander? Where do ye come from, lass? Spain? Italy?"

She shook her head. "Neither. America."

"America?"

"Yeah, you know. The US. That great big country across the sea?"

He'd never heard of the place but he let that pass. "Are yer kin nearby? It isnae safe for ye here. I will escort ye back to them—"

"I'm on my own," she blurted. Almost under her breath she added, "What the hell is going on? None of this makes any damned sense."

Finlay frowned. What woman would wander alone out here with all the strife that was brewing? It was obvious she was no spy, regardless of what Angus and his band of fools might claim, yet there was clearly more to her than met the eye.

He reached out and gently placed his hand on her shoulder. "What's yer name, lass?"

ELEANOR STARTLED AT the sudden contact. A shot of fear hurtled through her and she gathered herself to run. But as she looked up, she found herself staring into clear green eyes the same shade as the fresh spring grass and, inexplicably, some of the tension eased out of her.

"Eleanor," she heard herself answer. "My name is Eleanor Stevenson."

Her rescuer inclined his head. "I'm Finlay."

She gave him a weak smile. "Finn for short?"

An odd look crossed his face. "Finn?" he said softly. "My brothers used to call me that."

The man was maybe a handful of years older than herself. He was tall enough that she had to tilt her head back to look up at him and had the strong, toned build of an athlete. Dark hair, shiny like a raven's wing, framed a face with sharp cheekbones and full lips. A light dusting of stubble covered his chin. With a jolt she realized he was strikingly handsome.

But he wore the same traditional Scottish dress as the men who'd abducted her and they'd deferred to him, despite his altercation with Balloch.

She stepped back, suddenly wary. "How come you knew those men? Who are you? Who were *they*?"

"I've told ye who I am," he replied with a frown. "The men who were chasing ye are Lord Alasdair Stewart's soldiers. They took ye for a MacAuley spy." His eyes narrowed. "Were they right, lass?"

"No they were not!" she snapped. "I've no idea what you're talking about! I'm no spy! Why would you even *think* such a thing? Has everyone around here gone crazy?"

"Why else would a lass be wandering the woods alone, claiming she has no kin?"

"I got lost, that's all!" Oh hell! How had her day ended up like this? "I went walking from Achfarn and lost my bearings. I approached those men because I thought they might help me. More fool me, eh?"

The man—Finn—stared at her. He seemed to be weighing up her words, deciding if she was telling the truth.

Finally, he nodded. "I believe ye, lass. I will escort ye back to Achfarn although I dinna know the place. Where does it lie?"

Eleanor almost sagged with relief. Finally, somebody was going to help her! Drawing in a shaky breath, she swiped her forehead with the back of her hand and then looked around, trying to figure out where she was. She recognized nothing, of course. In her mad flight from Angus and his men, she'd lost all sense of direction.

"I...I...think it's north," she said at last. "We travelled for at least an hour – and we were riding."

Finn frowned. "Then it will take much longer to return afoot. Is there aught else ye can tell me about the place?"

"It's a small village," she said, desperately trying to think of landmarks. "There's a pub and a post office and a village shop. That's all." Then she remembered the hollow oak tree she'd stepped through. "But there's a stream that runs nearby that goes through a grove of oak trees. They're all gnarled and hoary, like they're really old. There are about ten of them on the side of the hill and one has a hollow trunk."

Finn suddenly paled. "Ye mean Brigid's Hollow?" he said sharply. "That's a place of the Fae. What would possess ye to go there, lass? Have ye lost yer senses?"

Eleanor blinked, a little rattled by his reaction. What did he mean 'Fae'? And why was he so freaked out by a grove of oak trees? Actually, no. She didn't want to know. All she wanted was to get back to the village, give a statement to the police, and then climb into bed.

She pulled in a deep breath. "Look, it doesn't matter. If you can't get me to Achfarn, just point me in the direction of a phone-booth and I'll take it from there."

There he went again, looking at her as though she was speaking some alien language, his eyebrows pulling into a frown and puzzlement reflecting in his clear green eyes. Then he shook his head.

"Nay, lass. I will see ye safely back to yer home, I give ye my word. And I know the way to Brigid's Hollow."

Was she imagining it or did a shadow of unease pass across his face as he said that name? It was so fleeting she couldn't be sure.

Finn checked the dagger at his belt and adjusted the bow slung over his shoulder. "This way."

With one last look around the clearing, Eleanor followed him. He led her onto a woodland trail that was wide enough for them to walk side by side. Silence descended, punctuated only by the call of birds.

Finn, she noticed, moved through the undergrowth effortlessly, leaving not a footprint in the damp earth and not disturbing a single twig. Eleanor, in contrast, found herself blundering along beside him like an awkward child, pushing branches out of her way and tugging on her clothing when it snagged on brambles.

Who was this guy? And what the hell was going on up here in the Highlands?

She looked at him sidelong. His expression was stern, his eyes scanning the woods continually as if alert for danger.

"Can I ask you a question?"

His green eyes flicked to hers. "Aye, lass. Although I canna guarantee I'll be able to answer it."

"Why do you wear traditional dress?"

"Traditional dress? What do ye mean?"

"You know, the tartan and all that. You and those men are the first people I've seen wearing it since I arrived in Scotland. I didn't think anyone bothered with it anymore."

"I dinna follow ye, lass," he replied. "Why would I not wear my clan's colors? To my knowledge even King James still wears his clan plaid."

Eleanor blinked and came to a halt. King James?

She paused, thinking. Neither Finn nor the men who'd abducted her seemed to have heard of half the things she mentioned. They had no idea what she meant by police or cell phone. They looked askance at her clothing as though she was dressed scandalously. They all wore traditional dress and carried weapons.

A terrifying possibility reared in her mind. What if she hadn't hit her head as she'd told herself? What if she wasn't suffering from amnesia or hallucinations? What if it was something else entirely? What if—?

No, she thought savagely. *Don't be ridiculous. There's a rational explanation for all of this. Everything will make sense as soon as you get back to Brigid's Hollow and from there to Achfarn.*

As they walked Eleanor strained her eyes and her ears for any sign of civilization. Over the brow of the next hill they would see a village glittering in the distance. Round the next bend in the trail they would find a road and hear cars. But they didn't. As they walked and the afternoon began to wear away they saw not another soul. They could have been the only people in the world.

Finn halted abruptly. He squinted at the sun which was beginning to touch the horizon. He seemed troubled.

"What is it?" she asked.

He glanced at her. "We canna reach Brigid's Hollow tonight. There's still a mighty long way to go."

"But...but..." Eleanor replied, panic clenching her stomach again. "We haven't passed a bed and breakfast or a hotel or anything. Shouldn't we keep on walking?"

He shook his head. "Nay, lass. This is dangerous country. I willnae risk blundering into an enemy patrol in the dark." His frown deepened. Almost to himself he added, "Ye never know who might be abroad in the darkness. We'll camp here and set out again at first light."

Eleanor looked around at the broad meadow they were walking through. The grass was ankle high with yellow wildflowers scattered throughout. "Here?" she said dubiously.

"Aye," he replied. "We'll move into the trees so we have a bit of cover from the wind. I can hear a stream in that direction so at least we'll have fresh water." He fixed her with a penetrating gaze. "Dinna worry, lass. I willnae harm ye nor let harm come to ye. Ye can trust me. I give ye my word."

Eleanor stared at him. Finn stared back, unblinking, and Eleanor felt something shift inside her. Her breath caught momentarily and a tingle walked all the way down her spine. She'd never met this man before today but for a reason she couldn't explain, she felt as if she *knew* him, like she'd known him her whole life.

She suddenly remembered the images Irene MacAskill had shown her through the archway. Three men standing in a circle of standing stones. One of them turning towards her, a man with night-black hair and eyes the color of spring grass...

She gasped and shook her head to push away such foolish notions. "Fine," she muttered, suddenly unsettled. "Whatever."

She followed Finn into the trees to a relatively sheltered spot beneath the spreading boughs of a huge silver-skinned beech tree. Here the ground was open, littered with dried leaves from last year's fall.

Finn dropped his pack to the ground and began collecting up firewood. From nearby Eleanor heard the gurgle of a stream.

"I'll go get some water."

Finn nodded and Eleanor grabbed the leather water bottle and made her way to the stream. It was wide and shallow with a gravel bottom and Eleanor could see tiny fish darting around beneath the surface. She knelt on the turf-covered bank and dunked the water bottle, allowing it to fill. She caught sight of her reflection and paused.

"What are you doing here?" she said to herself. "You should never have listened to Irene MacAskill. Maybe then you'd be back in your city apartment right now instead of being shunted back in time and into this crazy place."

As the words left her lips, she froze. Her heart began to thump in her chest. *Back in time.* Why had she said that? What a ridiculous thought!

Is it? a little voice said in the back of her head. *All the clues are there, you've just been refusing to acknowledge them. Finn wearing traditional dress and carrying antique weapons. Finn not understanding half the words you say and looking at you askance when you said you were from America. He mentioned King James. Scotland hasn't had a King James for hundreds of years!*

The realization hit her with the force of a gunshot. *She was in the wrong time*! It was the only explanation. The arch must be a portal of some sort and it had sent her back in time! Eleanor had never believed in such things. She was a scientist; she dealt in cold, hard facts. But her scientific training also led her to look at the evidence in front of her eyes and that evidence only led to one conclusion.

Oh god, she thought as panic twisted her stomach. *Oh crap, oh crap, oh crap.*

Breathe, she thought, forcing herself to take deep, steadying breaths. *Think it through. The archway brought you here. The archway can take you home. Finn is taking you to that archway so you'll be home tomorrow. There's no need for panic.*

Okay, she thought, pushing away the fear that battered at the corners of her mind. *You can do this. You've got it.*

She finished filling the water skin then had a quick wash from the stream. The water was icy cold and it helped to clear her head a little. Splashing her hands and face, she rose and walked unsteadily back to the campsite.

As she approached, she saw that Finn had started a fire and was seated on a log he'd dragged over. Eleanor paused by a tree and watched. Finn had his back to her and wasn't aware of her watching. He'd taken off his shirt and sat naked to the waist. A large, swirling black tattoo covered one half of his muscled back. The pattern was one of interlocking coils and the sight of it made her vaguely uneasy.

Finn gasped suddenly and Eleanor saw he was dabbing at a long cut in his upper arm with a bloody cloth.

Eleanor blinked. He was hurt and she hadn't even noticed. *Some doctor you are,* she scolded herself. Finn had walked all day with that wound and hadn't said a word. Damn him! Did he want it to get infected?

She cleared her throat and stepped out into the open. Finn's head whipped round, his hand going to his dagger, but he relaxed when he saw it was her. Without a word, he returned to cleaning his cut.

She set down the water bottle. "Let me take a look."

"It's naught," he replied. "I'll be done in a moment."

The firelight cast a ripple of shadow across his torso. His chest was tightly muscled and he had a six-pack that any gym-addict would have been proud of. But this wasn't what had caught Eleanor's attention. His body was covered in scars. They showed white against the golden tones of his skin. Some were cuts and stab wounds obviously made by blades but others were puckered like burns. Holy shit. What had been done to him?

Putting on her best doctor's voice she said, "Let me look. I can help."

Before he could protest she laid her hand on the meat of his arm. He looked up and their eyes met. For an instant all the thoughts flew right out of Eleanor's head.

"Here," she said, gathering herself. "Move this way so I can see better."

"There isnae need to fash, lass," he replied. "It's only a scratch. I've had far worse on the battlefield."

"Only a scratch?" Eleanor said, scowling. "Are you serious? It's sliced into the muscle and it looks like there's some dirt in there. Do you want to get gangrene and septicaemia? No? Thought not. So let me see what I can do."

He relented, allowing her to probe the wound. "Ye know something of healing, lass?"

She hesitated. How much did she dare reveal? "Yes," she admitted. "I'm a doctor."

"A doctor? Ye mean ye've studied at one of the Italian universities? How is that possible? Ye are a woman."

"Yes, well, attitudes are a little different where I come from," she muttered. "Now hold still."

Surprisingly, he did as she instructed. She pressed her fingers to the wound carefully. She could feel Finn watching her. Jeez, did he have to do that? His nearness and the feel of his skin under her fingers was making it difficult to concentrate.

"I need to clean it," she said. "Do you have any alcohol?"
"Aye, in the bag."

Eleanor inspected the bag's contents and came out with a small bottle of whisky. She uncorked it with her teeth.

"This might sting a bit."

She tipped the whisky over the cut, flushing out the dirt and the crusted blood. Finn gritted his teeth but didn't make a sound. When it was clean she doused the cloth in the alcohol and used it as a bandage. It was far from ideal but under the circumstances it was the best she could do.

"Why didn't you tell me you were hurt?" she asked as she wound the bandage tightly around his arm.

"There wasnae any need," he replied. "It will quickly heal."

"You still should have told me. After all, you took the wound for my sake."

He raised an eyebrow, a faint smile on his face. "I stand corrected, my lady. I will do so in the future although it's a damned waste of good whisky if ye ask me."

Eleanor wasn't sure if he was mocking her. She finished tying the bandage. "There. That should do for now. I'll check it in the morning."

She stepped back but Finn caught her hand.

"My thanks," he said softly.

Her hand felt tiny in his huge one and his skin was warm and rough with callouses.

Eleanor swallowed thickly. "You're welcome."

Flustered, she snatched her hand back and turned away, busying herself by grabbing the water bottle and taking a long drink. Finn pulled on his shirt and tied his plaid over his shoulder. When he was dressed he moved over to the fire and lowered himself to the ground, sitting cross-legged on his cloak. After a moment's hesitation Eleanor seated herself on the bedroll on the other side.

"I dinna have much in the way of food," Finn said, pulling over his pack. He rummaged around inside and came up with some strips of dried meat. "My apologies," he said with a shrug. "I didnae expect to have company." He tossed a strip to Eleanor who caught it deftly.

"Jerky?" she said with a smile. "My favorite. How did you know?" She took a bite and chewed mechanically. It was as tough as old leather and incredibly salty but it tasted good.

Silence settled between them, broken only by the crackling of the fire. "Can I ask you something?" she said.

He glanced at her over the flames. "Aye?"

She gathered her courage. "What year is this?"

His eyebrows shot up. "What year? How could ye not know such a thing?"

Eleanor floundered, searching for an excuse that wouldn't give her away. "I...um...we use the Gregorian calendar in my homeland," she blurted. "I was wondering if you used the same dating system here."

"It's 1543. Does that answer yer query?"

"Yes," she said quickly. "It does."

Her mind whirled. 1543? She'd gone back in time by hundreds of years! She looked around, suddenly wary of the shadows beyond the firelight. What dangers might they hide in this time?

"Dinna worry," Finn said, as if reading her thoughts. "The fire will keep woodland creatures away and there havenae been wolves or bears in these parts for many years."

"I was thinking more of the human type of predator," she replied.

"I willnae let harm come to ye."

He said it with such easy confidence that Eleanor didn't doubt him. She remembered the ease with which he'd defeated Balloch and the way he'd faced down four mounted warriors. Who was he? Why did he have that tattoo on his back and why was he covered in scars? There was more to Finlay than met the eye, she was sure of it.

She regarded him as she chewed on her dried meat. "What's your story?" she asked at last. "Do you live around here?"

He glanced at her. He was silent for so long she thought he wouldn't answer. Finally he said, "My base was Dun Marig. In the foothills of the mountains to the north."

Eleanor noticed that he said 'base' rather than 'home'. "Was?" she asked. "It's not anymore?"

"Nay," he said, shaking his head. "The MacAuleys captured it. Lord Stewart has made his headquarters in a manor house to the east—" He stopped abruptly, his eyes narrowing. "Why do ye want to know?"

"I was just making conversation," she replied, holding up her hands in surrender. "Sorry. I'll keep my mouth shut."

Finn sighed. "Ah, my apologies, lass. I have nay right to snap at ye. It seems that suspicion has become a way of life these days."

She waved away his apology. "Don't worry about it. I guess I'd be a little grumpy too if I was having to escort a complete stranger miles out of my way."

He looked at her, meeting her gaze across the fire. "Grumpy?" He smiled faintly. "I assume ye mean bad-tempered? Well, it isnae escorting ye that is making me 'grumpy', I can assure ye."

He looked around, eyes scanning the darkness beyond the firelight. His bow was leaning against a tree trunk within easy reach and he'd taken out his dagger and driven it into the log he sat on. It was made of a strange metal that looked like bronze or copper. Finn might claim they were far from any trouble but if the nearness of his weapons was anything to go by, he was still alert for danger.

"What's going on around here?" she asked. "It looks like I've stumbled into some sort of conflict. Who are the MacAuleys? And why was it assumed I was one of their spies?"

"The MacAuleys are a large and powerful clan," he replied, his voice strangely dispassionate. "They hold land to the west of the mountains all the way to the sea. They've allied with the MacConnells and sent a force against Lord Alasdair Stewart who holds land along their borders. There have been a few skirmishes already and it willnae be long before battle is joined. Aye, lass, ye have stumbled into the middle of a whole heap of trouble."

Fabulous. Not only had she been sent back in time, she'd been sent back right into a war!

"And Lord Stewart?" she asked. "Who is he? The man you work for?"

Finn's expression tightened. "Aye," he muttered.

"Right. Great. Why did I ever listen to Irene MacAskill?" Eleanor breathed to herself.

To her surprise, Finn's head came up suddenly. "What did ye say?"

She looked at him, a little startled. "I said I wish I'd never listened to Irene MacAskill."

His eyes flashed. "Ye know a woman called Irene MacAskill?"

"Yes," she replied. "Although I doubt you know her. She's from...well, from a long way from here, just some old woman I met."

"Just some old woman? Hardly. How do you know her?"

"Um...I don't exactly," Eleanor said, puzzled by his reaction. "I met her a couple of times. First in my homeland and again at the oak glade in—what did you call it? Brigid's Hollow?"

Finn surged to his feet. "Tell me everything!" he demanded. "Every word she said to ye!"

His skin had gone pale. There was a look on his face that Eleanor couldn't quite decipher. Fear?

"I...um..." Eleanor stammered, startled by his sudden intensity." She prattled on about destiny and fate but didn't make a whole lot of sense. Why are you so interested?"

Finn's jade eyes fixed on hers, his nostrils flared, and his hand strayed to the hilt of his dagger. He suddenly looked like a man who was either ready to flee for his life or fight for it. The hairs rose on the back of Eleanor's neck.

"What is it?" she asked, scrambling to her feet and backing away a step. "You look like you've seen a ghost. Do you know the woman?"

But that was impossible. He couldn't know her. Irene was from the twenty-first century. Wasn't she?

"Woman?" Finlay said in a voice so soft Eleanor could barely hear it. "She is no woman."

"What are you talking about?" Eleanor replied with a nervous laugh. "Of course she is! What else would she be?"

His eyes found hers. "Fae."

The word dropped between them like a stone. The prickling on the back of Eleanor's neck intensified. *Fae.* Something about that word sent a cold shiver right through her. How the hell could Finn know Irene MacAskill? Unless...

Unless she travels through time too, she thought. *Unless she is one of these 'Fae' Finn seems so frightened of.*

She shook her head. "Look, I only met her a couple of times. First she turned up in my doctor's office back in the US and then she was standing by the oak grove when I went walking. I barely even spoke to her and I'm sure it's coincidence that she turned up right before I got lost."

"There are no coincidences where the Fae are concerned," Finn replied. Almost under his breath, he added, "I should know. Damn the lot of them. What are they up to now?"

Eleanor crossed her arms. "Are you going to tell me what this is all about? You look like you're going to faint."

Finlay passed a hand across his face and when he removed it he looked a little calmer. He blew out a breath and took his hand away from his dagger hilt.

"Tales of the Fae are woven into our history as surely as the blood that runs in our veins. They are fairy creatures, immortal and ancient beyond our ken. It is said they founded Alba countless millennia ago and they reside here still, out of sight of mortals—except for those few who choose to meddle in mortal affairs." He fixed Eleanor with that piercing gaze. "Those like Irene MacAskill."

Eleanor gave a shaky laugh. "Irene, a fairy? Are you serious? Why would you even think that?"

"Because I met her too," he said quietly. "Only a few hours before I met ye. Like I said, there are no coincidences where the Fae are concerned."

Eleanor stared at him. She tried to recall everything Irene had said but her thoughts scattered like leaves in the breeze. She hugged her arms around herself, suddenly cold, despite the campfire. None of this made any sense. Surely it was all just some big mistake?

"I have no idea about Fae. All I want to do is go home." She hated how shaky her voice sounded.

Finlay regarded her for a long moment. Then he nodded. "Aye. Mayhap ye are right and it is merely chance that she crossed yer path." He gestured to the bed roll. "Get some sleep, lass. We'll leave at first light. If the weather holds we should reach Brigid's Hollow by midday tomorrow."

Eleanor nodded dumbly. She was suddenly exhausted and slumped down onto the bed roll. Finlay seated himself by the roots of a tall beech tree and leaned back against the trunk.

"What about you?" Eleanor asked. "You need rest too."

He shook his head. "I'll keep watch for a while. Dinna worry, lass. Sleep."

Using her arm as a pillow, Eleanor lay down and closed her eyes. The last thing she saw as sleep reached up and pulled her under was the firelight dancing in Finlay's green, green eyes.

Chapter 5

In only moments the lass's breathing evened out as she fell into sleep. Finlay wasn't surprised. She must be exhausted. The ordeal she'd been through today would have taken its toll on even the most seasoned of warriors and the lass was an outlander, lost and alone in a country far from her own.

He glanced at her. Her fiery colored hair spread out around her head like a halo and the firelight made it glint like burnished copper. Her creamy skin was smooth and her full lips were open slightly as she breathed deeply in sleep.

Finlay felt something stir inside. Lord, she was a beauty. She had a fiery temper to match her complexion and a bravery he'd rarely seen in a lass.

Who was she? And why had she burst into his life so suddenly?

Irene MacAskill. It all came back to that strange old woman. Why had the Fae—for Fae he was certain the old woman was—decided to meddle in his life once again? Hadn't they taken enough from him? Why would they not leave him be?

He realized he'd grabbed his dagger and was holding the hilt so tightly that his knuckles had gone white. He forced himself to relax. Curse Irene MacAskill and her damned meddling! And curse him for getting involved with the Fae in the first place!

Ye entered yer bargain willingly, a voice said in the back of his head, *knowing the price. Would ye do things differently given the choice?*

He knew he would not. He and his brothers had made their choice, the only choice they could to save their clan. Finlay would sacrifice his life a thousand times over to save his people.

Ironic then isn't it? whispered that ever-present little voice. *That ye now serve the man who wants to destroy them?*

That old, familiar guilt opened inside like a rotten flower. For a moment it was so strong that he gasped from the pain of it and squeezed his eyes shut as he pushed back the bleakness that threatened to swallow him. That way lay madness.

Aye, he'd traded away his life and for what? To become a traitor?

I had no choice! he thought bitterly.

He breathed deeply through his nostrils as pain flared down the length of his spine. His tattoo was beginning to burn. He'd been too long away from his master already, too long in obeying his orders. Hound, the men called him. It was an apt nickname.

Gritting his teeth, he growled, "Nay, ye willnae have me this time. I *will* see the lass safely home regardless of what ye do to me. I will keep at least one oath in my miserable life."

He leaned against the tree trunk, teeth bared against the searing pain. Above him an owl alighted silently on a branch and gazed down at him with huge round eyes before gliding silently off into the woods. Something rustled in the undergrowth and the striped head of a badger poked through the branches of a bush, saw Finn sitting there, then turned and disappeared back the way it had come.

In his youth Finlay had loved nights like this. He'd often gone out alone, normally avoiding some chore, and instead spent hours walking the land around Dun Ringill. As the youngest of the three MacAuley brothers he'd been free of the burdens of leadership imposed on Logan, his eldest brother, and the strictures of captaining the garrison like his middle brother Camdan, and as a result Finn had valued his freedom above all else.

Yet he'd agreed to a bargain that made him a slave.

His tattoo burned, turning his back into a sheet of fiery pain. Finn pushed it to the back of his mind, refusing to let it consume him. Instead, he did the thing he always did when his curse threatened to devour him, the only thing that brought him any relief.

He began to sing.

ELEANOR'S SLEEP WAS troubled by bad dreams. From the moment her head hit the mat, exhaustion swept up and swallowed her. But it was not rest. She found herself plunged into nightmare, the same nightmare she'd experienced over and over since that fateful day.

"Mom!" Eleanor cried, pointing. "Look!"

Without waiting for her mom's reply, Eleanor pelted over to the shop window, staring longingly at the dress displayed inside. It was perfect.

Eleanor turned when she realized her mom hadn't followed her. Annie Stevenson was leaning on the wall a few paces away, looking decidedly pale, one hand pressed against her chest.

"Mom, are you okay?" Eleanor asked.

Annie smiled. "Sure I am, honey. Just having one of my funny turns, you know how it is? I'll be fine in a second."

Eleanor hesitated. Then the lure of the dress became too much. "You have to see this dress! It's amazing!"

She turned back to the shop window and waited for her mom to catch up with her. But her mom never came and Eleanor heard a sudden thud from behind her.

That ever present guilt welled up inside. *No. Not again. I'm sorry!* Eleanor shouted into the void. *I didn't know what to do!* But the guilt wasn't interested in her excuses. It grabbed her, began pulling her down into darkness...

Then a sound intruded on the darkness. It was a voice, singing softly. Eleanor couldn't make out the words but the voice chased away the terror until the nightmare fragmented and blew away like sparks from a bonfire.

Eleanor opened her eyes. She was lying facing the fire which crackled merrily only a few feet away. Finn was sitting exactly where he'd been when she'd fallen asleep, his back against the tree, his long legs stretched out in front of him. His bow leaned against the tree and his dagger was driven into the earth by his side. He was singing.

His eyes were fixed on the darkness beyond the fire and he hadn't realized she'd awoken. For a moment Eleanor just lay there, watching him, listening. His voice was beautiful. Deep and rich, he would put most club singers to shame. She didn't understand any of the words, as they were in Gaelic, but there was something about it that spoke of longing and sorrow but something else as well. Hope.

Eleanor lay still, not wanting to disturb him, until finally he fell silent and stared out into the night with a faraway look on his face. Only then did she shift position. Finlay's eyes snapped to her and their gazes met across the flickering flames.

"My apologies," he murmured. "Did I wake ye?"

She shook her head. "That song. It sounded so sad. What was it about?"

Instead of answering he turned to stare into the darkness for a moment. "It's an ancient song sung by my people. It tells the story of a Fae woman who fell in love with a mortal man."

"What happened to them?"

He shrugged. "They spent a long life together and then he died. She lived on and became a guardian of the Highlands." He picked up a branch and started poking at the fire. "Get some sleep, lass. We have a long journey ahead of us tomorrow."

Exhaustion washed over her again. Her eyes slid closed and she drifted into sleep. This time there were no dreams.

ELEANOR AWOKE THE NEXT morning feeling stiff and sore. Her muscles ached from her flight through the woods and then the long trek with Finn. As she climbed gingerly to her feet, she found herself uncurling slowly like an old woman. Eleanor had always prided herself on keeping herself in shape and she could run ten kilometers with ease but it seemed the Highlands of the sixteenth century required a hardier disposition.

Stretching her arms over her head, she looked around. A pink smudge along the horizon told her that the sun would soon rise and already the chilly spring morning was alive with birdsong. The fire had died to embers which glowed in the still air and Finlay was crouching beside it. A small pot sat in the coals, bubbling softly.

"Good morning, lass," Finlay said with a small smile. "Would ye care for some tea?"

There were dark circles under his eyes and he looked weary, despite the smile. Jeez, had he slept at all? It took a moment for his question to penetrate Eleanor's still foggy brain and when it did the incongruous idea of sitting in the Highlands, hundreds of years in the past, whilst sipping tea made her shake her head. This place certainly was crazy.

"You know what," she said, wrapping her arms around herself to keep warm and then crouching by the fire opposite him, "a cup of tea sounds fantastic. My mom used to say that a cup of tea and a chat would solve all the world's ills." She smiled wryly. "Stupid, eh?"

"Nay, lass," he replied. "It sounds to me as though yer ma is a mighty wise woman."

Was, Eleanor thought. *Was a mighty wise woman.*

She watched as Finn lifted the pot from the fire with a forked branch and carefully poured the contents into a small pottery beaker which he handed to Eleanor. She took it with a grateful nod and wrapped her fingers around it, enjoying the warmth that seeped into her chilled bones. It smelled of a mixture of herbs and as she set it to her lips, she thought she detected mint and chamomile.

Finn drank his own tea straight from the small cooking pot and then rummaged in his bag and tossed her another strip of dried meat. He shrugged apologetically. "If we make good time ye will be home by midday and nay doubt be enjoying a good home-cooked meal."

"Home-cooked?" Eleanor said, raising an eyebrow. "You wouldn't say that if you'd ever tasted my cooking. As soon as I get back, I'll be driving to the nearest burger bar and having the biggest, greasiest, most unhealthy burger I can lay my hands on!"

Finn stared at her with an uncomprehending look on his face and Eleanor cursed inwardly. Dammit! She must watch what she said lest anyone suspect her origins. Who knew how the people of this time would react to the idea of time travel? For all she knew they would think she was a witch and try to burn her at the stake!

She busied herself drinking her tea and munching on the strip of jerky. Finn began eating his own breakfast. Silence descended, punctuated only by the chirping of the birds that flitted through the branches above them.

Eleanor found her thoughts turning towards home. Today she would return to the hollow oak tree, the arch through time, and home. The relief was so great that she felt a little giddy.

Finn finished his jerky, downed the last dregs of his drink, and then upended the pot over the fire to douse the flames. He rose to his feet, a slight grimace of pain twisting his mouth.

"We'd better get moving."

Eleanor climbed to her feet. "We aren't going anywhere until I've checked your wound."

He shook his head. "There's nay need. It's only—"

"Only nothing!" she snapped. "I won't have anyone under my care die because I didn't do my job properly!" *Not again*, that traitorous little voice in the back of her head whispered. *Never again.*

She pushed the voice away, crossed her arms, and raised her eyebrow at Finn.

He hesitated and then let out a sigh. "If ye insist."

He seated himself cross-legged on the bed roll and pulled off his shirt. Eleanor knelt by his side, unwrapped the makeshift bandage and gently probed the wound with her fingertips. She was relieved to find no sign of infection. The skin, although a little inflamed, did not feel hot and had scabbed over nicely. In fact, it was healing much more quickly than Eleanor expected.

"Good," she said. "It looks good. I'll re-bandage it but when you get home I want you to get your physician to have a look at it. If it starts to feel hot, you will need to apply a warm compress to help drain any infection."

He gave her a crooked smile. "Aye, my lady."

His eyes met hers and Eleanor was suddenly all too aware of how close they were. She cleared her throat and stood up abruptly.

"Right," she muttered. "Are we going to get out of here or what?"

"Aye, we are," he replied softly.

He stood and quickly pulled his shirt back over his head, wincing slightly as the fabric brushed his wound. He shouldered his pack, slung the bow across his back, and sheathed his dagger at his side. Then, with one last quick look around the campsite, he nodded at Eleanor and then led the way into the woods.

They made good time in the quiet spring morning and, as she strode along silently by Finn's side, Eleanor found her thoughts turning towards home. In a few hours she would be back in her normal life. She would be seeing patients, doing the dishes, setting the alarm clock and groaning in annoyance when it went off. So simple. So normal. So...so...empty. The sudden thought startled her.

Isn't that what you want? she asked herself. *This little jaunt into the past is addling your brain. The sooner you get home and leave all this behind, the better.*

She found herself glancing at Finn. He was unlike any person Eleanor had ever met. There was a quiet confidence about him, and yet she sometimes saw a glimpse of a deep sorrow in his eyes, quickly hidden. Yes there was more to him than met the eye but he must remain a mystery when she returned home and left him behind.

She asked Finn about the flora and fauna as they walked and he answered her questions patiently, smiling a little as though she was asking things any Highlander would have known since they were a child.

Eleanor didn't care. As she relaxed, she found herself enjoying Finn's easy company. He poked gentle fun at her when she slipped on a riverbank and went sliding down on her backside but then gallantly held out his hand and helped her to her feet before half-carrying her back to the trail.

They were walking through a copse off scraggly trees when Finn suddenly grabbed her and dragged her behind a tree. Eleanor yelped in alarm and Finn's hand clamped over her mouth. He pressed his finger to his lips to indicate silence.

Eleanor nodded to show she understood his warning. Slowly, Finn guided her to a gap between two branches that gave a good few of the meadow beyond and pointed.

Eleanor peered through the gap, trying to see what had caught his attention. Then she spotted it. A huge red deer stag was feeding in the meadow. He hadn't seen them and was completely relaxed as he grazed. He looked old, with a thick ruff of hair around his shoulders, scars from previous battles on his flanks, and a huge set of antlers that stretched out, attesting to his prowess.

For a reason she couldn't explain, Eleanor was suddenly reminded of Irene MacAskill. Like the stag, Irene was old and bore the marks of her age with easy dignity. And despite that age Irene radiated power and strength, just like the stag in front of her.

"Wow," she whispered. "He's magnificent."

"Aye," Finn replied softly." But I fear this year's rut will be his last."

His hand rested on her arm and he was standing so close his hip touched hers. It was the lightest of touches and Eleanor wasn't sure whether he was aware of the contact but she sure as hell was. The soft pressure of his weight made her heart beat a little more rapidly than it should. He was so near that she could smell the scent of pine needles wafting from his dark hair.

Eleanor swallowed thickly, thinking of how she should extricate herself from his hold. But she didn't move.

FINLAY TRIED VERY HARD to concentrate but it was almost impossible with Eleanor this close. He'd grabbed her without thinking, wanting to show her the stag in the meadow, but now he realized he hadn't released her and she hadn't asked him to. Her weight against him felt good, really good, and there was a faint scent to her, something between rose petals and lavender. He had no desire to move, to break the light contact between them, even though he knew he should.

Something stirred within him as they crouched together, watching the stag, sharing this secret moment. Something he couldn't quite name.

In the meadow the stag suddenly lifted its head, snorting in alarm. Then, with a flattening of its ears, it fled, pounding across the meadow and disappearing into the forest in the blink of an eye.

Finn tensed. He rested his hand on his dagger hilt and gazed in the direction the stag had gone, suddenly uneasy.

"What is it?" Eleanor asked. "What's wrong?"

He held up a hand for silence and slowly rose from his crouch. A noise carried on the air, coming closer. The drum of hoof beats. Finn drew his dagger, just as a mounted figure burst from the trees behind them, pulling his horse to a halt in a shower of mud.

Finn pushed Eleanor behind him and swung around to face the rider. The man's head was shaved to a fine black stubble and he fixed cold eyes on Finn.

"Finlay! There ye are!" the man snapped. "Lord Stewart sent me to find ye. Ye stand accused of desertion and the penalty is hanging!"

Chapter 6

Eleanor's heart thumped in her chest. Who the hell was this man? Where had he come from? Compact and muscular with a head shaved down to black stubble, he wore the same plaid as Angus and his men.

"Desertion?" Finlay snapped, his voice cracking like a whip. "What are ye talking about, Broag, ye damned fool! I'm here on Lord Stewart's business!"

"Really?" The man called Broag said. "Then why have ye not returned to give yer report? Why are ye wandering the wild with this lass?"

Other riders emerged from the trees. Eleanor counted at least six, all well armed and cold-eyed. They were leading a spare horse.

Finn scanned the men as though assessing his options. "Call yerself a tracker?" he growled at Broag. "Ye canna see what is right in front of yer eyes! Canna ye see that I'm taking this lass back to Lord Stewart right now?"

Broag narrowed his eyes. "Is that so? If she's a prisoner, why didnae ye just let Angus and his squad bring her back yesterday?" Seeing the look on Finn's face he nodded. "Oh, aye. They returned last night and gave a full account of what and who they'd encountered. Lord Stewart isnae best pleased his hound has refused to heel."

Finlay ground his teeth and a vein began to throb in his temple. Eleanor watched the two men with her heart in her mouth. What was Finn talking about? Taking her to Lord Stewart? He was leading her to the archway! He'd given his word!

"Angus?" Finn spat, his voice full of disgust. "Ye would have me leave the lass in his care? When he has Balloch in his squad? Would ye have the lass beaten and raped before Lord Stewart could question her?"

A sudden look of uncertainty crossed Broag's face. Then he shook his head. "It's fortunate then, isnae it that my men and I are here to escort ye and yer prisoner safely home?"

Finn waved a hand nonchalantly. "Aye, I suppose it beats walking. And ye brought me a horse I see. Most kind."

"Get her mounted up," Broag snapped. "Lord Stewart will have both our hides if we delay any longer."

To Eleanor's shock, Finlay suddenly grabbed her by the wrists, his grip hard enough to hurt.

"What are you doing?" she cried. "Let me go!"

Finn's face was an expressionless mask, his eyes cold. "Do as ye are told for once, woman!"

He uncerimoniously dragged her across the clearing to the spare horse. She resisted, pulling against his grip, but he was far too strong for her and he yanked her along as easily as if she was a child.

Reaching the horse he pushed her towards the stirrups whilst he held the horse steady with one hand.

"Get up."

Eleanor glared at him. What the hell was he playing at? She studied his face, searching for any hint of his intentions but that cold, expressionless mask didn't waver. He stared at her impatiently.

"Get on the horse," he snapped. "Or I will throw ye on myself."

Sudden anger flared in Eleanor's chest. "Go to hell!"

With a growl of annoyance he grabbed her elbow. She reacted instinctively, swinging her free hand in a punch at his face. Dimly, she was aware of the men gathered in a circle around them. They were watching this exchange intently. Almost nonchalantly, Finn caught her forearm before her punch could connect and then grabbed her around the waist. He lifted her as though she weighed no more than a doll and thrust her into the saddle.

He swung up behind her, settling easily into the saddle and then reached around her to grab the reins. The horse was huge and the top of its back seemed incredibly high to Eleanor. She clutched grimly onto the saddle horn with both hands as Finlay kicked the horse into motion and they rode from the clearing.

"What are you doing?" she hissed at Finn under her breath. "Where are you taking me?"

"Quiet!" he breathed in her ear. "Dinna say a word. Both our lives may depend on it."

She clamped her mouth shut and did her best to fight down the swirling fear in her stomach. Broag and his men surrounded her and Finlay in a broad circle, blocking any chance of escape.

She laughed bitterly to herself. Escape? Where exactly would she go?

Finn rode expertly, holding the reins lightly and steadying her every time she swayed in the saddle. For Eleanor, the ride was torture. The terrain was uneven and bumpy, the horses moved swiftly, and Eleanor's backside was soon bruised from being bounced around like a sack of apples. But she soon realized that a bruised backside was the least of her worries.

After riding for about an hour, they must have passed some sort of border because the wilderness began to recede to be replaced by small settlements, little more than isolated farmsteads and crofts. They looked abandoned, with no animals grazing in the fields and the doors to the cottages swinging open in the wind. Further on, they began running into mounted patrols. Each time the patrols would stop them, ask their business, and then wave them on their way.

At last they began to descend a sharp incline into a valley with a loch sparkling at its bottom. Around the shores of the loch Eleanor saw people milling around. Hundreds of people, perhaps thousands. They were housed in tents, giving the place the look of a shantytown. A large, stone building sat at the mouth of the valley. It was too small to be called a castle but bigger than a house. Its lower story was constructed of gray stone, its upper story timber, and a thatched roof covered the top. She could see no windows on the ground floor and the only door was reached by steps that led up to the first level. The windows were narrow, easily defensible. Eleanor guessed it must be some kind of fortified manor house. The large wall surrounding the house gave another clue.

They rode down a muddy trail and into the encampment. There were armed men everywhere. On a patch of cleared ground some were practicing fighting in close quarters. The clink of metal on metal and the grunt of exertion was loud enough to carry over the hubbub of the camp. Others were crouched around campfires, eating, drinking, and playing games of dice. Nobody paid Eleanor's group any attention as they skirted the banks of the loch and approached the manor house.

They were stopped at the gates by three heavily armed guards but were quickly ushered through when Broag explained who they were. They entered a cobbled courtyard. Finn pulled the horse to a halt and stable boys came running.

Finn dismounted and then held out a hand. Eleanor ignored the proffered help, and tried to dismount by herself. She swung one leg over the horse's broad back and kept a tight hold of the saddle as she slid ungraciously to the ground. She heard Broag's men snigger but Finn's arm suddenly went around her, steadying her and stopping her falling on her backside on the muddy cobbles.

She wrenched free of his grip and this made Broag's men snicker all the harder.

"She's a feisty one," Broag said. "I'm sure Lord Stewart will like her!"

The men's laughter sent a shiver right down Eleanor's spine.

"Come on," Finn snapped at them. "The sooner I get rid of this lass, the sooner I can get some food and ale."

Grabbing Eleanor roughly by the arm, he marched her up the broad steps to the door on the first level. Kicking it open, he dragged her into the dim interior. A wood-paneled corridor stretched ahead of her. Tapestries hung from the walls and the flagstone floor looked freshly scrubbed. Arched doorways marched down either side of the corridor, some closed, some open, and it was to one of these that Finn marched Eleanor.

From inside a voice shouted, "I dinna care if they have an army of Fae creatures and the king's best knights to boot! I *will* have their surrender or, by God, I will crush the whole stinking lot of them!"

There was a crash as if something had been thrown across the room and then two old men carrying rolled up parchment under their arms, hurried out, both looking flustered and hardly giving Finn or Eleanor a glance.

Finn strode through the door without knocking, pulling Eleanor behind him. Broag followed behind, taking a position by the door. Eleanor found herself in a high-ceilinged room. Narrow windows let in only a meager amount of light and candles burned in sconces on the walls. The room was sparsely furnished, with just a large table in the center strewn with documents and two chairs by the fireplace at the far end. A man leaned on that fireplace with his back to them, his hands gripping the stone mantelpiece until they went white.

"If ye bring me more bad news," the man growled without turning, "ye can damn well go back to where ye came from! I've had a belly full of it today!"

"Whether my news is good or ill is for ye to judge, my lord," Finlay replied.

The man spun at the sound of Finn's voice. His eyes widened and then he broke into a grin.

"Ah! Finlay, my faithful hound! So, Broag found ye then? My nephew claims ye deserted and ran off with some MacAuley spy!"

Finlay cocked his head. "And what do ye think, my lord?" His voice was quiet.

The man narrowed his eyes. He looked to be somewhere in his late forties and had narrow features and something of the aristocrat about him. His plaid bore the same pattern as everyone else, except Finlay, but his was thicker, the fabric richer and his fingers sported several golden rings. His dark hair was scraped back in a ponytail at the back of his head. He fixed a sharp, shrewd gaze on her and Finn.

"I think he was talking horse shit," the man replied. "We both know the depths of yer loyalty, dinna we, my faithful hound? Ye wouldnae risk all we have achieved together for the sake of one wench." His gaze sharpened. "Would ye?"

Finlay ground his teeth. "Nay, my lord."

A flash of triumph crossed the man's face and for an instant Eleanor saw undisguised malice shining in his eyes but it was gone in an instant. "So I wonder why ye didnae return yesterday as ye were ordered? And when ye finally do come back, ye bring this wench with ye?"

His gaze snapped to Eleanor and she felt a flash of fear. The man's eyes were as cold and dead as those of a snake. He watched Eleanor dispassionately, like a snake would watch its prey, deciding whether it would devour her whole or toy with her first. Lifting her chin defiantly, she gazed steadily at him, refusing to show any of the turmoil that twisted her insides.

Finn stepped forward. "I didnae return yesterday because I picked up the trail of Angus's patrol. When I found them I decided to relieve them of their prisoner as I didnae believe she would be safe with them and was bringing her here when Broag found us. Lady Eleanor Stevenson, may I introduce Lord Alasdair Stewart?"

"Lady Stevenson?" Lord Stewart said. "The MacAuleys are employing noblewomen as their spies these days?"

His mocking tone stung her to anger. "I am no spy, god dammit!" she snapped. "What is wrong with you people? Do I look like a spy to you? All I want is to be allowed to go home! I demand you release me!"

Lord Stewart's eyes widened momentarily in surprise. He looked her up and down, taking in her clothing. Then he gave her a slight, mocking bow. "My apologies, my lady. Yer accent is mighty strange. An outlander at a guess?"

"She's from America," Finn said. "Across the sea."

Lord Stewart glanced at him, annoyed that he answered for her.

"Yes," she replied, forcing her voice to steadiness. "I'm only a visitor in your land and have nothing to do with the MacAuleys or your damned war!"

Lord Alasdair Stewart stared at her for a long moment. "Ah, ye are good. The clothing, the accent, even the jewellery. Why, ye almost had me believing ye. But Logan MacAuley is a fool if he thinks I will fall for his ruse. Spies, my dear, come in all shapes and sizes."

"You're not listening!" Eleanor snapped. "Read my lips. I. Am. Not. A. Spy!"

A flare of annoyance crossed the man's face at her tone. Before he could speak Finlay cleared his throat.

"She speaks the truth. I questioned her thoroughly and I dinna believe she's a spy."

"Then why bring her here?" Lord Stewart growled. "If she isnae a spy, what value is she to me? Ye should have let Balloch have her, the lad needs his rewards after all."

Finlay's eyes flashed. He seemed to be struggling to keep his temper. "She is a doctor. She treated my wound with skill."

Lord Stewart's eyes sparked with interest. "A doctor? But she is a woman."

"And an outlander with ways different to our own. She claims in her homeland women are allowed to do all sorts."

Stewart stalked over to Eleanor, moving with the feline grace of a predator. He might wear fancy clothes and have the look of an aristocrat but Eleanor knew this man was dangerous. She stood her ground as he came to stand in front of her, his cold blue eyes studying her face.

"What would a trained physician be doing wandering a disputed border in the Highlands?" he asked quietly.

Eleanor got the impression that her fate depended on her answer. Swallowing thickly, she decided she would stick as close to the truth as possible. That way she'd be less likely to be caught out in a lie.

"I was invited here by the people of a settlement some distance away. They hadn't got a physician of their own and offered me a position in their community. I accepted. When

I arrived I decided to explore my new home. However, whilst I was exploring I got lost and your men found me."

"Exploring?" Lord Stewart snorted. "On yer own and without men-folk to escort ye? Did ye lose yer wits as well as yer path?"

"Where I come from," Eleanor stated coldly. "A woman is safe to go walking on her own without getting set upon by a band of unwashed louts!"

Stewart barked a laugh, the sound sharp and loud enough to make Eleanor jump. "Ha! Ye have more balls than most of my men! What was this settlement ye claim to come from?"

"It's called Achfarn," she replied. "Close to a grove of oak trees called—"

"St. Helen's kirk," Finlay cut in. "The lass told me it lies close to the ruins of St. Helen's kirk."

Eleanor looked at him sharply. Why was he lying to Stewart?

Stewart narrowed his eyes at Finn. Suspicion flared in them for a moment. Finn met his lord's gaze, unflinching, and after a moment, Stewart waved his hand dismissively.

"It hardly matters. Ye are on my land now and that makes ye my property." The cold gaze fixed on her again and he lifted her chin with the tip of his finger. "We shall see. If ye are a physician mayhap I can make use of ye. If not—" He shrugged. "Ye can entertain the men like the rest of the camp whores. Take her away." He stepped back, waving at Broag.

The man grabbed Eleanor by the arm. "This way, my lady."

"Wait!" Eleanor cried as Broag dragged her to the door. "What are you doing? Let me go! Finn!"

She twisted in Broag's grip to get a view of Finlay but he didn't even look in her direction. He was staring out of the window, no expression on his face at all.

She fought Broag's grip as he yanked her along the hallway to a stout wooden door. The man's fingers were like pincers pressing into her skin and her struggling only made him hold her all the tighter. He said not a word until he'd unlocked the door and pushed her unceremoniously inside.

"Want some free advice?" he growled. "Behave yerself and dinna anger Lord Stewart."

With that he left, slamming the door behind him and locking it. Eleanor stared stupidly at the closed door for a minute and then slowly looked around. She was in a small, sparse room. It might once have been a bedroom but no bed sat there now, only a musty pallet thrown into a corner. The walls were covered in mouldy plaster and the whole place stank of damp. The two windows were little more than arrow-slits, barely wide enough to get her arm through. No chance of escape that way. A fireplace sat against one wall, cold and empty, with a single candle on the mantelpiece.

Eleanor crossed to one of the windows and pressed her face up against it, trying to see out. A narrow slice of the army camp was all she could make out. Armed men strode everywhere and the only other women she spotted were scantily dressed and hanging around outside a rickety wooden structure little more than a hut. Even as she watched a man approached one of the women, threw his arm around her shoulders and allowed her to lead him into the hut.

Eleanor gulped. *And if not ye can entertain the men, like the rest of the camp whores.*

Her legs suddenly wouldn't hold her up anymore. She crashed to her knees on the hard floorboards, wrapped her arms around herself and cried.

Chapter 7

It took all Finlay's willpower to resist Eleanor's pleas as Broag dragged her from the room. She called his name, her voice full of fear and confusion. His muscles trembled with the effort of remaining still.

He schooled his face into that expressionless mask he'd developed over the years, letting none of his turbulent emotions show on his face. Instead, he stared through the window as Broag took her away, seeing nothing, hearing only Eleanor's cries disappear into the distance. If Stewart guessed that Eleanor was anything more than an annoyance to Finn he would find a way to use her against him.

The man said nothing but Finlay could feel him watching. Did he suspect the truth? Did he suspect that Finn hadn't been bringing Eleanor here at all but had been disobeying a direct order by taking Eleanor to Brigid's Hollow?

He turned to Lord Stewart. Scowling, he said, "If there's naught else, I'll take my leave. I've ridden a long way and I'm damned hungry."

Stewart held up a hand. "One moment."

Involuntarily Finn's fingers curled into fists and he forced himself to relax. Lord Stewart saw the movement and a smile flitted across his face.

"Oh, I see what's curling through yer veins right now, my hound," he said softly. "Ye are fighting the urge to strike me, are ye not? Ye have learned to school yer feelings well but ye canna hide them from me. I ken how much ye ache to plunge that bronze dagger of yers into my heart but we both know how that will end for ye, dinna we?"

Finlay said nothing. Hatred for this man seethed through his veins like molten metal. Aye, he would like naught more than to end his life. But he couldn't. His curse saw to that and the scars that crisscrossed his own body bore testament to how many times he'd tried, regardless of the cost.

"I am required to serve ye," he growled. "I am not required to like ye."

Stewart cocked his head. "Aye, but ye are required to follow my orders. If ye disobey me again, I will visit such pain on ye that ye will be reduced to a mewling babe, pissing his own breeches."

Finlay almost did it. He almost grabbed the dagger sheathed at his side and be damned with the consequences. Only the thought of Eleanor stopped him.

"Aye, my lord," he grated. "I'll keep that in mind."

"See that ye do. We'll soon be moving out and I would have ye by my side."

"Then it's true? Battle will soon be joined?"

"Aye," Stewart growled. "The bastards have us all but surrounded. Cornered like animals. Only the pass to the west remains open. We'll soon be forced to stand and fight."

Finn said nothing. Why had Stewart told him this? The man was normally taciturn and mistrustful. Was he testing Finn's loyalty?

"I trust ye know where yer true loyalty lies, Hound?" Stewart said, as though reading his thoughts. "I trust ye willnae be tempted to contact yer former... friends?"

Sudden anger flared in Finn's veins. "Still?" he snapped, his fists clenching and his lips pulling back from his teeth in a snarl. "After all these years? After all I have done in yer name? Still ye doubt me?"

He took a step forward, quivering with fury, and was pleased when Stewart stepped back.

"I have betrayed everyone," he growled. "Become the very thing I loathe because of ye. I should kill ye where ye stand!"

Stewart threw up a hand and searing pain exploded out from the tattoo on Finn's back. It was strong enough to drive him to his knees and for a moment he feared he would black out. But he fought it. Pulling breaths through his nose he climbed to his feet, staring at Stewart without flinching. He thought he detected a slight unease in Stewart's gaze.

Aye, ye bastard, he thought. *Ye canna break me, can ye? One day I will kill ye. Ye are right to fear me.*

Stewart flicked his hand and the pain disappeared, leaving Finn's limbs weak and sore. "Never forget who is yer master, Hound," Stewart whispered.

He nodded, dismissing Finn, who made his way to the door.

Stewart asked suddenly, "What is the lass to ye?"

Finn froze and then turned around slowly. He met Stewart's gaze and pulled the emotionless mask over his face. "She is naught to me but a pain the rear I am glad to be rid of. I have better things to do with my time than playing nursemaid to an outland woman who doesnae have the sense of a bairn. She's yer problem now."

Then, before Stewart could reply, he stalked through the door. He only hoped that Stewart didn't hear the lie in his voice.

ELEANOR LAY ON THE hard pallet, staring at the ceiling. Tears of fear and frustration rolled down her face. How the hell had she ended up here? How was she going to get out? The thoughts went around and around in her head with no answer emerging. Eventually she fell into fitful sleep.

She woke the next morning with a start. She'd fallen asleep fully clothed in an awkward position and her back ached. But a good night's sleep had left her calmer. She could think rationally. Get out of here. Get home. It was the only thought that kept going round and round in her head.

Damn this accursed place! And damn Irene MacAskill for bringing her here! Her anger warmed her a little and she sat up, examining the room, looking for any weakness that might aid her escape. She didn't find any. With the door locked, the windows were the only other exits and they were so narrow that not even a child could squeeze through.

With a small growl of annoyance she climbed to her feet and crossed to the door. Pressing her ear against the hard wood, she went very still and listened. She heard nothing from the other side and the only sounds that reached her were those of the camp coming through the window. No, wait. She tensed. What was that? Footsteps! And they were coming this way!

Quickly she pressed herself against the wall behind the door and waited. The steps halted outside her door and the key rattled in the lock. Her heart began to thump and she curled her fingers into her palms, digging her nails into her flesh and using the sudden pain to ground herself. This might be her only chance of escape. She had to take it.

The door swung slowly open and a guard stepped into her room. Eleanor darted through the door behind him and made a run for it down the corridor.

But she'd gone less than ten paces when a heavy weight slammed into her from behind sending her tumbling onto the hard flagstone floor. She landed with a yelp as arms like tree roots went around her waist and she was picked up and slung over a shoulder. She tried to scream but a hand clamped over her mouth as she was unceremoniously carried back to the room.

The guard kicked the door shut behind him and set her on her feet. Eleanor whirled to face him. Only then did she realize it wasn't Broag or one of his men. It was Finn.

"You!" Her open-handed slap caught him across the face, snapping his head to the side. "You lied to me!" She swung for him again but this time he caught her wrist before the blow could connect.

"Ye may strike me once," he growled. "Lord knows, I probably deserved it, but ye willnae strike me twice."

She glared at him, wondering if he was standing close enough for her to knee him in the privates and then make a run for it.

"Dinna even try it," Finn growled as if reading her mind.

Eleanor struggled, trying to break his hold, aiming kicks at his shins. Finlay slammed her back against the wall and pinned her there, his face only inches from her own.

"Be still, woman!" he hissed. "Somebody will hear this commotion and come to investigate! Stop fighting, ye damned wildcat! I'm here to help ye!"

"Help me? You lied to me! You said you were taking me to Brigid's Hollow and instead you bring me here! It's your fault I'm in this stinking place!"

His eyes glinted with anger. "What would ye have me do? Broag would have killed us both had I resisted!"

"So you just left me here, locked up like some criminal?"

"I couldnae see ye last night," he said. "How would that have looked? I told Stewart ye were my prisoner, remember? How many captors visit their prisoners? Now, I'm going to release ye. I would be grateful if ye dinna try to hit me again and instead listen to what I have to say. Can ye do that?"

She stared at him for a moment then nodded. He released her and stepped back a pace, crossing his arms over his broad chest and watching her.

Eleanor copied his gesture, crossing her arms and raising an eyebrow. "I'm listening."

"I need ye to trust me," he said. "I gave ye my word that I would get ye back to Brigid's Hollow and I intend to keep that promise. I will do all I can to keep ye safe whilst ye are here but ye must do as I tell ye. Understand?"

His gaze was clear and honest but she'd fallen for that once before. "How do I know you're not spinning me a line?" she asked. "How can I be sure you're not lying to me right now?"

"Ye dinna," Finn replied with a shrug. "Ye must follow yer heart."

Eleanor looked at him sharply. Follow her heart? That was exactly what Irene MacAskill had told her before Eleanor had stepped through the archway.

"I... I...don't know," she stammered. "I'm not sure what to think. What to believe."

Finn stepped closer. "I'm sorry, lass," he said softly. "I'm sorry ye were dragged into this. I canna change that now but I can swear that I will find a way to get ye safely home." He placed a finger under her chin and gently lifted her face to look at him. Eleanor found herself gazing into those deep eyes and a tingle went through her. "Do ye trust me?"

Her breathing quickened. Something subconscious answered that question. "Yes," she found herself saying. "I trust you. I must be crazy, but I do."

A sudden smile broke over his face. "Good. This camp will soon move and the army will ride into battle. When that happens I will find a way for us to slip away in the confusion. Until then ye must play yer part."

"My part? What do you mean?"

"Prove yerself useful to Lord Stewart," Finn replied. He crossed to the door and picked up a bundle that he must have dropped when he first came in. "Put this on. Whilst yer outland clothing may be acceptable in yer own land, here yer attire is a little...unusual... and will only draw unwanted attention."

Eleanor took the bundle. She untied it and shook out a long, copper colored dress. Glancing down at her skin-tight jeans, coat and boots, she realized that Finn was right. She needed to blend in and right now her clothing made her stick out like a sore thumb.

"Okay," she said, drawing in a breath. "Fit in. I can do that. Well, here goes."

She indicated for Finn to turn around and when he had his back to her she began stripping off her clothes. She felt awkward and vulnerable as she stood there in her underclothes but Finn was a perfect gentleman, resolutely staring at the wall and saying not a word.

Eleanor yanked the dress over her head and wiggled until it settled over her body. It was a perfect fit, hugging her slim waist and then flaring out down to her ankles. The arms covered her all the way to the wrists and the neckline was high enough to only show the barest slip of skin at the base of her throat. There were no zips, only a row of hooks on the back that Eleanor struggled to reach.

"Could you help me?"

Finn glanced over his shoulder, an uncomfortable expression on his face.

"I can't do up the back. Would you mind?" She gathered up her hair and held it out of the way for him.

Finn cleared his throat and for a moment looked scandalized that she would request such a thing but, perhaps realizing there was no other option, he stepped behind her and began fumbling with the hooks on the back of the dress. As he leaned down to get a better look, she felt his warm breath on the back of her neck and a shiver went through her. His fingers brushed her shoulder, the lightest of touches, but it sent goose bumps all the way down her arms.

"It's done," he said softly.

She turned around and found him so close that she almost bumped into him. Her stomach did a little flip. Jeez, what was wrong with her?

Finn's lips parted and for a moment he looked as though he would speak but then he cleared his throat and stepped back. Rubbing at the stubble that covered his chin he said, "Come. Lord Stewart wants to see ye."

Eleanor swallowed. "Right."

Finn led her from the room and up a winding staircase. At the top was a wide landing with four doors leading off. Finn knocked on one of these.

"Remember to go along with all I say or do," he said softly. Then he grabbed her arm roughly, pushed the door open, and dragged her inside.

"I've brought the lass as ye asked," he snapped in an annoyed tone of voice.

Lord Alasdair Stewart was the only occupant of the room, which seemed to be a private study. Up here, the windows were a little wider and Eleanor could see the valley spreading out below. Lord Stewart had his back to them, putting an object into a cupboard against the far wall. Eleanor only got a brief glimpse of it but it appeared to be some kind of metal implement with a long handle and a pattern of swirling metalwork attached to the end. It looked like the branding irons used to mark cattle. Stewart placed it into the cupboard carefully, as though it was precious, and then turned to face them.

Finn turned suddenly pale, his eyes fixed on the closed door of the cupboard. Alasdair Stewart watched his reaction closely and Eleanor thought she detected a slight hint of triumph in the lord's cold eyes. She glanced between the two men.

What is this? she thought to herself. *What's going on between these two?*

Finn pushed Eleanor towards Lord Stewart hard enough to make her stumble.

"If that will be all, my lord?" he said in a tight voice.

"Aye."

Finn spun on his heel and marched to the door. He didn't look at her and Eleanor forced herself to ignore him as he passed. She heard the door close behind him and she was left alone with the man who had become her captor.

Alasdair Stewart didn't speak for a long moment and merely stood looking at her, his eyes flicking over her new clothing, his expression calculating.

"What do ye think of my hound?" he asked suddenly.

The question was so unexpected that for a moment Eleanor floundered, caught off guard.

"You mean that lout that dragged me here?" she replied making her voice haughty. "What do you reckon? He's a brute and a mannerless oaf and I would thank you to keep him away from me!"

She snapped her mouth shut and glared at him, hoping she'd said the right thing. Finn had told her to follow his lead and he'd acted hostile towards her. Perhaps she should do the same. Stewart watched her for a moment.

"Aye, well, I dinna have the luxury of gentle servants, I'm afraid. My hound will have to do."

He shuffled over to a chair by the fireplace and slumped into it with a groan. A grimace of pain twisted his face and now that she saw him closer, Eleanor realized there were dark circles under his eyes.

"Why did you ask for me?"

"Is that how the master is addressed in yer homeland, my lady? Perhaps it is ye who is the mannerless lout. Ye will address me as 'my lord.'"

Eleanor drew a deep breath through her nostrils. "I'm sorry. Why did you send for me, *my lord*?"

"Ye claim to be a physician." He pulled up the kilt of his plaid to reveal his left thigh. A blood-stained bandage was wound around the meat of his leg. "Fix my leg and mayhap I will believe ye."

Eleanor heard the implied threat. *Fail to fix it and it will go badly for you*. She walked over to Stewart and knelt by his side. He leaned back in the chair, watching her carefully as he stretched out his injured leg. The bandage was dirty and who knew how much bacteria and other nasties were on that piece of material.

Gingerly she peeled away the bandage and tossed it into the fire. Beneath it, the top half of Stewart's thigh was a mess of crusted blood.

"I need water and a cloth."

Stewart waved to a dresser in the corner on which sat a pitcher of water and a large bowl with a cloth draped over the side. Eleanor fetched it, poured some of the cold water into the bowl, and began gently wiping away the blood and grime from Stewart's leg. Stewart grimaced in pain but made not a sound as she worked. Soon the water in the bowl had turned red.

She cleaned it diligently and was finally able to get a look at the wound. A slice had been taken out of Stewart's thigh, the cut clean and straight as though made with a sharp implement—a sword at a guess. The wound had been crudely stitched but now they were pulled tight over the swollen, shiny skin that had turned pink and sore with infection. It didn't yet smell, much to Eleanor's relief. Gangrene had yet to set in but if she was to save this man's leg, perhaps his life, she had to act quickly.

"Who patched you up?" she muttered. "It looks like a butcher has been at you."

"Angus," Stewart growled. "Both my physicians were captured by the MacAuleys. Just one more thing I owe Logan MacAuley for, along with this slice out of my leg."

"Well, the stitches need to come out, I'll have to drain the wound, clean it and then re-stitch it. And I'll need some supplies."

Stewart leaned forward and bellowed, "Get in here!"

A man Eleanor didn't recognise entered.

"Lady Stevenson will give ye a list of things she needs," Stewart said. "Ye will find them and bring them immediately. Understand?"

The man nodded. "Aye, lord."

Eleanor reeled off a list of supplies, substituting some of them—such as antiseptic—for what she hoped were sixteenth century equivalents.

The man left and Eleanor busied herself by heating water in a pot on the fire.

"Do you have a knife?"

Lord Stewart's eyes narrowed suspiciously and Eleanor rolled her eyes. "I'm not going to stab you with it. I need to take your stitches out."

Lord Stewart unsheathed the dagger at his side and held it out hilt first. Eleanor took it and dropped it into the pot of boiling water.

"Why are ye doing that?" Lord Stewart asked.

How was she supposed to explain about bacteria and infection to somebody from this time? "It's something we do in my homeland," she said. "We find if we clean the apparatus first it speeds healing."

There was a knock on the door and it opened to admit the guard, arms laden with the supplies Eleanor had requested. She nodded at the side board and he placed them where she indicated, giving Lord Stewart an odd look. He waved the man out irritably.

Eleanor inspected the sheet she'd asked him to bring. Yes it was clean, obviously freshly laundered, and would do for bandages. There were several needles and some strong thread along with a pot of honey and a bottle of whisky. She dumped the needles and thread in the boiling water alongside the dagger.

When she was satisfied it was sufficiently sterilised, she fished out the dagger and knelt by Lord Stewart.

"This will hurt. There's nothing I can do about that."

"Just do it," he growled.

Eleanor pressed the tip of the dagger under the first of the stitches and quickly sliced it. Stewart grunted in pain but said not a word. Eleanor quickly pulled out the stitch and then worked on the others. Pus and blood began oozing from the wound. She used the dagger to make a small incision at one end of the wound, and it began to flow more freely. Good. It would allow the infection inside to drain away.

"Hold that to your leg," she instructed Stewart, handing him a piece of the sheet she'd sliced off. "Use it to catch the blood but don't let it touch the wound. I'll be back in a moment."

Dropping the dagger back into the boiling water she took the bottle of whisky and pulled out the cork with her teeth. Alcohol could be used as a disinfectant and she hoped this local brew would do the trick. Returning to Stewart's side she gently probed the wound to check that all the infection had drained and then tipped the bottle of whisky all over it, flushing out the last of any nastiness.

Stewart hissed in pain but Eleanor ignored him, all her attention fixed on her work. As often happened when she was doctoring, she clicked into autopilot and her focus narrowed to only her patient and the problem in hand. A calmness came over her and she no longer saw a sixteenth century warlord who was holding her prisoner, or a grimy manor house in the middle of nowhere, she saw only an injury and the things she needed to do to fix it.

Having flushed out the wound, she took the needle from the pot of boiling water, threaded it, and then quickly stitched up the wound with small neat stitches, leaving it open at one end to allow any further infection to drain away. Lastly, she smeared it with honey as an antiseptic and wound a clean bandage tightly around the leg.

When she was finished she rocked back on her heels and looked at Stewart. His face was pale and there was a thin sheen of sweat on his forehead.

"You need to rest," she said. "If you move around too much on that leg you will reopen the wound and it will never heal properly. And keep your leg raised to reduce the swelling."

He snorted. "Rest? In case ye hadnae noticed, we're in the middle of a war, woman. Rest is the last thing I will be getting." He waved at the whisky bottle. "Any left in that?"

She handed him the bottle of whisky and he set it to his lips and knocked it back, guzzling the liquid as though it was water. When he was finished he dropped the bottle to the floor with a thump and sat back, wiping his mouth with the back of his hand.

"If you begin to develop a fever you must let me know immediately," she said. "Do you have any basil or garlic? It will help bring down fever."

He scowled at her. "Do I look like an apothecary?"

She sighed. So much for gratitude.

He struggled to his feet and limped to the door. Eleanor heard a muffled conversation from outside and Stewart returned a few minutes later.

Finn followed him through the door. He didn't look at her but scowled at Stewart instead. He held a half-eaten chicken leg in one hand.

"Aye?" Finn demanded. "What is it this time?"

Stewart glanced at Eleanor and she quickly schooled her expression into one of disdain, as though she wasn't pleased to see Finn at all.

"Ye've done well, Hound," Stewart said to Finn. "For bringing me such a prize. Lady Stevenson has a rare talent. I would hate that talent to be squandered. An army camp isnae a safe place for a lady, as ye know well. I am placing ye in charge of the lady's welfare whilst she is our guest. Ye will see that no harm comes to her and that she doesnae try to leave."

Finn's scowl deepened. "I am no nursemaid," he snapped.

"Ye are whatever I say ye are!" Stewart growled back.

For a moment Finn's eyes blazed. Then he lowered his gaze and nodded.

"Aye, my lord."

"Good," Stewart replied. "Escort the lady back to a guestroom." Stewart turned to Eleanor. "Ye will be my guest at dinner tonight, my lady."

It was clearly not a request. Eleanor's stomach tightened. Dinner? With this guy? She bit down the refusal that tried to spill out of her mouth and nodded.

With a dismissive wave Stewart turned away and Eleanor followed Finn out of the room. He pulled the door shut behind them and led her down the corridor. Only when they'd turned a corner did he speak.

"Are ye all right, lass?" he asked, his voice low and urgent.

"Fine," she replied. "I treated his leg wound, that's all."

Finn let out a long breath. "He thinks ye are valuable now. Stewart treats people well as long as they are of use to him."

Like you, you mean? Eleanor thought.

They reached the end of the corridor and Eleanor was surprised when Finn turned left instead of right.

"Where are we going? He told you to escort me back to my room."

"Ye are a guest now, remember?"

He led her up a rickety staircase that creaked alarmingly under Eleanor's feet and stopped outside a door. "I think ye'll find this more to yer liking."

He opened the door and Eleanor followed him inside. She halted, blinking in confusion. This was no bare room used to lock up guests. Instead this was a sumptuous bedroom with thick rugs on the floor, a large, canopied bed and freshly-swept fireplace. It was exactly the kind of thing she might have booked for a night in a swanky hotel.

"Well," she breathed. "There's an eye-opener if ever I saw one."

"There are still a few guestrooms in the place worthy of the name," Finn said.

She nodded. "I could almost believe I'm not a prisoner. Almost."

"It's some hours until the evening meal tonight," he said. "I will send somebody to draw ye a bath."

The evening meal. He meant dinner with Stewart. Oh hell. The thought of spending the evening in the company of that man made her feel queasy.

Finn strode to the door but paused with his hand on the handle. "Until tonight."

Eleanor swallowed and forced a nod. "Until tonight."

With that, he strode out. Eleanor slumped down on the bed, breathing deeply to clear her thoughts. For the second time that day she was left alone in her room, a prisoner in Stewart's household. But this time she didn't give in to despair. This time she had something she hadn't had the first time. This time she had hope.

She'd proven herself useful to Lord Stewart. He'd not thrown her in a cell or given her to the brothel. That was good. It was a start. Now all she had to do was win her freedom and find a way home. The thought was a daunting one but it wasn't as terrifying as it ought to be. Not when she had Finn to help her.

Chapter 8

Finn shut Eleanor's door behind him, locked it, and went in search of his squad. Hand-picked by Finn himself from the ranks of Stewart's forces, they were just about the only people Finn trusted in this god-forsaken place.

He found two of his trackers, Rob and Donald, exactly where he knew he would: playing dice in front of the kitchen fire. The two lads, neither older than seventeen, leapt to attention when he walked in.

"Is it true, sir?" Donald asked. "Did ye find a noble lady in the woods? A MacAuley spy?"

"Ye listen to too much gossip, lad," Finlay replied with a frown. "Aye, I happened across a traveler on my patrol but she isnae a MacAuley spy."

Donald seemed a bit disappointed by this. "Oh. Are we going out scouting? Do ye want us to go get the others? Duncan will probably be in the brothel by now but I can—"

"No patrol tonight," Finn cut in. "We have a more important duty. We've been tasked by Lord Stewart with keeping the lass safe. Donald, ye will arrange food and a bath for her then guard her door. Rob, ye will go and drag the others from the brothel and tell them to report to me before the evening meal. Over the next few days I want eyes and ears everywhere. Anyone mentions the lass, I want to know about it."

The two lads nodded and scrambled to their assigned tasks, leaving Finn alone in the kitchen. He breathed out slowly and thought back over the last few days. His life had taken a very sudden and very unexpected turn.

He knew he played a dangerous game, lying to Alasdair Stewart. If he discovered Finn's true intentions, his fury would be terrible, his retribution swift. Stewart wouldn't kill him, of course, although Finlay would probably wish for that before the end. No, Lord Alasdair Stewart had far more inventive ways to make Finn pay.

His fists clenched. *It will be worth it*, he thought. *It will be worth any pain to see Eleanor safely home again. It will be worth it to keep a vow after I've broken so many.*

He walked out of the kitchen and across the courtyard towards the stables. He was so caught up with thoughts of how he might get Eleanor safely out of the camp that he suddenly collided with somebody leaving the stable.

A heavy shoulder slammed into him and an angry voice growled, "Watch it, fool!"

Finn looked up to find Balloch glaring at him. The man's eyes widened as he realized who'd bumped into him and then his glare intensified, his fingers curling into fists.

Finn hadn't seen the man since their altercation in the forest the day he met Eleanor. Balloch was travel-stained and had splotches of blood all over his plaid—blood that didn't appear to be his own.

"Be so kind as to step aside," Finn said.

Balloch didn't move. Finlay sighed. He didn't have time for this.

"Ye seem to have forgotten yer rank, soldier," Finn said, keeping his voice pleasant but with a touch of steel. "Now kindly step aside."

Balloch grinned. "I dinna give two shits about yer rank. Ye havenae got Angus to back ye up now. I'm Lord Stewart's nephew and that means I outrank ye every time. Do ye know where I've been, Hound?"

Finn made a show of looking him up and down. "From the look of ye I'd guess ye've been trying to shave again. I've told ye before ye shouldnae try such complicated tasks."

Finn watched him closely, waiting for the telltale sign that he was about to lash out. With Balloch, violence never lay far below the surface. To his surprise, Balloch only grinned wider.

"I'll tell ye where I've been, shall I? A secret mission. One that will see the downfall of the MacAuleys."

He reached beneath his plaid and pulled out a tattered bit of material which he brandished in front of Finn like a trophy. It was drenched with blood but even so Finlay recognized the colors. The MacAuley plaid. He felt the blood drain from his face.

"Aye," Balloch said, his grin widening. "I thought ye might recognize it. Yet, it shouldnae bother ye to see the MacAuleys wiped out, should it? Traitor that ye are?"

Balloch's words sliced into him like blades. It was all he could do to keep his expression neutral, to keep the pain from showing on his face. Only long years of practice allowed his expression to remain cool. But inside, his stomach knotted. Traitor. Aye, he was that and more. What would his brothers think if they could see him now?

His eyes strayed to the blood staining Balloch's plaid. MacAuley blood. Had Finlay's kin died at the hands of Balloch today? Had his brothers?

Nay, he thought fiercely. *Balloch is baiting ye. He is a thug with all the imagination of a lump of wood. Stewart wouldnae trust him with any secret mission.*

He strode past Balloch, shoving him out of the way. The big man made no move to stop him but when Finlay had moved past, he said over his shoulder, "I hear ye brought the lass back with ye. Excellent. I've been looking forward to getting reacquainted with her."

Finlay froze in his tracks and then turned slowly. "If ye lay a hand on her, I will kill ye."

Balloch laughed and walked away without another word. Finlay watched him go, fury seething through his veins. Balloch was full of piss and wind, a spoiled bully riding on his uncle's influence. He wouldn't dare hurt Eleanor, not here, not while she remained a guest of Lord Stewart.

But if he does, Finn thought, *I will kill him. Nobody will hurt her. Not while I live.*

ELEANOR DOUBTED SHE'D ever felt this uncomfortable in her life. The dress was too tight, the chair too hard, the heat in the room stifling. But these weren't the reasons why she sat straight backed and tense, doing her best to hide the unease that coiled through her like a snake.

No, it was the hard, hungry eyes that watched her from all around the room. The raucous, ribald jokes aimed in her direction, quickly stifled when Stewart growled at the perpetrator, and of course, the presence of Alasdair Stewart himself sitting beside her, way too close for her liking.

When Stewart had said that she was to join him for dinner tonight she'd assumed he'd meant a private dinner—and that would have been bad enough—but this loud, brash feast in front of his men was far worse. She felt like a prize on display. Which, of course, was exactly what she was.

She glanced over her shoulder. Finn stood by the wall behind her chair. He didn't look at her, his eyes continually scanning the gathering, guarding her just as Stewart had ordered him to. His presence was just about the only thing making this evening bearable.

The hall of the manor house—the large room where she'd first met Stewart— had been turned into a makeshift banqueting hall. Long trestle tables had been laid out in a square around the room, leaving an open space in the middle. Stewart took pride of place on the head table by the fireplace and Eleanor sat on his right, Balloch on his left.

Eleanor did her best to ignore Balloch even though he kept grinning at her, obviously taking great pleasure in her discomfort. The rest of the tables were taken up by Stewart's men, his officers at a guess, although the term 'officer' was a very loose description to give to the dirty, rowdy renegades that sat eating, drinking, arguing, and occasionally fighting, at the tables.

Eleanor took a sip from her goblet. The wine, she was surprised to admit, was excellent, and the food that had been brought out so far was much better than she'd expected. Lord Stewart, it seemed, still clung to a few luxuries, even in the midst of war.

As she sipped, she glanced around the room, assessing. Even though it was loud, full of raucous laughter and ribald jokes, to Eleanor's mind the joviality seemed a little forced. The men ate and drank with gusto, as though this might be their last opportunity. She sensed tension beneath the bravado and it didn't take much for that to spill over into violence. Two fights had already been broken up, the combatants bodily thrown out of the hall and ordered to muck out the stables.

The men were worried, Eleanor realized. Finn had said that the army would soon be moving out, marching to meet their enemies, the joint forces of the MacAuley and MacConnell clans in battle. From Balloch's swagger and Stewart's calm arrogance, it seemed that he was in the ascendency and that the coming battle was a mere formality but now she began to wonder. Perhaps Stewart wasn't in as strong a position as he liked to portray. Perhaps he was on the defensive. That would explain how he'd manage to lose his physicians to the MacAuley raids.

"Not eating, my lady?" Stewart said, making her jump.

She had barely touched the plate of roast chicken that had been placed in front of her. The defiant part of her wanted to tell Stewart where he could stick his roast chicken but that would be foolish. She needed to keep him sweet. For now.

Without a word she began eating, mopping up the gravy with a slice of crusty bread.

Lord Stewart watched her eat for a moment and then said, "Tell me of yer homeland."

Eleanor nearly choked on her food. She swallowed and then croaked, "What do you want to know."

"Everything. But ye can start by explaining what kind of place allows women to train as physicians. Everyone knows that women are too weak of disposition for such things."

Oh, you reckon? Eleanor thought. Stewart was watching her keenly and she sensed that she had to tread very carefully here. She needed a credible story—one he would believe.

"Not all women," she said, meeting his eyes. "Only highborn women. My father is an important military man." This at least was true. He'd done several tours of duty as a colonel in the army and been away for most of her childhood. It was one of the reasons she'd barely known him. "He saw the merit in training his daughter to take care of his men's injuries."

To her relief, Stewart nodded as though he could understand the sense in such a measure. "Mayhap that is why ye have been parading around in men's clothing, looking hardly decent."

"Yes," Eleanor said quickly. "Pants...er...trews, I mean, are much easier to work in than a dress."

"And this father of yers, this man who saw the merit in training his daughter, he also saw fit to send ye across the sea on yer own, to an unknown land, did he?" Stewart's gaze sharpened and his eyes glinted with suspicion.

"I came here to help people," she said, unable to keep the annoyance out of her voice. "Is that so strange?"

To her surprise, he smiled. "I wonder if all women in yer homeland are as wilful as ye. Mayhap it comes from allowing them to do a man's job."

Eleanor opened her mouth to reply but was saved by a sudden commotion amongst the men. The musicians in the centre of the hall had come to the end of their song and were standing to receive the applause of the crowd. Except they didn't receive much applause. The men were shouting and jeering. Somebody even threw a chicken bone.

Lord Stewart sighed dramatically. "Ye canna find good musicians anywhere these days." Swivelling in his chair, he beckoned to Finn. "The entertainment is sadly lacking tonight, Hound. Ye will play for us. Something rousing, to stir the men's blood."

Finn flushed. Anger glinted in his eyes. "Nay. I willnae."

Stewart glared at him. "Aye. Ye will. That's an order."

He clenched his fist suddenly and a spasm of pain swept across Finn's face. Stewart opened his fist and the expression passed.

Eleanor glanced from Finn to Stewart and back again. What the hell? What had just happened? She watched, nonplussed, as Finn made his way into the centre of the hall. One of the musicians handed him a stringed instrument that Eleanor guessed was a lute, and then the two musicians fled, obviously relieved.

Finn stood alone in the centre of the hall, holding the neck of the instrument and staring into space as if deep in thought. The jeers around the hall intensified and Balloch suddenly shouted "Ho! He we go! The Hound is going to howl for us!"

This brought a round of laughter. Finn ignored it as he took a seat on one of the stools vacated by the musicians and began strumming on the instrument, picking out a few chords in a minor key that rang through the hall as clear as a bell. Then he began to sing.

As Finn's deep, clear voice filled the hall, the laughter died. The jeering fell away, to be replaced by rapt silence. Eleanor understood why. The song was in Gaelic and she understood not a word but even to her untrained ears she knew she was listening to a master at work. She remembered suddenly the night in the woods when she'd woken to hear him singing. Then he'd been singing under his breath, unaccompanied by any instrument and even then she'd been struck by the quality of his voice. Now she was stunned by it.

Deep and haunting, it filled the hall with sound. Perfectly in tune, perfectly in key, his voice seemed to swell like a wave until Eleanor felt as though she was being swept away by it. Although she didn't know the words, the song conjured up images in her mind's eye. She saw a loch sparkling under a silver moon. She saw a ring of standing stones silhouetted against the night sky. She saw dark bowers where no human had ever trod. She saw mist-wreathed clearings where no human ever would. Without knowing how, she realized it was a song about the Fae.

She risked a glance at Stewart. He was leaning forward, his hands steepled in front of him, watching Finlay intently. There was a look on his face she couldn't quite identify. Was it wariness? Unease? Did this song mean something to him?

She turned back to watch Finn. What was going on here? How could a man like him, work for a man like Stewart, a man he clearly hated? It made no sense.

Finn's song finally came to an end and he held the last note for a long time, allowing it to ring out and hold them all spellbound until it finally faded into silence.

Nobody moved for a moment. Then there came a thunderous banging as the men thumped their tankards on the table in appreciation and called for more. Finn obliged. He broke into another song, this one jaunty, quick-tempoed and obviously a drinking song.

"Ye appreciate my Hounds singing, I see," Stewart said.

Eleanor jumped. She'd been so caught up in Finn's song that she'd forgotten he was sitting next to her. "I...I...um never thought somebody like him would have a voice like that," she floundered.

"Aye," he agreed. "Some might think it was a gift given by the Fae."

Something about the way he said it sent a spike of alarm through Eleanor. "The Fae?" she laughed shrilly. "Everyone knows they don't exist!"

"Do they?" Stewart said quietly. "Then mayhap it is a talent passed down through his bloodline. Mayhap Finlay MacAuley inherited it from his ancestors."

Eleanor looked at Stewart sharply, sure she must have just misheard. "MacAuley? Did you say Finlay's clan name is MacAuley?"

Stewart raised an eyebrow. "Did my Hound not tell ye that detail? I'm nay surprised. Nobody wants to advertise the fact that he's a traitor. Aye, lass. He's a MacAuley. And not just any MacAuley, in fact, but brother to the laird of the MacAuley. The people we are fighting against. Over the years my Hound has been most useful in betraying his clan's secrets. And now he's going to be most useful in helping me to destroy them."

Eleanor stared at him, feeling suddenly cold.

"Ye can ever trust him," Stewart warned. "The man may have the voice of an angel but he is a liar and a traitor."

Something hard settled in Eleanor's stomach. No. It couldn't be true. Could it? Finn couldn't be a traitor. He couldn't be fighting against his own family. There must be some sort of mistake or Stewart was lying to her. But even as she thought this, she knew it wasn't the case. Finn had never told her his clan name but he wore a plaid in different colors to everyone else. Why was that? Unless it was his clan plaid, the MacAuley plaid. His brother's colors. The colors of the clan he was fighting.

Finn finished his song. Then he stood, put down the lute, and walked from the centre of the hall without a word. There was a chorus of shouting and banging of tankards on tables. Balloch cupped his hands around his mouth and made a howling noise like a dog. Finn flicked him a baleful glance before taking up his position behind Eleanor once again.

She resisted the urge to look at him. Her thoughts tangled around each other, becoming a confusing knot. Why had Finn kept his identity from her? And why was he fighting for Alasdair Stewart against his own family? It didn't make sense. Unless Finn really was what Stewart claimed: a liar and a traitor.

She took another sip of wine. Lord Stewart was talking to Balloch, paying her no attention. She risked a glance over her shoulder and found Finn watching her. Their eyes locked and her heartbeat quickened. She ripped her gaze away. Oh hell. She didn't know what to think. She didn't know what to feel.

Determined to keep a clear head, she drank no more wine but ate everything that was brought to her and listened. She listened to the conversations and banter of the men, trying to pick up anything that might be useful, anything that might help her figure a way out of this mess.

Finally, the meal came to an end. Suspecting that the men would now fall into even more drinking, dicing and general rowdiness, Eleanor told Stewart she was tired and that she'd like to go back to her room. Stewart waved her away irritably.

"Hound! Make sure the lady is escorted safely back to her chamber."

Finn gave a tiny bow. "As my lord commands. This way, my lady."

Eleanor followed him from the room and into the blessedly cool and quiet corridor outside. They walked in silence. Finn said not a word, did not even look at her. No candles had been lit and so the corridor was dark. When she glanced in Finn's direction she couldn't see much of him, except the glint of moonlight that reflected in his eyes. But she could feel him. His presence by her side was dark and brooding, like a thundercloud. She thought suddenly of the way he'd sang in the hall tonight, the beauty of his voice.

Liar. Traitor.

They reached her room. Somebody had been in and lit a fire, for which she was grateful. The spring night had turned chilly.

"One of my lads will keep watch on yer door," Finn said.

He turned to leave and Eleanor suddenly blurted. "Why didn't you tell me who you are?"

He froze, turned. "What?"

Eleanor looked up at him. "Lord Stewart told me you're a MacAuley. That your brother is the laird of the MacAuleys."

"Of course he did," Finn said under his breath. "That bastard."

"He also told me you can't be trusted. That you're a liar and a traitor. That you're fighting against your own family. Is it true, Finn?" She tried to keep her voice steady but it shook a little.

His gaze met hers and she saw anguish in his eyes. "Aye, it's true," he breathed, his voice barely above a whisper. "I am all those things and more."

Eleanor took a step back, her legs feeling suddenly shaky. Could she trust anyone in this god-forsaken place?

He reached a hand towards her but she backed away. "Why...why didn't you tell me? Why did you lie to me?"

He stared at her for a long moment. "Because if ye knew the truth ye would see me as everyone else does. As Stewart's Hound."

"I don't get it. It's obvious you hate Stewart. Why do you serve him?"

He glanced away, scrubbed a hand through his hair. "Because I havenae a choice."

"Of course you have a choice!" she replied. "He doesn't own you!"

Anger flashed in his eyes. "Ye dinna know of what ye speak, woman. I canna disobey Alasdair Stewart any more than I can stop breathing."

She shook her head. "I don't understand."

"Nor will ye," he snapped. "It's between me and him. I would thank ye to keep yer nose out of my business."

"Fine!" she cried. "I'll just be a good little girl and go along with everything you say, shall I? I'll just keep my mouth shut, do as I'm told and hope you weren't lying when you said you'd help me escape, shall I?"

His expression darkened. "My word is my bond. Do ye doubt me?"

"Damn right I doubt you! You've just stood there and admitted you've been lying to me! I trusted you, Finn! Now I don't know who the hell you are or whether I can believe a word you say!"

"I will keep my word to ye, Eleanor," he said. "With God as my witness, I willnae let any harm come to ye. I have broken many vows in my life but I will die before I break this one."

The pain in his voice was so strong that it twisted Eleanor's heart. Oh god. What had been done to him? She felt her anger melting away. How could she be angry at him for keeping secrets when she kept so many of her own? For a moment she longed to tell him the truth and to have it all laid bare between them. She ached to tell him the truth about why she'd come to Scotland, of the terrible, gut-wrenching guilt she was trying to outrun, of Irene MacAskill sending her back in time. But she couldn't tell him any of that. She dare not.

"Oh, Finn," she breathed. "What are we going to do?"

He laid a hand on her arm. "I dinna know, lass." His lips quirked in a crooked smile. "But I'm working on it."

Despite herself, she felt her lips tug into a smile in response. "Well, I suppose that will have to do won't it?" She looked up at him. "Oh, and by the way, you're one hell of a singer."

"One hell of a..." he looked puzzled. "I assume there's a compliment in there somewhere?"

"Yes," she said. "A big compliment. Where I come from you'd have been talent spotted years ago. Where did you learn to sing like that?"

He shrugged. "I am the third son. My eldest brother was trained to lead, my second brother, to fight. But the spoiled youngest son was allowed a little more freedom." He laughed lightly. "Some might say a little too much. I spent my childhood ducking out of chores and exploring the countryside with old Ham, the huntsmen. It was from him I learned how to track and use the bow. And my mother indulged me in my other passion: music. I spent every spare hour practising. I was the clan bard by the time I was fourteen years old." His voice was warm and there was a faint smile on his lips as he relived bright memories.

She smiled. "I wonder what you were like at fourteen. Breaking the hearts of all the clan girls, I'll bet."

Finn raised an eyebrow. "Hardly. That was Camdan's domain. I was a gangly youth forever tripping over his own feet."

Eleanor laughed lightly and Finn's eyes sparkled. His hand was still resting on her arm. Even through the fabric of her sleeve, she felt the warmth of his touch against her skin. A tingle walked up her arm as he watched her, firelight dancing in his eyes.

Eleanor opened her mouth to speak but instead her breath came out in a low gasp. Finn's lips parted and he stepped closer, bending his head towards her.

"Everything okay, sir?"

Eleanor jumped as Finn spun around with a curse. "Damn ye, Donald! What are ye doing sneaking around like a thief?"

A youth of around seventeen with a shock of red hair was standing in the doorway, looking a little sheepish. "Sorry, sir. I heard voices and after what ye said about guarding the lady, I thought I'd better check who it was."

Finn sighed. "Aye, lad. Ye did right. My apologies. Ye startled me, that's all." He looked at Eleanor. "Lady Stevenson, this is Donald MacTavish, one of my best trackers. He'll be guarding yer door tonight."

Donald flushed at the compliment and then dropped Eleanor an awkward bow. "An honor, my lady. Just call if ye need aught. I'll be right outside."

Eleanor smiled at him. "The honor is mine, Donald. And it's Eleanor. None of this 'my lady' business."

Donald's blush deepened and he dropped another bow. Finn smiled at the boy's embarrassment and then said, "Sleep well, my lady. Come, Donald, let's give the lady some peace."

Donald nodded and ducked out of the door. Finlay followed but paused with his hand on the jamb. He looked back, his eyes finding hers. For a moment Eleanor thought he would say something but he only gave a brief nod and then followed Donald out, pulling the door closed behind him.

Eleanor stood there for a moment, her heart racing. She squeezed her eyes closed, clenched her fists, and sucked in one, two, three breaths, until her pulse began to steady. For a moment there she'd thought Finn would kiss her. And for a moment she'd really wanted him to.

A sudden wave of exhaustion washed through her. It had been quite a day. The bed had never looked so inviting. She managed to struggle out of the dress and hung it on a peg on the back of the door. In only her under-shift, she climbed beneath the covers, lay down and closed her eyes.

In minutes, she was asleep.

Chapter 9

She awoke just as weak morning light was beginning to creep through the narrow windows. Eleanor took a minute to lie still, eyes closed, then with a sigh, she threw back the covers and swung her legs out of bed. The fire had died to cold ashes and there was a chill in the air. Still, she felt far more rested than she had expected. Her sleep had been deep and dreamless and she felt calmer, more determined this morning.

She had a plan. Last night, listening to the grumbling of Stewart's men at dinner, the glimmer of an idea had come to her.

She got out of bed, gave herself a bracing wash with the cold water in the basin, brushed her hair and teeth using the rudimentary implements Stewart had provided, and then dressed. She had nobody to help her into the gown so it took a while, but eventually managed to fight her way into the cumbersome garment. This done, she crossed to the window and squinted through the thin gap.

Below her the encampment spread out, a sea of tents stretching into the distance. Finn had said the men in the camp were dangerous and posed a threat to her safety, but if she played this right, they might just be her ticket out of the manor house.

There was a knock on the door.

"My lady?" Donald's voice called. "Are ye decent? May I come in?"

"Yes," she called. "And it's Eleanor, remember?"

The door swung open and Donald backed in, carrying a tray. He gave her a shy smile. "Finlay said to bring ye breakfast, my la...Eleanor."

"Did he now?" Eleanor replied. "That was very kind of him. And very kind of you to bring it for me."

He blushed to his hairline, set the tray on the bed and bobbed his head. "Do ye need aught else, my lady? I mean Eleanor. Do ye need aught else, Eleanor?"

"Actually, yes," she replied, giving him a smile. "Could you please let Lord Stewart know that I would like to speak to him at his earliest convenience?"

Donald paled slightly at the mention of Stewart's name. "I...of course. Enjoy yer breakfast."

"I will. Thanks, Donald."

The lad hurried out, locking the door behind him. On the breakfast tray Eleanor found a bowl of unsweetened porridge, some bread and butter, and a cup of small beer to wash it down with. There were no chairs so Eleanor perched on the end of the bed as she ate, making sure to finish it all, even though the porridge was a little bland without sugar to sweeten it. When she was full, she settled down to wait. Would Stewart even grant her an audience?

It wasn't long before she found out. Less than ten minutes later the door opened and this time Finn strode into the room. Her heart leapt at the sight of him. His hair had been washed and combed and fell onto his shoulders in midnight waves and he wore a crisp white linen shirt under his plaid. It clung to his muscled chest in a most distracting way.

"I am to escort ye to Lord Stewart," he said, fixing her with a puzzled expression. "He says ye requested to speak to him. What are ye playing at, lass? Didnae I tell ye to keep out of his way?"

"Good morning to you too," Eleanor replied, raising an eyebrow. "Yes, I know you said to avoid him but that's not going to work. We'll never get out of here if I'm confined to this room all day. If I can get Stewart to trust me, he'll give me more freedom, and if he gives me more freedom, we can get away."

Finn crossed his arms over his broad chest and frowned. "Win Alasdair Stewart's trust? And how, exactly do ye plan on doing that?"

She smiled. "You're just going to have to trust me, aren't you?"

His frowned deepened but he didn't say another word as he turned and led her from the room.

Lord Stewart was eating his breakfast when they entered his study. He looked up irritably, then waved for Finn to leave. Finn gave her a look as he went to wait outside that plainly said he hoped she knew what she was doing. Eleanor hoped the same thing.

Stewart took his time finishing his bowl of porridge, making Eleanor wait, before finally looking up. "I trust ye slept well?"

"I did."

"And yer accommodation is to yer liking?"

"It's fine."

"Then what can I do for ye? Spit it out. I'm a busy man."

"It's actually what I can do for you. I've come to check your wound."

He leaned back in his chair. "There isnae need for that. The wound is fine."

Eleanor drew a breath. Just as she had expected, Stewart was going to be a difficult patient. Well, she had plenty of experience with those.

"Oh? My apologies. I didn't realize you'd already had it cleaned and dressed this morning. Or that you already knew what to do to keep out infection. Or that you understood all about the dangers of gangrene and losing your leg. In that case, I'll trouble you no more."

She walked to the door but before she reached it Stewart called, "Wait."

Eleanor looked over her shoulder. "Yes?"

"Fine. Do what ye must but be quick about it."

Ignoring his curt tone, she bade him sit back. Kneeling by his side, she unwound the bandage and inspected his wound. It looked clean and had no smell. She quickly cleaned it with the supplies she'd used yesterday then wrapped a fresh bandage around the cut.

"It's healing well and the stitches should be ready to come out within the week."

Stewart glanced at her. His dark, cold eyes held a wary look, as though he was suspicious of her motives.

"Ye may go."

Eleanor didn't move. "Actually, there is something else."

He raised an eyebrow. "Oh?"

"You have a camp full of fighting men outside these walls and no physician to take care of them. How many wounded do you have in your ranks?"

"That isnae any concern of yers," he snapped.

"I'm a doctor!" she snapped back. "Would you let your men die for lack of a physician?" His nostrils flared in anger and she wondered if she'd gone too far but she plowed on anyway. "Let me tend to your wounded. I might be able to save some of them."

Stewart said nothing. She could see his thoughts turning behind his eyes. He didn't trust her—she doubted he trusted anybody—but he was weighing this against the possibility of having more fighting men to throw against the MacAuleys.

"Hound!" he bellowed. "Get in here!" Finlay stepped into the room. "Ye will escort the lady to the camp. Take her to the hospital tent and see that she has all she needs." He leaned forward, his grip tightening on the arms of his chair. "And Hound? Ye will see that she doesnae cause any trouble."

Eleanor heard his implicit threat—*see that she doesn't try to escape.*

Finlay's eyes flicked to Eleanor's then back to Stewart. "Aye, my lord."

Stewart waved them both away irritably. Eleanor followed Finlay out the door.

"I dinna like this," Finn muttered. "Do ye know the type of men ye will be administering to? Murderers, rapists and thieves most of them."

"That may be," Eleanor replied. "But it's not my place to decide who deserves medical treatment and who doesn't. I took an oath to help any who need it—even Stewart's men."

Finlay led her to the manor house's large door. Eleanor paused on the landing outside, looking out over the busy courtyard below. It felt good to be outside again, with the wind tugging at her hair and the fresh smell of the Highlands filling her nostrils. Even so, she balked at the sight of so many fighting men, men that carried weapons, men wound almost to breaking point with the thoughts of the coming battle.

Finlay glanced at her, raising his eyebrow in a question. She nodded, took a deep breath, then followed him down the steps into the courtyard. Finn paused long enough to call two of his trackers down from their guard duty on the wall and then instructed them that they were to guard Eleanor whilst in the camp. Eleanor recognized Donald and Finlay introduced the other as Rob. More dour that Donald, he didn't smile, but gave Eleanor a respectful nod.

Finn led the way to the main gate, striding by Eleanor's side with Donald and Rob falling into step behind. The gate guards didn't challenge them as they passed through and Eleanor guessed that Lord Stewart's command to allow her into camp had already reached them.

As she walked towards the camp Eleanor put her shoulders back and lifted her chin, forcing herself to walk as though she was confident even though nerves wriggled in her stomach. She tried not to stare as they passed the hut that served as a brothel, even though the line of men waiting outside watched her with hungry eyes as she went by. Finlay glared at them, his hand resting on one of his daggers and so the men did no more than stare.

They entered the camp proper. It was a muddy, messy place full of dirt and unpleasant smells. The avenues between the tents had been churned into a quagmire and the tents themselves were ragged, damp things that no doubt did very little to keep out the Highland weather. Men sat outside their tents either singly or in small groups, sharpening weapons, playing dice or swigging from whisky bottles. Their hard gazes sprang to Eleanor as she passed and she had more than one ribald comment shouted in her direction.

Finlay though, was a solid presence by her side and his glare kept the men in check so she arrived at a larger tent without mishap. This tent was set a little apart from the others and there was a wide ring of open space around it as though the men were reluctant to go any closer.

Finlay ducked under the tent flap and held it open for her. As she stepped inside the stink of infection hit Eleanor almost like a physical blow.

Placing a hand over her mouth, Eleanor looked around. The interior was dimly lit by a single brazier standing in the corner and in the dim light she made out twelve crude pallets laid out around the tent. Each held an occupant.

Some of the patients were unconscious, others awake and moaning in pain. Eleanor's stomach tightened. The old, familiar self-doubt came racing to the surface.

I can't do this, that voice whispered in the back of her mind. *I'm not good enough. I'll do something wrong and somebody will die. This was a terrible idea.*

Whenever she'd worked on trauma before there had always been an older, more experienced doctor supervising and decisions that might mean the difference between someone's life and death hadn't been hers to make. She'd shied away from having that responsibility ever since...ever since that day.

She turns around. Her mom has gone pale, clutching at her chest...

Eleanor gritted her teeth, pushing the memory away. *You can do this,* she told herself resolutely. *You have to. There's no one else.*

"Eleanor?" Finn said. "Is something wrong?"

Eleanor realized that she'd closed her eyes, curled her hands into fists against her sides and was gasping for breath. She opened her eyes, forced herself to relax. "Fine. Everything's fine. Who's in charge here?"

A man walked from the far side of the tent. Eleanor recognized the dour, bearded face of Angus, the man who'd been in charge of the group who captured her.

"What are ye doing in here?" he demanded, wiping his hands on his blood-stained apron. "What's going on?"

"Lord Stewart has given the care of the wounded into my hands," Eleanor replied.

Angus looked her up and down. "Ye? A woman? Is this some sort of jest?"

Finlay stepped up beside Eleanor, his hand on his dagger hilt. "Are ye questioning Lord Stewart's orders? The lass is a physician. Stand aside. That's an order."

Angus looked from Finlay to Eleanor, his face folded into a scowl. He untied the apron and threw it to the floor.

"Whatever ye say, *sir*. If ye can do aught for these poor bastards, I wish ye luck. They're beyond my skill to heal. I only did a little barber surgeon work under my da. These need a proper healer."

With that, Angus stomped out of the tent.

Eleanor looked around and drew in a breath. "Okay. First, open the tent flaps and pin them back so we can get some fresh air and better light in here."

As Donald and Rob ran to do her bidding, Eleanor rolled up her sleeves.

"Right. Let's get started."

FINN WATCHED ELEANOR in fascination. She worked confidently, diligently, assessing each patient in turn using something she called 'triage' and then treating them in the order of severity. Finlay stayed by her side as she cleaned wounds, stitched gashes, set broken bones, gave pain relief, and quietly but confidently gave instructions for ongoing care.

Who was this woman? There was no trace of the uncertain, frightened woman he'd discovered running from Angus and his men. This woman was confident, self-assured, utterly in control as she quietly issued orders to Donald, Rob and even Angus who wandered back in and who, for a wonder, obeyed her instructions without question.

Finlay had never seen anything like it. At Dun Ringill they'd had a healer, old Morag, who was well versed in the setting of broken bones or the delivery of a babe, but even she didn't exude the quiet confidence that Eleanor did as she concentrated on her patient, her expression intent, her lips pursed slightly as she went to work on fixing the problem before her.

It was highly unusual for a woman to have such skills. As far as he knew only the great Italian universities might equip somebody with the knowledge she exhibited and yet only men were admitted entrance to those hallowed halls, and only the very rich could afford the services of those who graduated from them. Yet here Eleanor was, ministering to the lowliest soldier in a renegade army.

Who was she really? She'd come from Brigid's Hollow, a place of the Fae. She'd met Irene MacAskill, one of the Fae. She spoke and behaved and displayed a bravery unlike any woman Finn had ever met. There was something he was missing. She was keeping something from him, he was sure of it. But for the life of him, he couldn't figure out what that was.

Eleanor worked diligently for several hours, the sleeves of her dress rolled up and her hair tied away from her face in a plait. Two of the men were beyond her aid, with wounds that even Finlay could see would take their lives by the morning. For these two Eleanor gave them tincture of poppy for the pain and then sat quietly and talked with them for a while. Under her gentle care the men's expressions eased and they began talking about their lives, the lives they'd lived before they fell on hard times and found themselves fighting for the renegade Lord Alasdair Stewart.

Finlay stood back, arms crossed over his chest and watched in silence. His admiration for Eleanor grew. Would he behave as bravely if he was being held by the enemy in a land not his own?

Eleanor patted the soldier's hand and then stood. "He's asleep. He needs to be given more poppy in four hours and somebody should stay with him."

Angus nodded, his bearded face filled with something Finlay had never expected to find there: respect. "Aye, my lady. I'll see to it. Trevor took an arrow for me some years back, seems the least I can do is keep him company as he goes to meet his maker."

Eleanor nodded then pressed her hands into the small of her back and stretched. "I'll check on the others tomorrow."

They left the tent. Once outside she staggered and would have fallen if Finlay hadn't darted forward to catch her. He lifted her gently back to her feet.

"What is it, lass?" he asked. "Are ye well?"

"Just tired," she murmured.

The sight of her, wisps of hair coming free from her plait, skin pale from exhaustion, sent a pang right through him. He wanted nothing more than to scoop her up in his arms and carry her to safety.

But he couldn't. He could sense people watching them, felt feral eyes tracking his every movement.

In a voice harsher than he intended he snapped, "Stand up. Ye mustnae show any weakness, lass. Remember where ye are. Ye are among predators who will attack if they smell blood."

Eleanor swallowed, pulled in a deep breath. Then she pushed away from Finlay's grip and straightened. Brushing a stray strand of hair back from her face she said, "It's fine. I'm okay now."

Aye, her hair might be dishevelled and there might be a thin sheen of sweat on her brow. Her dress might be creased, the arms rolled to the elbows. Even so, in that moment, her beauty struck Finn like a physical blow. She wore that beauty with ease, as though she wasn't even aware of it and this only made it all the more powerful to Finn.

"Come," he said gruffly. "Let's get back."

FINN MADE TO WALK OFF but Eleanor caught his arm. In truth, she was exhausted and would love to sink onto her bed and sleep. But she couldn't return to the house yet.

"Wait. I need some supplies." She held open the leather bag Angus had given her so Finn could see the meagre contents inside.

"What kind of supplies?" Finn asked with a frown, glancing at the campfires and the men seated around them.

"Well," Eleanor replied, pursing her lips in thought. "Poppy would be a good start. It can be used for all sorts of pains. Then there's comfrey to stop bleeding and help with breathing problems. Oh, and yarrow if we can find it. That's good for wounds and helping circulation. And garlic, of course, which is good for just about anything."

Not for the first time since arriving here Eleanor gave a silent thanks to the room-mate she'd had at medical school. Donna had been very much into alternative medicine and had lectured Eleanor endlessly on the benefits of reiki, acupuncture, herbal medicine and a whole host of other things. Thank god she'd listened, otherwise she'd be well and truly stuck right now.

Finn's frowned deepened. "I dinna like it. We've been out here too long already. Mayhap it's time we returned to the manor house."

"Look," Eleanor said, planting her hands on her hips. "Lord Stewart asked me to treat his men. How am I supposed to do that if I don't have anything to treat them with? You're a tracker aren't you? You know the woods around here better than anyone. Surely you can help me find what I need?"

Finn hesitated for a moment then nodded. "Aye. Come, then."

He walked close by her side as they strode through the camp, weaving between tents and campfires. Finn stared down any men he thought might cause trouble, his hand resting on the handle of his bronze dagger. They reached the edge of the camp without incident and passed into the thick woodland that surrounded the manor house.

After the noise and stink of the camp, the woodlands were like a balm. Green, and bursting with life, they were a million miles away from the melting pot of anger and resentment that made up Stewart's army. Eleanor breathed deeply, finding herself relaxing for the first time in days. Finn too seamed more at ease, his shoulders losing some of their tension as he walked silently by her side.

Eleanor looked around. She could see nothing but an endless expanse of trees reaching into the distance. There was not another person in sight.

"Couldn't we just slip away now?" she said to Finn. "There's nobody here but us. Would anyone notice if we made a run for it?"

Finn glanced at her. He took her arm and guided her behind the wide trunk of an oak tree and pressed his fingers to his lips for silence. He pointed into the trees. Eleanor followed the line of his outstretched hand but saw nothing.

"Watch and wait," Finn said.

Eleanor concentrated. At first she saw nothing but a tangle of leaves and branches but then something shifted and she made out a man standing there. He'd kept so still he'd been barely visible.

"Stewart's pickets," Finn said by way of explanation. "Guards posted to keep a watch for the enemy—and on anyone leaving camp. They're posted all around here. We wouldnae be able to get past them without being seen."

Eleanor breathed out slowly. She could have walked right past the man and not even known he was there. The sight of him underlined just how dangerous a situation Eleanor had found herself in. What would have happened if she'd come out here without Finn?

She nodded and she and Finn left their hiding place and skirted wide around the picket. Finn led her along a gurgling stream which eventually reached a flower-filled meadow. The sun had broken through the clouds and late afternoon sunshine bathed the meadow in a warm glow.

"Poppies," Finn said, pointing at the red wildflowers filling the meadow. "And unless I'm mistaken there's some yarrow growing over by the stream. If ye want garlic and comfrey we'll have to go further into the wood where it's shady."

Eleanor nodded, staring at the meadow in delight. Oh what she wouldn't give for a nice picnic right now! With a good bottle of wine, of course.

She walked out into the knee-high grass, delighting in the feeling of the warm sun on her skin, and began harvesting the poppies. Finn stood at the edge of the meadow, arms folded across his chest, looking around warily as if he expected something to jump out at them any minute.

Eleanor raised an eyebrow. "You know, this would go a lot quicker if you gave me a hand rather than standing there on sentry duty."

He frowned, looked about to object, then seemed to think better of it. He strode into the grass and began collecting the delicate flowers in those big hands of his. Eleanor bent to her work and they worked side by side in silence.

"I can see why you like it out here," she said after a while.

"Like it? What do ye mean?"

She gestured at the landscape. "You seem far more at home out here than you do at Stewart's camp. I can understand why. It's so...so peaceful."

"Aye," Finn breathed, looking around the sunlit meadow. "It is. When I was a lad I used to spend most of my time outdoors. It makes me feel..."

"Free?" Eleanor supplied.

"Aye. Something like that."

His eyes met hers and Eleanor went very still. A bunch of poppies dangled from one hand, suddenly forgotten as she found herself trapped by Finn's gaze. His eyes were as green as the grass they trod upon, full of something that made Eleanor's heart begin to thump. For a frozen moment they stood staring at one another, the only sound the roaring of Eleanor's blood in her ears.

Then Finlay suddenly crossed the distance between them in two long strides, caught her around the waist and jerked her hard against him. His mouth descended on hers, hot and insistent. And Eleanor responded. Oh god, she responded.

The poppies fell unheeded from her hand as she snaked her arms around him, pulling him close as her lips parted to accept him. Searing heat flashed through her and she moaned as his tongue slipped between her lips. His warm breath enveloped her, his hard body pressed against her in a way that all but robbed her of her senses. She could barely breathe, barely think as they kissed, hard and long and deep. The torrent of desire that had been building since the first moment Finn had walked into her life broke free and swept her away.

She had no idea how long the kiss lasted. It might have been a year or less than a heartbeat but eventually, finally, Finn lifted his lips from hers and Eleanor sagged in his arms, breathless. Finn held her tight and gazed down into her eyes. Eleanor felt trapped as surely as a fly in amber.

"I'm sorry, lass," he said, not sounding sorry at all. "I shouldnae have done that."

"Shouldn't you?" Eleanor said breathlessly. "I don't know. Maybe you should do it again, just so I can check."

Finn smiled, his eyes sparkling. He lowered his face towards her but before his lips could touch hers there was a sudden snap of a branch nearby. Finn sprang away from her, spinning towards the sound and whipping his dagger from its sheath.

But it was only a wood pigeon landing awkwardly in a bush nearby. Finn breathed out and Eleanor pressed a hand against her racing heart. If that had been one of Stewart's men... She glanced at Finn and saw the same concern written on his face.

"That was too close," he said. "Lord above, what were we thinking?"

Despite the danger, Eleanor found herself grinning. "I'm not sure there was much 'thinking' involved."

He smiled, his eyes suddenly full of mischief. "Nay, lass. I think mayhap ye are right."

The look he gave her made her heat rise. Holy shit, how she wished he'd kiss her again.

But she knew that was dangerous. Anyone could be watching. So, doing her best to ignore the way her stomach was doing somersaults, she resumed gathering poppies. After a moment Finn joined her, so close she could hear his breathing.

Oh god. This was going to be a long afternoon.

Chapter 10

The wind caught Finlay's hair and sent it streaming out behind him, a chill bite to it that seemed to deny the onset of spring. He squinted into the wind and stared out from the watchtower. The sun had fallen low in the sky and it would soon be dark. He and Eleanor had returned to the manor house several hours ago. He'd escorted her back to her room and come up here onto the ramparts to think.

Before him, the landscape of the Highlands rolled out like a map, the heather-clad hills dotted with sparkling lochs and rugged, snow-capped mountains in the distance. Somewhere out there lay the meadow where he'd kissed Eleanor.

The memory sent heat rushing straight to his groin. He'd never experienced anything like the all-consuming desire he'd felt as his lips had found hers. He knew he shouldn't have done it. He knew it was dangerous and reckless but he couldn't bring himself to regret it. Lord help him, he knew he'd do it again given the chance.

He turned suddenly as he heard footsteps on the stairs and Donald came puffing to the top, leaning with his hands on his knees as he caught his breath.

"What is it, lad?" Finn demanded, alarmed. "What's happened?"

Donald straightened, his face as red as his hair. "Came to tell ye," he gasped. "A scouting party is getting ready to depart to the south."

"The south?" Finn asked. "What is the point in that? The enemy lie to the north and west."

"Aye," Donald replied. "That's why I came to tell ye. They aren't scouting for the MacAuleys. It's something to do with Lady Eleanor."

"Lady Eleanor?" Finn asked, his heart suddenly thudding. "Where is the scouting party now?"

"At the gate. They were getting their horses ready when I came so they might not have left yet."

Finn didn't wait for him to finish the sentence. He bolted for the stairs and took them two at a time. He sped through the grounds of the manor house but slowed when he reached the courtyard before the west gate. Pressing his back against a stack of empty barrels, he peered around them. Sure enough, two men were waiting impatiently with their mounts. They were lightly provisioned to allow for speed and stealth. The fact they were leaving just as it was getting dark confirmed that this was a covert mission.

Both men turned as a third figure approached them. It was Alasdair Stewart.

"Ye are prepared?" he asked the men.

"Aye," one of them answered. "Angus has told us where he found the lass and even drawn us a map. Dinna worry, my lord, we'll find her trail and discover where she came from."

Stewart nodded. "See that ye do. I want answers. I dinna trust Lady Eleanor Stevenson. There's more than meets the eye to my esteemed physician—I dinna like people trying to deceive me." He reached into his tunic and pulled out a piece of parchment which he unrolled and showed to the men. "This is a map of the area she was found in. Do ye see aught of interest?"

The men squinted at it. "Looks like empty wilderness to me," one of them said.

"Exactly. Without any mention of the settlement she said she came from. Which means she was lying. In fact, the only thing of any note in the area is this." He pointed to a spot on the map.

The men paled. "Brigid's Hollow," one of them breathed whilst the other made the sign against evil.

"Aye. Find her trail and follow it back to its origins. If it leads back to Brigid's Hollow I want to know—immediately. Ye will tell nobody of yer mission. Ye will report directly to me when ye get back. Understood?"

"Aye, lord."

The men took the map, mounted their horses, and rode out the gate. Stewart watched them go for a moment before spinning on his heel and striding back into the manor house.

Pulse racing, Finn hurried into the stables and quickly saddled a horse. Curse it all! Finn should have guessed Stewart wouldn't take Eleanor's story at face value. The man was as cunning as a lighthouse rat and trusted precisely nothing and nobody. What worried Finn the most, however, was how he'd made the connection between Eleanor and Brigid's Hollow. What had the man discovered? Did he know more about Eleanor than he let on?

Finn climbed into the saddle and kicked the horse into motion. The guards on the gate paid Finn no heed as he galloped through. It was not unusual for him to go riding at all hours. The sun had sunk behind the hills and darkness was falling. He slowed his horse to a walk and scanned the trail for signs of the men.

As he'd expected, they did not keep to the main road, instead turning off and making their way across country. Their trail was easy enough to follow, a narrow track where their horses' hoof prints were clear in the mud. There had been little rain recently and if Angus's directions were accurate, they'd soon pick up Eleanor's trail.

And where will it lead them? Finn wondered to himself. If her trail did lead back to Brigid's Hollow rather than this Achfarn place she'd told him she came from? What would that mean?

The unease deepened. He'd suspected Eleanor was keeping something from him, something important. Now, it seemed, Alasdair Stewart suspected the same.

He shook his head. None of this mattered. All that mattered was keeping Eleanor safe and helping her escape from Stewart's clutches. Protectiveness flared in him as he remembered how soft and small her hand felt in his, how warm her smile. Then something else: heat as he recalled the silky feel of her lips on his, the roundness of her breasts as they pressed against his chest...

Aye, he would protect Eleanor Stevenson with his life.

It wasn't long before he spotted the patrol ahead, moving steadily south. They had lit torches, thinking there would be nobody to see them at this late hour. Fools. The light bobbed through the darkness like a firefly, advertising their presence to anyone who might be watching.

Finlay growled under his breath. Any tracker under his command would have been severely reprimanded for such lack of discipline. Still, it made it easy for him to follow. He stayed well back, so that they didn't hear the thump of his horse's hooves or the jingle of his tack and wrapped his dagger in cloth so that the newly risen moon didn't reflect off it.

Like this, they traveled for several hours. All the while Finn's senses were alert, eyes scanning the darkness, ears pricked for any sound that didn't belong. They'd passed through the picket lines of Stewart's sentries a while ago and were now in the no-man's land south of Stewart's holdings. Out here there would be brigands and worse, flourishing in the lawlessness that inevitably came when there was clan conflict.

Up ahead, the patrol reined in their horses. From the way the torch bobbed he guessed they'd dismounted and were busy scanning the ground. Finlay pulled his horse to a halt, dismounted, and tethered it out of sight behind a tree. Taking his bow from the saddle, he slung it over his shoulder and proceeded on foot. Moving silently as only one who has spent years walking the wilderness could, he padded through the darkened wood, using only the pale moonlight to guide him and circled around towards the patrol from the east. He crept to within twenty meters of the pair and then hunkered down behind a tree to observe.

They had dismounted in a wide clearing. A cold fire-pit sat in the center, with logs pulled up around it. The two men were careful where they put their feet as they inspected it to avoid trampling any footprints.

"This is the place," one of them said. "Angus said they were eating around the fire when the lady approached." He knelt and examined the ground, holding the torch high. "These footprints must belong to Angus and his men. See the size of them? But here's a set of smaller ones." The man straightened and began following the line of footprints to where they led out of the clearing. "Look, they're as clear as day. Lucky we've not had any rain to wash them away, eh?"

"Aye," his companion grunted. "Lucky us. Being sent on a fool's errand in the middle of the night. What more could we ask for?"

"Ye are just sore ye've not been able to visit yer whore tonight. She'll still be waiting when ye get back."

The second man scowled. "Aye, and the sooner we finish this mission the sooner I can get back to her."

The first man glanced at the ground, then at the map. "The tracks lead south west, just like Lord Stewart said they might. Towards Brigid's Hollow."

The second man whistled under his breath and made the sign against evil. "Right. Can we go home now?"

"Ye heard what Lord Stewart said," the other man replied. "He wants us to track the lass's trail and find out where she came from. Her trail leads *towards* Brigid's Hollow but that doesnae mean it doesn't branch off and go some place else. Do ye want to return to Lord Stewart and tell him we didnae follow the trail to the end? I never took ye for a superstitious bastard." He grinned. "Dinna worry, I'll protect ye from the fairies."

"And I'll wipe that grin from yer face if ye dinna shut yer hole," growled the other.

They returned to their horses and, leading the beasts this time, began heading south. Finn watched them go, biting his lip. He longed to follow them but it was no longer safe for Eleanor at Stewart's manor. He had to get her out before those two returned to make their report. He counted to a hundred slowly to give the men plenty of time to get away and then edged carefully out of his hiding place and towards the campsite. His eyes scanned the ground, the moonlight giving enough light to see by. Eleanor's prints were clear, as were those of Angus and his men. Something glinted in the grass by his feet. Puzzled, Finn crouched for a closer look. It appeared to be a small, flat silver box with glass covering one side. Carefully Finlay reached out and picked it up. It was very light and the glass on one side had cracked, probably when it was dropped.

Turning the thing over in his hands, he frowned. He'd never seen anything like it. What was it? And how did it get here? Was it something of Eleanor's?

He tucked the strange device into his saddle bag, climbed into the saddle and set his heels to the horse's flanks. Despite the danger of galloping in the dark, he sent the beast thundering along the trail.

He had to get back to Eleanor before it was too late.

ELEANOR SLEPT THE SLEEP of the exhausted and woke early the next morning with a heavy feeling in her limbs. As she opened her eyes to the pale morning light, she felt restored, invigorated. The light coming through the windows seemed a little brighter, the air smelled a little cleaner and Eleanor felt...alive.

Finn's face flashed into her mind, a handsome face with dark, sparkling eyes and a crooked smile. Then hot on the heels of this, she remembered the feel of his lips on hers, the soft warmth of his kiss, the heat of his breath, the touch of his hands on her skin...

She wanted more of it. She longed for his smile, his touch. In Finn's presence, the world seemed full of endless possibilities.

What is happening to me? she thought. *I have no idea. But I like it.*

Eager to start her day, Eleanor climbed out of bed, went through her morning ablutions and attempted to dress. God in Heaven, how women in this century managed this every day was beyond her. Give her a pair of jeans, a flannel shirt and a stout pair of boots any day of the week! But the difficulties of dressing couldn't dampen her mood and she found herself humming— humming!—as she brushed her hair and tied it back in a plait.

There was a knock on the door and Eleanor jumped to her feet, her stomach doing a little somersault, expecting Finn. But it wasn't Finn who stuck his head around the door, it was Donald.

The lad shuffled his feet awkwardly. "If it please ye, my lady," he muttered. "I've brought yer breakfast."

Eleanor craned her head to look behind him. "Thanks. Where's Finlay?"

Donald carried a tray into the room and placed it on the bed. "He went out on a mission last night. He isnae back yet."

A jolt of alarm went through Eleanor. Finn had gone on patrol? In the middle of the night? Towards enemy forces? Oh god. What if... what if...

He will be fine, she told herself. *He knows what he's doing.*

She forced a smile onto her face. "Thank you, Donald. You've been most helpful. I'll be sure to tell Finlay when he gets back."

Donald blushed to his hairline and then gave an awkward bow before backing out of the room. Eleanor turned to her breakfast but found that she had little appetite. Her thoughts turned to Finlay. Where was he? Would he be all right out there on his own? If anything should happen to him...

She swallowed thickly. Damn it. With a cry of frustration she dropped her spoon onto the breakfast tray and pushed it aside. This wouldn't do. Standing, she strode to the door, yanked it open, and hurried out. Donald, who'd been leaning against the wall, came alert with a startled yelp and hurried to catch up.

"Where are ye going, my lady?" he stammered. "Finlay told us we weren't to let ye leave—"

He cut off as Eleanor rounded on him and fixed him with a glare. "*Let* me leave?"

The boy swallowed. "That is...um...we are to ensure ye dinna come to any harm while he's away. He thought it best if ye remain inside today."

"Did he? How kind of him. Unfortunately, my patients don't have the luxury of waiting around until Finn decides it's safe for me to see them. I'm going down to the kitchen garden now to gather some herbs. You can either come with me or stay here. Which will it be?"

Donald licked his lips. "I...I think I'll come with ye, my lady."

"Let's go then."

She knew her way around the manor house by now and took the corridor that led towards the back of the house and the servant's staircase that led down to the courtyard. She and Donald crossed it and entered the little gate that led into the kitchen garden. It had been sorely neglected and there was a riot of weeds growing amongst the herbs but there was still plenty she could make use of. Crossing to a patch of wild garlic growing under the window, she knelt and began harvesting it. In the right dosages it could be useful in treating diarrhoea and other stomach problems—many of which were rife in Stewart's army.

When she had enough she placed it in her basket and stood. She must ask Stewart to allow her somewhere to make her cures. Maybe there was a disused outhouse somewhere or a storeroom in the manor house she could appropriate. She also needed to go on another foray into the woods to gather poppies and hemlock for pain killers. Her stomach did a little flip at the thought. A perfect excuse to be alone with Finn.

With Donald at her side, she left the kitchen garden and headed back towards the manor house. They rounded the corner of the bakehouse and Eleanor, deep in thought, almost collided with someone coming the other way. She stumbled back, mumbling an apology, but the words froze on her tongue as she found herself looking into the cold eyes and mocking grin of Balloch Stewart.

He was stripped to the waist and his muscled torso was covered in sweat, probably from a bout on the sparring ground. Spotting Eleanor, his grin widened and he raised an eyebrow.

"There's nay need to apologize," he drawled lazily. "I canna blame ye for wanting to get me alone."

The mocking tone of his voice made her seethe. She'd met plenty of men like him at home—arrogant men who saw women as nothing more than a trophy to hang on their arm. Cocky, arrogant and convinced of their own superiority, men like Balloch thought they could take whatever they wanted.

"Excuse me," she said, forcing her tone to civility. She began to move around him, Donald at her side, but Balloch stepped into her path.

"Going so soon? Mayhap ye should stay a while longer. Send yer page on his way and we can get to know each other a little better."

She glared at him, even though her heart was starting to race. She didn't like the look in his eyes. "I don't think so. Good day."

She shoved past but his hand snapped out and snagged her elbow. "Dinna walk away from me, woman," he growled. "We have unfinished business. What was left unfinished in the woods will be finished now."

"Let go of me!"

Eleanor tried to yank free but Balloch's grip was like iron, his fingers digging into her skin hard enough to hurt. She aimed a kick at his shins but he merely laughed it off.

"Take yer hands off the lady!" Donald cried. Taking his duty to protect her all too seriously, the youth had drawn his sword and held it out threateningly. Even so, his eyes were round with fear.

"Run away, little boy," Balloch growled at him. "This is grown-up business."

Donald, to his credit, stood his ground. "Release the lady or I'll...I'll..."

"Ye will what?" Balloch asked, turning his baleful gaze on the youth.

Then, quick as a flash, he lashed out with his free hand and punched Donald square in the cheek. The blow was powerful enough to send the lad crashing into the bakehouse wall where he slid to the ground, unconscious.

"Donald!"

Eleanor struggled and kicked, trying to break free of Balloch's grip but her efforts only seemed to please him more.

"You bastard!" she growled at him. "He's just a boy!"

Balloch grinned. "That's it. Fight me. It will just make this even more pleasurable."

He yanked her through the door of the bakehouse. There was nobody else in the small room, and the oven in one corner was cold. Eleanor considered screaming but they were far from the manor house and she doubted anyone would hear her. Besides, she suspected that's what Balloch wanted.

Balloch rammed her against the wall hard enough to make her gasp. With a desperate cry, Eleanor swung her free hand at his face but he caught her wrist nonchalantly and pinned her arms above her head with one meaty fist. He ran his other hand down her side, his touch sending a sliver of fear right through her body. No. No! This was not happening!

He leaned close, pressing himself against her and whispered, "I'm going to enjoy this."

Eleanor screwed her eyes tight shut, trying to fight the panic that had turned her insides to water. Balloch's stink was all around her, the weight of his body pressing her against the wall, the sound of his excited breathing heavy by her ear.

Then a howl of rage tore through the air. Eleanor opened her eyes to see Finlay standing in the doorway. His eyes blazed, his face twisted in a mask of white-hot fury. He launched himself at Balloch who released Eleanor and turned to meet his attack. Finlay punched him hard enough that Eleanor heard the crack of Balloch's nose.

Finlay followed, grabbed Balloch by the shoulders and rammed him against the wall, just as Balloch had done to Eleanor. He rained punches into the man's gut, and Balloch doubled over, grunting at each blow.

Eleanor watched in horror, her hands covering her mouth, her stomach twisted into knots. She saw Balloch's foot come lashing out and cried a warning.

"Finn, watch out!"

Too late. Balloch's foot caught the back of Finn's ankle and tripped him. He went crashing to the ground and Balloch followed him, stamping down towards his face with one booted foot. Finn rolled out of the way and came back to his feet fluidly, facing his opponent with a snarl on his face.

"What's wrong?" he growled at Balloch. "Dinna ye like victims who fight back?"

"I'll kill ye," Balloch bellowed, wiping a trail of blood from his nose. "I'll kill ye and leave ye for the crows!"

With a roar of rage he charged at Finlay. He caught him around the waist and his momentum took them both crashing through the door to sprawl onto the courtyard outside. Eleanor followed them, trying desperately to think of a way she could make them stop.

But both men were in the thrall of blood lust now and they scrambled to their feet and began circling, each searching for an opening. Finn looked not in the least winded but Balloch's face dripped blood and his shoulders heaved with exertion. There was a flicker of uncertainty in his eyes as Finn stalked him.

Then Eleanor heard footsteps and turned to see three other men running over. Balloch saw them too and the uncertainty evaporated to be replaced by a wide, cocky grin.

"Perfect timing, boys," he called. "Ye can join me in bringing this hound to heel."

The three men, obviously Balloch's toadies, spread out in a circle around Finlay. His eyes flicked to them and Eleanor didn't see any fear in his eyes, only a calm acceptance.

She had to help Finn. But how? Maybe she should run to the manor house and get help but the fighting men blocked the exit from the courtyard. Biting her lip, she looked around. There. A broom was propped against the wall, its handle stout and thick. Grabbing it, she smashed it against her knee, snapping off the end with the bristles, leaving a long, smooth staff.

Balloch's toadies attacked. As they threw themselves at him, Finn moved, ducking under their clumsy blows then pivoting to land a kick into one man's knee, a punch into the face of another before spinning away to give himself room for a roundhouse kick into Balloch's stomach. Then he took three steps back, opening up a gap.

It was the space Eleanor needed. "Finn! Here!"

She tossed him the staff. He caught it deftly, twirled it a few times to get the weight and then turned back to the fight. The men had drawn weapons now and steel glinted in the sunlight. Their expressions had become cold, raw fury. Eleanor knew they were beyond reason now and they would show Finn no mercy.

Please help him, she prayed, not knowing to who or what she prayed. *Please don't let him get hurt. I couldn't bear it. Oh god, Finn.*

Chapter 11

Finn felt a strange calm settle over him. It was the same calm he experienced when out tracking in the woods alone. All his thoughts seemed to stop, his past and future fell away and there was only the now. This moment. The moment that might mean the difference between his life and death.

Balloch and his toadies were furious now. He could see it in the way their lips twisted back from their teeth. He could see it in the way their faces had turned red and the way their shoulders were hunched. They were men ready to kill.

So be it. He'd always known there would be a reckoning with Balloch one day. Today was that day.

A cold stab of fear like a sword blade had gone right through his guts when he'd seen Donald laying unconscious by the bakehouse. He'd paused only long enough to check the lad was all right before hurrying into the building, knowing what he would find there and praying to every Fae, every god, every friendly spirit, that he wasn't too late.

He'd always thought himself a rational man. A man who thought through his actions. A man who considered consequences before he acted.

As it turned out, he was none of those things.

When he'd seen Balloch pinning Eleanor to the wall, his stinking frame pressed against her, his hand roving over her body as if he owned it, all rationality had disappeared. White-hot fury erupted and the only thought in his mind was that he would kill this man who'd tried to hurt her. He would kill him and enjoy doing it.

That rage had not abated. His fists ached to meet Balloch's flesh, to inflict on him the pain he'd planned to mete out to Eleanor. But now his calm detachment had cooled the rage to a slow-burning ember, one that allowed him to think rationally.

He looked around, assessing his options. The four men circled him, blocking all avenues of escape but that hardly mattered. Finn had no intention of trying to escape. He breathed deeply, rocking onto the balls of his feet, ready to move in any direction.

A red-haired man called Robert lunged at him with a roar, his blade angling straight for Finn's stomach. At the same time, as Finn's attention was pulled to Robert, he sensed Balloch move as well, coming at him from behind. Finn shifted. He brought the staff around to meet Robert's thrust, slamming the hard wood against the blade and ripping it from the man's grip. Then he ducked, rolled, and Balloch's blade went singing through the air where his neck had been a moment ago. He came to his feet and pivoted, ramming the heel of the staff into the paunch of Patrick, a blond-haired man who'd attacked from Finn's left.

Dimly, he was aware that a crowd was beginning to gather, no doubt alerted by the sound of fighting the way wolves would scent blood. But he paid the onlookers no heed. All his attention was fixed on his opponents.

Finlay swayed and ducked and counter-attacked, keeping them at bay with ease. He had always been quick. Only Camdan was a better fighter than Finn and even he had often struggled to keep up with Finn's lightning reflexes. From his center of calm detachment Finn could almost sense his opponents' moves before they made them and so they laid not a single blow on him whilst they were quickly covered in cuts and bruises from where his staff struck them.

"What are ye playing at?" Balloch roared to his toadies. "This isn't ring of roses, ye damned cowards! Will ye let one man best ye? Kill him, damn ye!"

As if chastened by his taunts, the three toadies attacked in unison, each coming from a different direction, each with murder in his eyes. Finn stilled, assessing who would reach him first. Then, just as Robert swung a punch at Finn's kidneys, he dropped to one knee, ducking under the punch and smashed the end of the staff into Robert's knee with a crunch. Robert crashed to the ground with a howl, rolling around and clutching his wounded knee.

Finn sensed someone approaching from behind, and reversed the staff, driving it behind him so it connected with Patrick's stomach. Rising, Finn swung the staff in an arc, its end connecting with Patrick's chin hard enough to snap his head back, send his eyes rolling in his head, and lay him out unconscious next to Robert.

Finn's neck prickled in warning and he threw himself to the side just as a blade came whistling through the air. It was such a wild swing that it took Balloch's third lackey, a man Finn didn't know, staggering to one side and Finn took advantage of the man's loss of balance by bringing the staff crunching down onto the wrist of his sword arm. The man yowled in pain, his fingers springing open and sending the sword crashing into the dirt. Finn smacked him across the back of the head, knocking him unconscious.

That left only Balloch. Finn turned to face him. The man's face was almost purple with rage, his eyes glinting with hatred. He looked at his downed comrades and his lips pulled back in a sneer.

"Want a job doing, do it yerself," he growled. "Useless bastards."

Around him Finn heard the jeering of the crowd and guessed that most of the manor house had gathered to watch this fight. Whether they were cheering for Balloch or himself he didn't know. Nor did he care. His gaze was fixed on Balloch.

"Ye know," Balloch said conversationally. "Ye should have let me have her. Let her know what it's like to have a real man. I'm sure she would have enjoyed it. Eventually."

Finn's control slipped. The rage that lurked just beyond his circle of calm reared up, threatening to shatter his composure. He fought it. Balloch wanted him to lose control. He would not fall for the trap.

"Ye are honorless," Finn said, his words clear and calm. "A disgrace to yer name. And I'm going to kill ye."

The words had the desired effect. With a roar, Balloch gripped his sword two-handed and charged at Finn. Finn let him come, waiting until he could see the white of Balloch's eyes. Only then, when the tip of Balloch's blade was only inches from his chest, did he step nimbly out of the way, grab Balloch's sword arm to yank him close, then squarely head-butt him in the face. Balloch staggered back, his sword arm drooping, and Finn hammered the staff into his wrist, knocking the weapon from his grasp. In a flash Finn swept Balloch's legs out from under him, then, as the man collapsed to the ground, he drew his bronze dagger and knelt on his chest, pressing the sharp blade against Balloch's throat. All the while he felt a calm, icy detachment.

Looking down into Balloch's eyes, wide and fearful now, he hissed, "I told ye one day there would be a reckoning. That day is here."

He tightened his grip on the dagger, preparing to strike, when a cold, clear voice rang out, cutting through the hubbub of the crowd.

"Stop."

And just like that Finlay couldn't move.

Pain flared down his back as his tattoo, the mark of his bargain, came roaring to life. He felt it burn white-hot on his back. As it did so the iron jaws of his curse came down on his will like the teeth of a man-trap.

No! he thought desperately. *No!*

He fought frantically to move but his muscles would not obey him. Their control no longer belonged to him, but to another. He shifted his eyes to the left and saw Lord Alasdair Stewart standing there, holding a bronze branding iron in his left hand. His cold, hard eyes were fixed on Finn.

Finn pulled his lips back in a rictus snarl and fought. With every sinew in his body he tried to move, tried to fight the power of his curse. His muscles strained, his lungs filled to bursting, the tendons in his neck stood out like ropes. It was no good. His curse held him as securely as if he was bound with iron chains. He glared at Stewart, black hatred bubbling in his stomach like bile.

Lord Stewart stepped forward. His eyes flicked contemptuously to Balloch. "Get up, ye worthless excuse for a Stewart."

Balloch scrambled out from beneath Finn and backed off, watching his uncle warily. Stewart's gaze returned to Finn.

"This ends now," he said loud enough for everyone to hear. "No MacAuley will lay hands on a Stewart. Not again. Not ever."

Balloch limped to his uncle's side. His face was a mass of bruises and blood crusted his nostrils. Finlay's stomach constricted with hatred. If he went anywhere near Eleanor...

"Call yerself a Stewart?" Lord Alasdair growled. "Ye allow yerself to be bested by a MacAuley?"

"It isnae my fault—" Balloch began.

"Quiet! I willnae listen to yer excuses. Ye willnae allow a MacAuley to lay hands on ye again. It is time this hound was taught his true place—and ye will be the one to do it. Dinna worry, I think my hound will find he is suddenly very obedient."

Stewart gestured at Finlay and spoke a word under his breath. Obeying the silent command, Finlay's body surged upright, forcing him to stand and face Stewart. Balloch looked at his uncle uncertainly.

"Hit him!" Stewart snapped. "Or should I fetch one of the stable hands to do it for ye?"

Anger twisted Balloch's face. He stepped forward, clearly wary, but when Finn didn't move—couldn't move—he grew in confidence. With a growl, he landed a punch into Finn's stomach that knocked the breath out of him and doubled him over with a grunt. Slowly, he straightened. Balloch backed away, expecting Finn to counter attack but when none came, that familiar cocky grin spread over his face, the grin that made Finn want to kill him. He swung at Finn's face and he was powerless to step aside as Balloch's fist connected with his chin. Finn's head snapped to the side and the iron tang of blood filled his mouth. A second later another blow cannoned into his temple, throwing him off balance. Finn staggered and the ground suddenly came rushing up to meet him.

He lay on his back, staring up at the sky as a boot crashed into his ribs, one, two, three times. Pain exploded along his nerves and it was suddenly difficult to breathe. He tried to curl into a ball but even this respite was denied him.

He heard Eleanor screaming and managed to move his eyes enough to see her struggling in the grip of three men, desperately trying to reach him.

Nay, lass, he thought. *Dinna come near. I am cursed, don't ye see? Stay away.*

Blow after blow rained down on him. Balloch was going to kill him, Finn realized. Finally Stewart had tired of his hound and he was going to let his nephew kill him. Not the beating of course. Stewart knew that no amount of physical violence could break Finn's curse. But all it would take was for Balloch to draw his dagger—with iron in the blade—and plunge it into Finn's chest.

There would be nothing he could do to stop it. An ignominious end for the once-heralded youngest son of Clan MacAuley. No noble death in battle for him. No glorious sacrifice that the bards would sing of. Instead he would choke out his last breath in a muddy courtyard. If he had the strength, he would have laughed.

But then Stewart spoke suddenly. "Enough."

The blows stopped and Finn sucked in a breath that felt like hot needles piercing his lungs. Blood dripped slowly from his nose to pool on the ground by his face. It was bright red, like holly berries.

"I think my hound has learned his lesson." Stewart's voice cut through the air like a knife. "Ye will leave, all of ye."

Finn managed to lift his head enough to see the crowd dispersing. Balloch, his shoulders heaving, gave Finlay a final glare and then stomped off in the direction of the house. Only Eleanor remained, being restrained by Stewart's guardsmen, and Donald, who still lay unconscious by the bakehouse.

Stewart came to stand over him. His expression was emotionless. He could have been looking down at an insect. Finlay breathed deeply, pushing away the pain enough to get control over his limbs. He felt the curse loosen its grip and he was finally able to move – barely. Gritting his teeth, his lips pulling back in a snarl of effort, he slowly pushed his tortured body to its knees. From there he forced his screaming muscles to uncurl into a standing position. Blood rushed to his head and for a moment he thought he might faint but he curled his hands into fists, digging his nails into his palms and used the pain to steady himself.

I am a MacAuley, he thought. *I willnae show weakness in front of this bastard.*

It took every shred of willpower, every ounce of self-control he'd learned through the long years of training under his father and elder brothers to keep himself standing, to lift his chin and meet the eyes of his torturer. He pulled his torn lips back in a smile and was rewarded when Lord Alasdair Stewart paled slightly.

"I owe ye my thanks," Finn croaked, the effort sending a line of blood spilling down his chin. "I never quite understood why ye hated me so much. Now ye've helped me understand. Ye dinna hate me at all, do ye? Ye fear me."

"Fear ye?" Stewart spat. "What do I have to fear?" He stepped forward, put a finger under Finn's chin and stared into his eyes. "Remember, Hound, ye are mine. Only death can free ye. Yer life belongs to me. Until I see fit to end it."

Suddenly Finn remembered standing in a ring of stones with his brothers. It was dark and from that darkness a voice spoke to him, a malevolent voice filled with glee. "The bargain is made. In payment, I take yer life, but ye willnae die, darling of the MacAuley Clan. Ye, who of all yer people long for freedom, will instead live yer life as a slave. Only death will free ye."

Snapping back to the present, despair washed through him like bile. He was a fool to fight. Only pain and suffering lay that way.

As if guessing his thoughts, Stewart smirked then turned and snapped at Eleanor, "Ye will heal him. I want him fit and ready to fight." Then he waved to his guards and hurried away.

The world seemed to contract around Finn and there was a roaring in his ears. The last thing he remembered as blackness took him was Eleanor catching him as he fell.

Chapter 12

Eleanor clung to Finlay's hand, fingers wrapped tight around his. She leaned forward, staring at his face as he lay unconscious on the bed in a tiny room of the manor house.

"Wake up, damn you," she growled. "You will wake up. Hear me?"

She'd done all she could for his injuries. She'd bathed his bruises, cleaned and stitched his cuts, dribbled poppy juice into his mouth for the pain, and wrapped tight bandages around his chest. But she was afraid that wasn't enough. She suspected he had several broken ribs and if one had punctured his lung...

Damn this time and its lack of medical facilities! If she'd been in the twenty-first century, she would have ordered an MRI, seen exactly what was going on inside Finn's body, sent him for surgery and fixed whatever the problem was. But here she didn't even have a stethoscope so, although she'd pressed her ear to his chest to listen to his breathing, she couldn't tell if his lungs were damaged or if there might be any internal bleeding.

She brought his hand to her face and pressed it against her cheek. Tears squeezed from her eyes.

Images played through her mind. Images of Finn stepping between her and Balloch. Images of Finn fighting to protect her. She'd never been so relieved to see anyone as when he'd stepped into the bakehouse. And she'd never been as terrified as when Alasdair Stewart had ordered Balloch to beat him.

She shook her head. Why did Finn allow that to happen? He was more than a match for Balloch. Why hadn't he defended himself? Why had he done exactly what Stewart had ordered him to, even to the point of letting Balloch beat him half to death?

She drew a deep breath, unwilling to follow where that thought might lead. Finn hadn't stirred for hours and the sun had climbed in the sky. Nonetheless, it was gloomy inside the tiny room. A single candle burned in the corner, throwing flickering light across the contours of his face.

After the fight, Stewart had ordered his men to bring Finn into this sparse room but since then the only people who'd been in were Donald, who'd been brought in with Finn, and the rest of Finn's command, who'd been pale and wide-eyed seeing their commander comatose and bleeding. Eleanor had put them to use in fetching the supplies she needed and had then examined Donald to find he only had a mild concussion. Once he'd woken, she'd ordered Rob to take him to the kitchen and saw he got a good meal before retiring to his bed.

Finlay suddenly stirred and she leaned closer. "Finn? Can you hear me?"

His eyelids fluttered then his eyes slowly opened. He stared blearily up at the ceiling for a moment but then his gaze cleared and he looked around, taking in his surroundings before his eyes finally settled on her.

Relief washed through Eleanor. It was so strong that for a moment dizziness overcame her and she feared she might faint. *Oh God. Thank you. Thank you, thank you, thank you.* Suddenly she could breathe again. Suddenly there seemed to be color in the world again. If Finn had died...

She clamped down on that thought.

A smile crept across her face and tears gathered in the corners of her eyes. Clasping his hand against her chest she whispered, "You came back to me."

His gaze strayed to her fingers gripping his own firmly. "Aye, lass," he whispered, his voice hoarse and raspy. "Ye brought me back. Ye gave me the strength."

"You did that yourself. How do you feel?"

A ghost of a smile played across his face. "Like I've been wrestling with a bear." Then his gaze sharpened. "And ye? Donald?"

She shook her head. "I'm fine, thanks to you, and Donald just has a concussion. He'll be okay after some food and rest."

"Good," he breathed. "That's good."

He extricated his hand from hers and wedged his arms under him. Then, to her surprise, levered himself up into a sitting position, wincing at the pain. She ground her teeth. He should be lying down and resting.

He looked around at the room and then peered at the window as if measuring the position of the sun. "How much time has passed?"

"It's almost midday. You've been unconscious for several hours."

"Has a patrol come back recently? Two men, dressed as trackers?"

"I've no idea," she replied, surprised by this sudden change in topic.

"Nay, they wouldnae have time to get there and back again, even if they galloped the whole way and they didnae look like they were in a hurry."

Eleanor frowned. She had no idea what he was talking about. "Okay. Whatever. You need rest. I'll get some food sent up for you and then you need to—"

"Has Stewart asked to see ye?" he demanded. "Asked any strange questions?"

"Finn, I haven't seen or heard from Stewart since the incident this morning. And it's just as well because next time I lay eyes on that bastard I'm going to kick him right where it hurts. He's a monster, Finn. He has to be stopped. I almost hope the MacAuleys take him out during the battle—and that goes against everything I've ever believed as a doctor."

It was Finn's turn to frown. "What do ye mean 'battle'?"

"Can't you hear it? The camp is in an uproar. Broag came to tell me a little while ago that Stewart has ordered the army to move out. They're marching to meet the MacAuley and MacConnell forces. Broag reckons there'll be a battle the day after tomorrow."

Finlay paled at the news. She could almost see the thoughts forming behind his eyes. Would his brothers be there? Would he have to face them?

He passed a hand over his face and let out a long breath. "The patrol will probably be back tomorrow and if the Lord is smiling on us, they'll come back to an empty manor house and have to follow the army. That buys us some time."

"Finn," she said, schooling herself to patience. "I've no idea what you're talking about. What patrol?"

His eyes snapped to hers. "The patrol that Stewart sent out to investigate yer story. That's why I wasnae here this morning. I followed them, all the way back to the place where ye first met Angus and his men."

Eleanor felt the blood drain from her face. Her stomach flipped over. Oh god. "Why...why would he do that?"

Finn slipped a hand inside his shirt and brought out an object which he held out to her. "Mayhap ye should tell me."

The flat, oblong object was smeared with dirt and cracked all over but Eleanor still recognized it. Her cell phone. At the sight of it sitting in Finlay's palm her heart began to race, thumping against her ribs as though she'd been running.

Finn's eyes were fixed on hers, stern and unyielding. "The time for secrets between us is over, Eleanor. If we are to get out of here, I must know the truth. What is this thing? It's like naught I've ever seen before. Why is Stewart so interested in where ye came from? What does he suspect?"

Eleanor's thoughts whirled. She'd been so stupid! Did she really think she could practise modern medicine in this time and not arouse suspicion? Did she really think she could rely on such a flimsy back story to cover the truth? Alasdair Stewart was no fool. And neither was Finlay. His gaze was unblinking as he watched her, waiting for her to speak.

I can't tell you! she wanted to shout. *What am I supposed to say? I'm from the future. Nothing to worry about. I just thought I'd pop back in time hundreds of years for a quick vacation. Is that all right with you?*

He'd think she was insane or a witch. Possibly both. She cast around, desperately trying to think of something to say, anything that would deflect him. Her eyes alighted on the lines of his tattoo as it curled over the top of his shoulder.

"You're a fine one to talk about secrets!" she blurted. "You want honesty between us? Fine! Then how about you tell me what hold Alasdair Stewart has over you?"

He stared at her. Then blinked and looked away. "I dinna know what ye mean."

"Don't you? I've been doing a little digging of my own whilst you've been unconscious. Maybe you can tell me whether the story Rob told me of the cursed MacAuley brothers is more than a child's tale. Maybe you can tell me if I'm stark raving crazy or if I really did see that tattoo of yours glowing like molten metal? Maybe you can tell me who you really are, Finlay MacAuley!"

"Ye shouldnae listen to gossip," he muttered.

"I'm not listening to gossip," he said. "I'm asking you."

"Ye are trying to deflect my questions," he replied. "I'm not a fool, lass. What I want to know is why? What are ye hiding? Why willnae ye trust me?"

Trust? Was he serious? How could she *not* trust him after all he'd done for her? After what they'd shared? She longed to tell him everything, for it all to come spilling out and be damned with the consequences. But it wasn't that simple. The truth about her time-traveling would endanger him as much as it would endanger her. How could she put him at risk like that?

What choice do you have? a voice said in the back of her mind. *I can't tell him!* She thought desperately. *I just can't.*

FINN WATCHED ELEANOR. There was a crease between her eyebrows and her large, luminous eyes were full of worry. He wanted to reach out, pull her to him and kiss her until the worry evaporated from her beautiful face. But he knew he could not.

A gulf lay between them, one that neither could cross. It was a chasm made up of secrets, of half-truths and things left unsaid.

Oh, how he longed to tell her everything. How he longed to have it all laid out between them, the truth, no matter how dark and painful it might be.

But she would turn from ye if she knew the truth, a voice whispered in his head. *And she would be right to do so. Why would she want aught to do with ye? Traitor and liar that ye are?*

Then he heard Irene MacAskill's voice, the words she'd spoken to him that day in the woods. *There is always a way back, lad. Destiny has a way of leading us safely home if we go astray—as long as we have the courage to listen when it calls.*

Courage? It seemed he was running low on that lately. Dare he take the risk of her hating him?

Aye, he thought. *I'm done with secrets. She deserves the truth.*

Pulling in a sharp, quick breath, he threw back the bed covers and swung his legs over the edge of the bed.

"What are you doing?" Eleanor cried in alarm. "You're not well enough to be out of bed!"

Finn gritted his teeth and climbed to his feet, taking a few steps away from the bed. Sharp, stabbing pains ripped through his chest and back, making him grimace and grit his teeth. He breathed slowly, one, two, three breaths, and the pain slowly began to fade.

Eleanor stared at him, her mouth forming an O of surprise. "You have broken ribs! You shouldn't even be able to stand!"

Finn crossed to the window and stood looking out through the narrow gap. In the valley beyond the manor house the camp seethed like a kicked ant's nest as men packed up and got ready to move out. So. This was it. In two days' time he would finally meet his brothers in battle.

Eleanor didn't move but Finn felt her presence behind him, heard her breath as it hissed in and out of her chest. He screwed his eyes tight shut for a moment, gathering his courage, and then turned to look at her.

"By morning I will be healed, with no trace of injury."

"Don't be ridiculous," she replied. "Nobody heals that quickly. It's not possible."

He drew a deep breath, forced himself to meet her eyes. "It is if ye have Fae magic running through yer veins."

Silence descended. From outside came the shouts of men, the barking of dogs, the snorting of horses. But inside the room all was still.

Finally, she shook her head. "There's no such thing," she said at last, rising to her feet. Her eyes glinted with something. Anger? "You expect me to believe such crap? Why are you risking your recovery by telling yourself such nonsense? I haven't spent hours treating your injuries only to see you keel over from internal bleeding because you wouldn't rest!"

"Ye wanted the truth did ye not?" he snapped back, taking a step towards her. "Sometimes the truth isnae what we want to hear. Sometimes it's ugly and twists us up inside. Ye wanted to know who I really am? Very well. I am cursed, lass. Those stories ye've heard about me? They are true. All of them."

She stared at him, her nostrils flaring, her chest heaving as his words settled in.

"The Fae," she muttered. "Magic. Curses. Irene MacAskill. Brigid's Hollow. This is all crazy. Crazy." She pulled in a deep breath. "And your tattoo? Why was it glowing?"

"It isnae a tattoo," he replied. "But a brand. A mark that shows I belong to the Fae. Or in this case, to the man who bargained with them for my soul."

Eleanor passed a shaky hand over her face and then wrapped her arms around herself as if she was suddenly cold. "Hell. Hellfire and damnation. None of this makes any sense." She lifted her chin to look at him. "You better start from the beginning."

He nodded. "Aye. I suppose I better." He rubbed at the stubble on his chin and then blew out a breath. Tell her everything? Where was he supposed to begin?

"I've already told ye I was bard and tracker for my eldest brother who became laird after my father. I was out on one such tracking mission several years ago when I spotted a fleet of ships crossing the Irish Sea, heading for Dun Ringill. It was a fleet of raiders, come to sack my home, burn what they couldn't carry off, and terrorize my people."

He shook his head at the memory. It had been a bright, clear day, and as he stood on a cliff top the sight of those sails in the distance had sent a chill right through to his heart.

"The MacAuley is, and has always been, a strong clan. But even we didnae have the strength to stand against such numbers. We knew that if we met them in battle, we would lose. In desperation, we turned to other means. My cousin, Eoin, was learned in the ways of the Fae and he suggested a pact with them, a bargain for the power to defeat our enemies." He clenched his fists, the muscles standing out in his arms as he remembered that meeting in his brother's solar. The meeting that changed the course of his life forever. "So my brothers and I went to the stone circle at Druach and there we met one of the Fae. He agreed to our bargain: the power to defeat our enemies in exchange for the lives of my brothers and me."

He raised his eyes to look directly at Eleanor. "It was a bargain we made gladly. What worth are three lives compared to those of our clan? The Fae kept his word. We were imbued with a power I canna explain. I willnae describe what my brothers and I did that night but when dawn rose, the Irish fleet was destroyed."

Memories assailed him. A feeling of euphoria, of invincibility. Blood and pain. Terrified screaming.

He closed his eyes, pressing his hand across them, trying to drown out the memories of that night.

"I don't understand," Eleanor said softly. "You said the Fae kept his bargain but you're here. You're alive."

"Aye," he said, turning to look at her. "Because we didnae envisage the treachery of the Fae. In payment the Fae took our lives but he didnae kill us. He cursed us. Cursed to be forever outcasts, scraping a half-life on the edges of the world. And for me? For the spoiled youngest son who valued his freedom above all else? My curse was to have that freedom taken away. To become a slave. To have my soul sold into the keeping of another."

"Stewart?" she breathed, as realization dawned. "I saw him locking away something I took to be a branding iron, the kind used on cattle. Oh god! It has the same design as your tattoo! Why the hell didn't I realize this earlier? It wasn't for use on cattle was it?"

"Nay, lass," he said softly. "It is the thing that binds me to Alasdair Stewart. He holds the strings of my soul and makes me dance like a puppet whenever he chooses. That's what ye saw in the courtyard this morning and that's why I'll be healed come the morrow. Stewart knew Balloch's blows wouldnae kill me. Only the touch of iron can do that. It is anathema to the magic of the Fae."

"So that's why you carry a bronze knife and arrows?" she said, her eyes widening in sudden understanding. "You can't carry iron."

"Aye."

He watched her closely, gauging her reaction. He'd never talked about this with anyone. Other than Alasdair Stewart, only his brothers, Logan and Camdan, knew of his curse, and even they didn't know what form it took. It effected them all in a different way, robbing each of them of the very thing that made them who they were. Such was the cruelty of the Fae.

He couldn't tell what Eleanor was thinking. Her face was pale, her breathing rapid as she thought through all he'd told her.

"What's Stewart's role in all this? You made a bargain with the Fae, not him. So how come he controls the curse? And how come he hates you so much?"

"He hates my entire family," Finn said softly. "And he has reason to." He scrubbed a hand through his hair, gathering his thoughts. "Ye have to understand, lass, the Highlands can be a dangerous place. We are far from the king's justice and peace is maintained through strength. Sometimes that strength can be brutal.

When I was a boy, Alasdair Stewart lived with his mother in a village on the border between my father's lands and that of our neighbors, the Campbells. When I was around ten and Alasdair Stewart maybe double that age, his mother, a village healer and wise-woman, was accused of being a witch. I dinna know where the accusation came from but Alasdair rode to petition my father in Dun Ringill. He begged him to intervene, to save his mother. My father went with him to the village and held a trial. He listened to the village priest's evidence against the woman, the witnesses who accused her of bewitching them. Alasdair spoke in his mother's defense, but my father, perhaps to keep the peace, perhaps due to pressure from the Church, found in favor of the villagers. Punishment of Stewart's mother was handed over to the priest. She was burned as a witch. Alasdair Stewart cursed my father and vowed revenge. He vowed that one day he would destroy my father's family as my father had destroyed his."

He drew in a deep breath and looked directly at Eleanor. "After the death of his mother, he joined forces with a man called Robert MacGregor, an outlaw and people trafficker running his operations out of the mountains. In the lawless border lands they flourished and Alasdair Stewart became a rich man. He bought himself lands and a title, put on a facade of respectability. And he knew of the Fae. Maybe he got the knowledge from his mother, I dinna know, but he made a bargain with them, and in payment he was given my life, to do with as he pleased. He had his revenge on my father—at least in part. But destroying me would never be enough. Only the destruction of my clan would satisfy him. Two years ago my brother Logan broke his curse and returned to the lairdship of the MacAuley, my brother Camdan did the same a year later, and together they turned their attention to the outlaws along their borders. They routed MacGregor and his crew from their mountain lair and now their attention has turned to Alasdair Stewart. The MacAuley and MacConnell forces outnumber Stewart's and they would have won long before now if not for the bargain Stewart made with the Fae. If not for me."

He gritted his teeth as the old, familiar shame washed through him. He forced himself to continue. "If not for my help, my knowledge of the MacAuley strategies, the make-up of their forces, the likely lines of attack and retreat, my brothers would have defeated Alasdair Stewart long ago." He met her gaze. "So ye see, lass. I am everything they say I am. I am a traitor and a liar. Ye wanted the truth? Now ye have it."

He couldn't bear to look at her. He couldn't bear to see the revulsion in her eyes. He turned away, placed his hands on the window sill and looked out, head hanging as though waiting for the executioner's axe.

FINLAY TURNED AWAY from her, rested his hands on the window sill and hung his head. His torment was evident in the hunch of his shoulders, the rigidity of the muscles in his back.

Eleanor ached to run to him, ease away that tension, tell him everything would be okay. But she couldn't tell him such a lie. Everything was most definitely *not* okay.

Holy crap, what was she to do with everything he'd told her? A maelstrom of thoughts and emotions churned inside her, each chasing the other, making her pulse drum in her ears.

She found her eyes drawn to his tattoo. It was quiet now, just a normal black tattoo swirling down his back in a Celtic design of whorls and loops.

It's not a tattoo though is it? she thought. *It's a brand. The mark of his bargain with the Fae. Oh, Finn. What has been done to you?*

She realized suddenly that she didn't doubt his story at all. She knew in her bones that everything he said was true, as crazy as it sounded. It all made sense now. The way he'd reacted when he found out she'd come via Brigid's Hollow, a place of the Fae. The way he did Alasdair Stewart's bidding, even though he clearly loathed the man. The reason he, a MacAuley, worked for the enemy against his own people.

He was as trapped as she was.

Anger began to simmer in her belly. Anger at Alasdair Stewart. Anger at the Fae who tricked him. Anger at the world in general for allowing this to be done to him.

Softly, she walked over to stand behind him. He didn't turn to face her. She raised her hand and ran it softly over the lines of his tattoo, drawn to the strange, swirling design. His skin felt warm, the muscles underneath hard with tension but it felt like a normal tattoo, not something that marked him out as cursed.

He pulled in a soft intake of breath and turned to face her. "Lass," he breathed, his voice more like a moan.

She reached a hand towards his chest but he caught her hand before she touched him.

"Nay," he breathed. "Ye shouldnae do that. Ye should stay away from me."

Stay away from him? Did he not realize that staying away from him was no longer an option for her?

She drew in a deep, steadying breath, and made a decision. He was right. The time for secrets between them was over. She brought her other hand up between them and held out her palm. In it rested her cell phone. She held down the button to turn it on and the cracked screen lit with a light brighter than the candle.

Finlay's eyes widened. "What the—?"

Eleanor flicked to the file that contained her photos. There wasn't much battery left and she had to make Finn understand before it died forever. She scrolled to photos of her home city. She held up images of cars, of landmarks, of streets busy with people.

Finn watched in silence, his expression one of wonder. Mirroring her words from earlier, he said, "Start from the beginning, lass."

"It's called a cell phone," Eleanor replied. "Where I come from virtually everyone has one. They're electronic devices that we use to talk to each other over great distances. And they can be used for lots of other things too, such as taking photographs—captured images like a painting."

"I havenae ever seen such a thing."

"No, you won't have. Nobody has," she replied. "Nor will they. At least not for another several hundred years."

She looked up at him, saw the puzzled expression on his face. No going back now. "Finn, I'm from the future," she blurted. "From the twenty-first century. When I stepped through Brigid's Hollow it brought me back in time."

She held her breath, watching his reaction. For the longest moment he said nothing at all. Then he glanced to the cell phone in her hand and back to Eleanor's face.

"That isnae possible," he began. Then he barked a sudden, bitter laugh. "Isnae possible? What am I saying? I, who know all too well that aught is possible where the Fae are concerned. Ah, lass, ye should have told me sooner. Ye should have trusted me with this."

"Then you believe me?"

"How can I not? I've just seen the evidence in front of my very eyes."

Relief flooded through her, so strong that her legs went weak. Finn believed her! And he didn't look as though he wanted to run a mile or burn her at the stake!

"I...I wanted to tell you," she said. "I just didn't know how. And let's face it, that kind of knowledge would hardly endear me to your people. You told me not twenty years ago a woman was burned as a witch."

He gazed down at her, the look on his face becoming intense and penetrating. "This changes naught, lass. I made a vow to get ye home and I will keep that vow. I swear on my family's honor."

She smiled. "And I vow I'll do whatever I can to help you get free of Alasdair Stewart. I guess we're in this together then, eh?"

His fingers curled around hers, holding her hand tight. "Aye, lass. We're in this together."

Eleanor's heart fluttered. He was looking at her like that again: that way that made it seem they were the only two people in the whole world. Silence descended, just the call of men outside and the pounding of feet somewhere else in the house. In the room, all was still.

Instinctively, Eleanor reached out and placed her hand against his chest, against the hard contours of his pecs where the bruises were already fading to yellow. She felt his heart beating beneath her palm.

She glanced up, found him gazing down at her. His eyes had gone dark, the candlelight playing across the angles of his face. His breathing was a soft, steady in-and- out that made his chest rise and fall under her hand.

"Eleanor," he whispered.

Her name on his lips sent a tingle all the way down her spine.

He bent his head and covered her mouth with his own. It was what she'd been waiting for ever since that first kiss in the meadow.

She leaned into him instinctively, pressing herself against his chest as his arms circled around her, his palms pressing into the small of her back. His lips moved insistently against hers and she responded. Desire flared through her body, goose bumps riding up her skin as the kiss deepened. Finlay's tongue moved between her lips, forcing them open and then ravishing her tongue with his own.

She gasped as Finn's lips moved down to her chin, then her neck, leaving a trail of fire along her skin. She threw her head back, giving him whatever access he wanted, just as long as he didn't stop touching her.

Then, with a growl, Finn grabbed her around the waist, spun her around and pinned her against the wall. Eleanor tangled her fingers in his thick, soft hair and their lips met in a passionate dance, his body felt hard and unyielding as it pressed her against the stone and she welcomed every inch of him touching her.

His breathing was becoming ragged and she could feel his desire for her in the hardness that pressed against her stomach. Lord, the feel of it nearly undid her. She wanted this man. She wanted him more than she'd ever wanted anything. A desperate, urgent need took her, and she ran her hands down his back, her fingers trailing across the bunched muscles beneath the skin, wanting to feel every inch of him, wanting...wanting...

Somebody banged on the door.

Finn sprang back, hand going to his belt where his dagger would be but Eleanor had removed it when he was brought in. She glanced at him, eyes wide, but he was watching the door, tense as a coiled spring.

The banging came again. "Lady Eleanor?" a voice called. "I've come to escort ye on yer rounds."

Eleanor breathed a sigh of relief. It was Angus, not Stewart. "I'll be out in a minute," she called, pressing a hand against her chest to still her thumping heart.

She glanced at Finn, reading the same concern written across his face. That was close. If Angus had walked in and found them like that? Or worse still, Alasdair Stewart?

Finn took her hand. "Ye must go," he breathed. "Act normal and dinna alert Stewart's suspicions."

"What about you?" she asked. "You need to rest."

"There isnae time for that," he replied, shaking his head. "I will return to my command and find out what's happening. In the confusion of the army moving out we might just find the cover we need to slip away. I'll come find ye later." He looked at her. "Tell me, lass, is there aught incriminating about yer origins that Stewart's patrol might find at Brigid's Hollow?"

"Yes," Eleanor breathed. "Dammit, yes! My watch—a device to tell the time. I dropped it when I came through the arch."

"Then we'll have to hope the patrol doesnae find it. Or if they do that we're long gone by the time they catch up with Stewart. Now go, before Angus comes in here looking for ye."

She nodded, began to walk off, but he suddenly pulled her back, caught her up, and kissed her long and deep.

Eleanor was a little breathless when he released her.

"Be careful," he said.

Eleanor nodded. "You too."

With that she headed out the door, the taste of Finn's kisses lingering on her lips.

Chapter 13

The man winced as Eleanor delicately probed his head wound. There was a tear in his scalp, not deep, but it bled profusely, as scalp wounds often do.

"How did you do this?"

The man gave an angry glance at his companion who sported a swelling around his eye that was quickly turning purple.

She sighed. "Let me guess. You were fighting?"

Their sullen silence was all the answer she required. Great. This was all she needed. It was the third injury she'd treated today caused either by fighting or drunkenness.

She washed out the wound—non too gently—and then applied a poultice of comfrey, yarrow and honey to keep out infection.

"You'll be fine," she told him. "It's already starting to scab over but don't scratch it and please don't get into any more fights."

The man nodded. A big bear of a man with a shaggy red beard and hands like hams, he ducked his head respectfully as he climbed to his feet and shuffled off, his companion at his side.

Eleanor placed her hands on her hips and looked around. Several paces away stood her two guards lounging against a stack of crates. Eleanor didn't recognize them. Stewart had appointed new guards since Finn's fight with Balloch and members of Finn's command were no longer allowed to escort her.

Around her the army was settling down for the night. They had decamped from the manor house that afternoon and marched for many hours, stopping only as the sun began to set. The men were edgy, tense, knowing that they were marching to meet the enemy. She wasn't surprised that fights and drunkenness had broken out and she was glad of the two burly guards that Stewart had assigned her, despite the way they leered at her and made crude remarks.

She turned at the sound of footsteps approaching her make-shift medical station. A man ran up to her guards, spoke urgently in low tones, and hurried off again.

One of the guards came over, a skinny man with one ear missing and a row of teeth that any horse would have been proud of. He jerked his thumb. "Lord wants to see ye."

Eleanor ground her teeth. "You'd better lead the way then."

She grabbed the leather bag containing her supplies and allowed the guards to escort her through the camp to its northern edge where Stewart's tent had been set up. It was more like a pavilion and once inside she saw it was divided into two rooms by a fabric curtain, one room for meeting with his officers, one for sleeping. The guards led her into the back room where she found Alasdair Stewart seated on the edge of a camp bed.

Eleanor bridled. Hot rage came bubbling to the surface, quickening her breathing and sending her pulse hammering. This was the man who'd allowed Balloch to beat Finn senseless. This was the man who'd made Finn a slave, stopped him from returning to his family, and turned him into a traitor. Oh, how she longed to land a fist into that twisted face of his!

But she schooled herself to calm, forced her face into an expressionless mask. Why did he want to see her? Had the patrol he sent to Brigid's Hollow returned? Had they found something incriminating about her? The thought made fear coil in her belly.

"You asked for me?"

He glanced at her, his face gray with pain. He was holding a wad of cloth against his thigh. It was red with blood.

"Ye took yer time," he snapped. "The ride has reopened my wound. See to it."

Eleanor hesitated. The thought of laying hands on this man, of helping him, was almost more than she could bear. But she couldn't refuse. She was a doctor wasn't she? She'd sworn an oath to help any in need, even if that person was a monster who caused untold suffering.

She hefted her bag of supplies and knelt by Stewart's side. She glanced up at him as she removed the wadded cloth and found him watching her with hard eyes. Pointedly she looked away, concentrating on her task. She no longer cared whether Stewart suspected her true origins. He needed her and so for the time being he wouldn't do anything to harm her. Or so she told herself.

Wiping away the blood, she sucked a breath through her teeth. "You've burst your stitches," she snapped. "Didn't I tell you to avoid excessive movement?"

"Aye, ye did," he snapped back. "But I dinna take orders from a woman. Ye will remember who ye are addressing!"

"I'm addressing my patient," she replied, glaring at him. "And I suggest you get used to taking orders from a woman or this wound is never going to heal!"

He ground his teeth, anger flaring in his eyes, and for a moment Eleanor thought she'd gone too far. Then he looked away. "Just patch it up so that I can swing a sword come the battle."

Eleanor cleaned out the wound with alcohol, re-stitched it, smeared the wound with honey, and applied a fresh bandage.

"Is there anything else?"

Stewart stood, stretching himself experimentally, a slight grimace escaping him as he pulled the new stitches.

"That will do." He grabbed her arm and marched her to the tent's entrance.

"Ye will escort the lady back to her tent," he instructed the guards.

Eleanor followed her guards through the camp. She couldn't help but look for Finn as she walked but she knew she wouldn't find him. She'd not seen him since this morning, not since a whispered conversation when he'd told her he was going out scouting the MacAuley lines.

She concentrated on the path, not wanting to trip on any tent ropes or slip in the mud. They'd almost reached the small, patched tent she'd been given when a sudden ripple of alarm passed through the camp. The sound of shouting came from somewhere to the north. The men seated around their campfires jumped to their feet, grabbing for weapons as cries rose of, "A raid! To arms!"

Eleanor's two guards fumbled to draw their weapons and swore under their breath as their comrades all went running off into the night. One of them pushed Eleanor towards her tent.

"Stay here," he growled.

Then he and his companion sprinted after their fellows. For the first time in what felt an age, Eleanor was left alone. She cocked her head, listening. She could hear the commotion to the north: men shouting, the neighing of horses, the clink of steel on steel. Her heart thumped.

A MacAuley attack! But a full-on attack or merely a skirmish? Would her guards come racing back any minute? For the first time since she'd arrived she was unguarded. Free.

She looked around, mind whirling. Could she make her escape now whilst Stewart and his men were distracted? No. Stewart set perimeter guards around the camp and she would be unlikely to get through. And besides, she would not leave without Finn.

Her eyes settled on Stewart's tent. It stood maybe a hundred paces away, a silhouette against the night lit only by a single lamp burning inside. She bit her lip, thinking. Then she made her decision.

Keeping low, she hurried between the tents, skirted around campfires, and approached Stewart's tent. A single guard stood on duty outside, holding his sword and staring anxiously northwards, paying little attention to any danger closer to home.

Treading carefully, Eleanor moved around the back of the tent and listened. No sound came from within and she guessed Stewart had gone to see what the commotion was all about. Adjusting the strap on her medical bag so it sat against her back like a rucksack, she threw herself onto her belly and squirmed under the canvas wall, coming out in Stewart's bedchamber. She was breathing heavily, heart hammering, and forced herself to take long, slow breaths. The lamp had almost burned down, casting the empty room into shadow but it was strong enough to illuminate a cedar wood chest in one corner.

She padded over to it and gently, slowly, untied the leather clasps that held it closed. Grasping the lid, she slowly lifted it, pausing when it suddenly let out a low creak.

She waited for one, two, three heartbeats, expecting any minute to hear the guard come inside to investigate the noise. He didn't.

After a long, tense moment, Eleanor opened the lid all the way and examined the contents of the chest. A velvet drawstring bag lay inside. At the sight of it Eleanor's heart almost jumped into her throat. She'd guessed right! She'd seen this bag once before, when she'd first been ushered into Lord Alasdair Stewart's presence, he'd been locking it away in a cupboard. Carefully, almost afraid to touch it, she reached in and took it out.

It was heavier than expected. She untied the drawstrings, revealing a long bronze implement with a hand-grip at one end and a pattern of swirling metalwork at the other.

Finlay's brand.

Quickly pulling the drawstring tight, Eleanor hurried to the rear of the tent and was about to leave when a voice suddenly spoke out of the gloom.

"Going somewhere?"

Eleanor almost jumped right out of her skin. With a cry of alarm she spun to see Balloch standing there. His arms were folded and he wore his usual lazy grin.

"Ye know," he said conversationally. "My uncle doesnae take kindly to thieves."

"I'm no thief!" Eleanor spat. "This doesn't belong to Stewart. I'm returning it to its rightful owner!"

Balloch took a step forward and Eleanor stepped back, her back pressing against the tent wall. A feral look lit Balloch's eyes.

"There's nobody here to help ye now, lass," he said. "They're all off fighting this raid. It's just ye and me now."

Eleanor swallowed. "There's a guard outside. If I scream, he'll come running."

"*Was* a guard outside," he corrected her. "I sent him on his way. When I saw ye sneaking in here, I just had to know what ye were up to. Now put that bag down and lie on the bed. If ye dinna struggle I promise not to hurt ye too much."

"Go to hell," Eleanor snarled.

Balloch pouted, putting on a hurt look. "Now ye've hurt my feelings." He shrugged. "Never mind. I suppose we'll have to do it the hard way."

He lunged at her, his hand closing around her forearm. Eleanor reacted instinctively. She swung the bag towards him and the heavy metal brand inside clunked into the side of his head with a crack that echoed through the tent. Balloch's knees gave way and he crashed to the floor, his eyes rolling back in his head.

Clasping the drawstring bag to her chest Eleanor ran to the door and fled into the darkness.

FINN FLITTED THROUGH the trees like a ghost, stalking his prey. His quarry had no idea that he was shadowing their movements like a predator, watching, waiting.

Call themselves trackers? Finn scowled. He would never give men as sloppy as these a place in his command.

The two men—the patrol Stewart had sent out to investigate Brigid's Hollow—were walking their horses, following the obvious line of march that Stewart's army had taken. The wide swathe of churned up ground wasn't hard to follow. Even a bairn would be able to track the army's passage.

Finn had been keeping pace with them for over an hour now, gauging their speed, their mood, trying to figure out if they posed a threat to Eleanor. They were not hurrying and from their pace it would be several hours yet before they caught up with the army. If he measured it right, they would arrive after midnight.

Three shapes materialized out of the darkness in front of the patrol. "Stop right there!" one called. "Name yerself or ye'll feel cold steel through yer gut."

Finn took cover behind a thick screen of hawthorn bushes and peered through the branches. He recognized the newcomers as some of the outlying pickets of Stewart's army, sent to guard his rear from being flanked.

The patrol from Brigid's Hollow halted. One of them leaned forward, peering through the gloom.

"That's young Martin unless I'm mistaken! I'll forgive ye for not recognizing me, dark as the Devil's arse out here, but I'll thank ye not to get in our way. We have important news for Lord Alasdair Stewart."

"Sean?" Martin replied. "What are ye doing out here? We weren't told to expect ye riding into camp."

"Lord Stewart has to explain everything to ye now, does he?" Sean growled. "He sent us on a mission and we have something very important to bring to his attention." He patted the pocket of his shirt. "Now stand aside."

Finn's blood ran cold. Something important? Had they found something that would give away Eleanor's origins?

"Aye, very well," Martin replied, his tone surly as he and his fellows pulled aside to let Sean and his companion pass. "Nay need to be bad-tempered about it."

"Aye, well ye'd be bad tempered if ye'd been riding for four days without a soft bed or a hot meal," Sean replied as he stomped past.

Finn watched for a moment longer and then silently slid from behind the hawthorn bushes. Sean and his companion didn't bother to pick up their pace. Despite their griping about hot food and a warm bed they seemed in no particular hurry to get back to camp. Finn didn't blame them. Who would want to return when they might be forced into battle on the morrow?

Finn considered his options. He could ambush them. He could easily take them down, leave their bodies in the woods and Stewart would never hear what they'd found. But Finn was no murderer.

The only option was to get Eleanor out of camp now, while there was still time. Moving wide of the patrol, Finn broke into a run, pelting through the dark landscape as swift and fleet as a shadow.

He approached Stewart's camp from the east and, as he reached the first tents, he frowned to himself. If the number of tents was anything to go by, Stewart didn't seem to have the number of fighters Finn expected. If he had, the MacAuleys wouldn't have been able to mount a raid without warning. Something didn't feel right. Why did there seem to be fewer warriors here than there were back at Stewart's manor?

Scowling to himself, he pushed all such thoughts from his mind and approached the meeting point he'd agreed with his men. As he entered the clearing he found Donald, Rob and Duncan waiting for him, sitting their horses with hunched shoulders, tension written across their faces.

They spun as he strode towards them, weapons sweeping from their scabbards.

"Easy," he said to them. "It's only me."

They let out relieved breaths. Donald, Finn was pleased to see, seemed to have fully recovered from his beating at Balloch's hands although he had a black eye to show for his troubles.

"Report," he barked to his men.

"It's as ye guessed," Rob replied. "The MacAuley forces have taken the northern ridge, the MacConnells the valley below, controlling the water source and blocking any retreat.

Stewart's forces hold this hillside and the trees will make it hard for the MacAuleys to guess our numbers."

Finn nodded. "And Stewart?"

"I tailed him as ye commanded," Donald said. "He rode out to inspect the pickets then went into his tent. He called Lady Eleanor to tend his wound then he got called away by the skirmish."

"And Lady Eleanor?" Finn asked. "She's safe?"

"Aye," Donald replied. "Last I saw, her guards were escorting her back to her tent but I left to follow Lord Stewart."

Finn nodded. He looked around at his men, at their eager, honest faces. They were good men. Honorable and loyal. They deserved better than the fate he'd led them to, better than to serve in a renegade army under a man like Stewart.

"Ye've done well, all of ye," he said. "Now, back to yer posts. Watch and report back to me if Stewart returns to camp."

They nodded, wheeled their mounts, and trotted off into the night. Finn watched them go for a minute and then drew a deep, steadying breath. This was it. The MacAuley raid might just provide the cover he needed to get Eleanor out of the camp. He must act now, before Stewart restored order.

He ran to the camp and approached Eleanor's tent. No glow of candlelight came from inside and no guards stood outside. He frowned, unease tingling down his spine. Something was wrong. Ripping aside the tent flap, he strode inside. It was empty.

His stomach contracted. Where was she?

Going back outside, he knelt in the mud, forced his mind into a tracker's calm, and looked for clues. There weren't many. The ground had been churned by the passage of many booted feet but he finally found a set of smaller tracks leading away from the tent and towards the woods that surrounded the camp.

Quickly, he ran to the horse lines, untied his horse and led it into the woods, following the tracks. Urgency bit at his heels. Time was running out. The jaws of the trap were closing. He must find Eleanor before they snapped shut.

ELEANOR STUMBLED THROUGH the woods. The darkness under the trees was thick, the shafts of moonlight hardly penetrating the canopy. She cursed herself for a fool. What the hell had she been thinking? She was no woodswoman. What was she doing wandering around like this?

The thick undergrowth had snagged her dress more than once, scratched at her face and hair, and she was pretty sure she was going around in circles. Off to her left, less than half a mile away she could see the light of burning campfires. She had a vague notion that if she could find the camps outer guards—pickets Finn called them—then she'd find Finn or at least Donald or one of his other men as they'd been assigned this duty for the night. But she hadn't found them and instead spent the last hour blundering through the woods and not getting anywhere.

Any sane person would return to the camp but the thought of Balloch sent a cold shiver down her spine and spurred her deeper into the woods. The velvet sack hung over her shoulder and she was damned sure it was getting heavier by the minute.

Somewhere ahead she heard movement. Eleanor froze. There it was again. A faint rustle as something brushed against a branch. Her heart began hammering. Was it Balloch? Her only weapon was the metal brand so she hefted the sack, grabbing the heavy bronze through the velvet and holding it up like a poker.

Sudden movement behind her. She yelped, whirled, and swung the brand with all her might.

A hand caught it.

"Easy, lass. Ye damn near took my head off," said Finn with a lopsided smile.

Eleanor gaped for a second. Then she dropped the bag and threw herself at him, wrapping her arms around his neck and burying her face in his hard shoulder.

"Thank God it's you!"

He held her close for a moment then pushed her to arm's length. "Lord above, woman, ye know how to give a man a scare. What are ye doing out here? When I found ye gone from the tent I feared the worst."

"Change of plan," she muttered. "I had to make a run for it. How did you find me?"

He held out a scrap of material that looked like the hem of her dress. "I'm a tracker, remember? Yer trail wasnae hard to follow once I found this on a branch near camp." His eyes fell to her wrist, to the mark where Balloch had grabbed her. His expression darkened.

"What is that?" he demanded. "Has somebody hurt ye?"

She shook her head. She didn't want to talk about it. "It doesn't matter. What matters is this." She grabbed the velvet bag and opened it, revealing the brand inside. It glinted like burnished copper in the moonlight.

Finlay's eyes widened and he stepped back a pace. He reached out a hand as though he might touch the cool metal but then snatched it back.

"How did ye get that?"

"I stole it. From Stewart when he got called away, but, holy shit, Finn, we're in trouble now. I knocked Balloch out with it and when Stewart finds out I've got it they'll both be on our tails. We have to get out of here. Now."

Finn nodded. "Agreed."

A rustle sounded behind them and they spun, Finn's hand going to his dagger. Donald and Rob rode into the clearing and dismounted.

"They've beaten off the raiders," Donald blurted. "The men are returning to camp. They'll arrive any minute."

Finlay swore under his breath. "Stewart?"

"Unharmed," Donald replied, his eyes flicking to Eleanor. "It willnae be long before they discover Lady Eleanor isnae in her tent. Ye need to leave now, sir."

"I know that," Finn replied. "Curse it all! They'll pick up our trail easily."

Donald and Rob shared a look. Then Rob grinned. "Nay, they willnae," he said. "Because we'll make sure they dinna. We'll cover yer tracks so they canna pinpoint which direction ye've gone, then we'll cut the horses loose, send them stampeding to the west. It'll cause chaos. More than enough cover for ye to get away."

Finn shook his head. "Nay. It's too great a risk."

"Any greater risk than riding into battle against the MacAuleys?" Donald asked. "Ye are our commander. Our friend. I would most likely have starved had ye not taken me into yer command and taught me to be a tracker. If I can repay that favor then I will. And besides, we willnae let Lady Eleanor come to harm."

Donald's voice was firm, resolute, and he suddenly no longer looked like an unsure youth but a confident young man determined to see this through. By his side Rob nodded to show he felt the same.

Finn strode over and laid a hand on each lad's shoulder. "I willnae forget this. If by some miracle we all come out of this alive, I will find ye, and repay this debt."

He pulled Donald into an embrace, slapping the lad on the back, then doing the same to Rob. Eleanor, feeling tears gathering in her eyes, kissed them both.

"Please stay safe."

They nodded, then without a word, turned and disappeared into the night.

Finn watched them go for a moment then took her hand and led her over to a thicket where a horse was tethered, saddled and loaded with Finn's weapons. The horse lifted its head, snorting a greeting.

"Easy, boy," Finn said softly, taking the reins and leading him out of the thicket.

Finn grabbed Eleanor around the waist and hoisted her into the saddle. A second later, he swung easily up behind her, the saddle creaking as he settled his weight. He held her close with one arm across her stomach, grabbing the reins with the other. Clucking lightly to the horse he nudged him into motion through the dark wood.

The horses' hooves, Eleanor noticed, were wrapped in leather, meaning they made not a sound against the forest floor nor left behind much in the way of hoof prints in the thick leaf-litter. If they were lucky, and if Donald and Rob were able to hide their tracks, there was a chance, just a chance, that Stewart wouldn't find them.

They'd managed to escape Stewart's clutches but now they were on the run for their lives. Something told her this was far from over.

Chapter 14

Finn felt as tense as a bowstring. As he crept slowly through the woods, he started at every little sound, jumped at every shadow. He peered into the dark with wide eyes, his ears straining for the slightest hint of anyone nearby. He heard only the night time sounds of the forest.

He knew this was deceptive.

He'd instructed Eleanor to wait with the horse in a holly thicket several hundred yards behind whilst he carried on alone. Somewhere around here were Stewart's perimeter guards and it was imperative he and Eleanor got through unseen. If they didn't, they would have no chance of escape.

Finn halted and went very still, back pressed against a tree, and listened. Somewhere an owl hooted and rustling in the undergrowth indicated some night time predator out looking for a meal. For a while he detected nothing untoward, but his neck prickled, warning him that something was nearby. This area, with its thick ground cover would be the perfect place for Stewart to set his pickets. They could observe anyone sneaking around the camp without being seen themselves.

So Finn waited. Several tense minutes later a sudden break in the clouds let through a shaft of moonlight. It caught on something that flashed in a thicket up ahead before being quickly stifled. Finn smiled grimly. He recognized the flash of a metal blade.

Moving silently and swiftly, Finn crept up on the thicket. As he drew closer, he made out the silhouette of a man standing in the dark, so still he was barely visible. Finn drew his dagger and crept forward on cat's paws until he stood directly behind the man. He tapped the guard on the shoulder, then, as the man spun in alarm, smacked him in the temple with the hilt of his dagger. The guard's eyes rolled back in his head and Finn caught him as his legs buckled, lowering him silently to the ground.

Finn looked around, checking he hadn't been seen. Satisfied, he dragged the guard deeper into the thicket then hurried back to Eleanor. He nodded to indicate he'd dealt with the picket and they mounted in silence. Moving carefully, they wove their way past the unconscious guard and out into the unguarded woods. Finn let out a sigh of relief but didn't relax his vigilance.

What was happening back in camp? he wondered as they rode. Had Stewart discovered they were missing yet? Likely. He only hoped Donald and Rob had managed to create a diversion to slow Stewart down.

In front of him Eleanor was sitting upright, her shoulders tense, her eyes scanning the woods. She hadn't said a word since they'd left the clearing. It had been a tense and terrifying night but she was free. They both were. His eyes strayed to the velvet sack tied to the saddle. He struggled to comprehend what she had done. How had she managed to get the brand away from Stewart? It was protected by Fae magic. Only its master, Alasdair Stewart, could touch it, and yet Eleanor had been able to snatch it from right under his nose. It made no sense.

He knew he was holding Eleanor tighter than was strictly necessary but he couldn't help himself. Balloch had almost hurt her again and he would die before he let anything else happen to her. So he clutched her tight, fierce protectiveness filling him.

The clouds parted and the starlit sky allowed him to navigate their route and keep them traveling well into the night. When the moon finally set, he pulled the horse to a halt on the summit of a wind-swept hill to inspect the land behind them for any signs of pursuers. He saw none and decided it was safe to stop for the night.

He'd scouted this area many times and knew of an isolated croft, recently abandoned when news of the impending battle had spread. If Finn had his way they would keep traveling, putting as much distance between them and their pursuers as he could. But Eleanor looked exhausted and needed rest. It would do for one night.

He nudged the horse into a trot down a wide trail between the towering peaks of two bald hills. As they rounded a bend in the valley bottom he finally saw it: a small, lonely cottage with a barn standing out the back. Finlay slowed the horse to a walk, alert for danger. But the croft was deserted, the windows of the little cottage gaping like dark eyes in the night. He reined in the horse.

"We'll stay here tonight."

ELEANOR FELT EXHAUSTED. It took a supreme effort not to doze off in the saddle and she was pretty sure that Finn's tight grip was the only thing that kept her falling off the horse. She was mighty glad when he pulled the horse up by a deserted cottage and announced they were going to stop for some rest.

He dismounted and made a circuit of the tiny house. "The roof has fallen in," he announced. "We'll have to sleep in the barn."

Eleanor nodded. She didn't give a damn where she slept as long as it was warm and dry. Awkwardly she swung her leg over the horse's back and slid to the ground, staggering a little. Finn caught her arm, steadying her.

"This way."

He took the horse's reins and Eleanor followed him into the barn. There was space inside for several horses although it was empty now. A ladder led up to the hayloft. Finn saw to the horse whilst Eleanor pulled off the saddle bags, slung them over her shoulder, and climbed the ladder into the hayloft. A thick bed of dry hay still filled the space. Right now it looked as good as a feather bed in a plush hotel.

She dropped the bags and began rifling through the provisions. There wasn't much, only what Finn had been able to grab before he left on his scouting mission. She found a skin containing weak ale, some hard biscuits, a round of cheese wrapped in muslin, and some dried meat. Eleanor unwrapped the muslin and used it to lay out their supper.

The ladder creaked as Finn made his way up. He seated himself cross-legged in the hay opposite her and she handed him some food. He took it with a nod of thanks and they ate together in silence, punctuated only by the sound of the horse munching on his nose-bag below.

It was a cold night and Eleanor cursed herself for not thinking to bring a cloak. Her dress certainly wasn't designed for camping and the icy air sent shivers across her skin.

"We canna risk a fire," Finn said, noticing her discomfort. "If we're being tracked, it would give away our position. And besides," he smiled wryly. "It isnae a wise thing to do in a hayloft."

Eleanor nodded. "Are we safe here do you think?"

"We aren't safe anywhere," he replied with a shake of his head. "And we willnae be as long as we remain on Stewart's lands. Get some sleep. I will keep watch."

"N...now, that sounds like a g...great idea," Eleanor stammered, her teeth chattering.

A frown of concern creased Finn's face. He moved close, kneeling in front of her. "Ye are freezing," he said. "Here."

He hitched her dress up to her knees and began rubbing her calves. "Yer skin is like ice, lass. Why did ye not say anything?"

"B...bigger things to worry about than my cold f...feet."

A ghost of a smile quirked his lips. "Aye. Fair enough."

"You're g...good at that," Eleanor said, leaning back on her hands. His touch felt good. Really good. Already she was beginning to warm. "If you l...lived in my time you'd make one hell of a masseur."

"Really? I dinna have the first clue what they might be but I'll choose to take it as a compliment."

Eleanor laughed and some of her tension uncoiled. There was something about Finn that made her relax, despite the situation. He had an easy way about him, a way of putting her at ease and making it seem like everything would be all right.

He continued to rub her calves, working up towards her knees and Eleanor had no desire to stop him. Her muscles began to thaw and a warmth to spread through her, one that she was sure had more to do with Finn's proximity than anything else. She felt the roughness of his skin against hers, the callouses on his fingers from his years of working with a bow.

He paused suddenly and looked up at her. Their eyes met. Eleanor froze.

WHAT WAS HE DOING? What had possessed him to touch Eleanor like this? Didn't he realize the effect it would have on him? Apparently not, because now Finn found himself staring at her, captured by those beautiful eyes. His palms tingled where they touched her skin.

This was hardly decent, his hand resting just below her knee like this, her dress hiked up, revealing tantalizing glimpses of a pale thigh. Yet he couldn't bring himself to move away. Desire stirred within him, heat rippling through his body like an ember glowing in a blacksmith's forge.

Eleanor had gone very still, staring at him. A strand of hair in front of her face stirred with her breath. Lord help him, but she was the most beautiful thing he'd ever seen. The sight of her, tousled and breathless, stirred his blood, sending it roaring to life.

If he was any kind of honorable he would back off. He would take himself over to the other side of the hayloft, or even better, take watch downstairs with the horse. That would be the sensible thing to do. But Finn was no longer sensible where Eleanor Stevenson was concerned. He could barely think straight for the rampant desire running through him.

Ye shouldnae be doing this, a voice in the back of his head warned him.

But he didn't listen. He didn't back away. Instead, he found himself scooting closer, placing his hands on either side of her face and kissing her.

HE WAS KISSING HER. Oh god, he was kissing her again. Eleanor had a nanosecond to process this before desire sparked in her veins, just as it had when they'd first kissed in the glade, just as it had the second time in Finn's sick room.

His touch was electric. A jolt went through her from top to bottom and her blood roared to life, sending tingles racing along her nerves.

Finn kissed her softly at first, his hands to either side of her face but then, as she responded, moving her lips against his and letting out a soft moan, his kiss deepened, became harder, more insistent. He bit her lip, teased her lips apart and forced his tongue into her mouth. She let him, allowing her desire for this man to rampage through her.

She placed her hands against the hardness of his chest and pushed him backwards until he was lying in the straw. She followed him down, not breaking their kiss for a second. His fingers trailed the length of her spine to her waist and he lifted her easily, onto him so that she straddled his waist, her dress riding up past her knees, the hardness of his desire pressing against her in a way that sent her thoughts spinning out of control.

Conscious thought evaporated. All she knew was that she wanted this man, wanted him more than she'd ever wanted anything. She tugged at his shirt and Finn obliged her by pulling it over his head and tossing it away. With a low hiss she ran her hands over his naked chest, the tips of her fingers tracing the contours of his muscles and the slightly raised lines of his scars. The edge of his tattoo peeked over one shoulder.

Finn watched her, his eyes dark, his hands resting lightly on her waist. Then he grabbed her, pushed her onto her back in the hay and began kissing her neck, her shoulders, his lips trailing a line of fire across her skin. At the same time his hand found her inner thigh and worked its way upwards.

Eleanor gasped, arching her back as his touch found its way to the warm core of heat between her legs and gently began to massage. What was he doing to her? It was too much. She couldn't stand it. Surely she would break apart.

But she didn't. Finn brought her to the edge of losing control and stopped, leaving her teetering on the brink, gasping for more.

"Nay, lass," he growled. "Not yet. Not until ye are mine."

He reached under her, grasped the hooks of her dress, expertly unfastened them then pulled down the dress. Eleanor wriggled out of it and yanked hard at Finn's plaid, desperate to have nothing between them but heat. Finn kicked away their clothing and Eleanor had a second to take in his glorious naked body before he was pushing her down into the hay.

He nudged her knees apart and then dropped his hips atop her. His weight pinned her down and she felt a sudden explosion of fire as, with one hard thrust, Finn drove himself into her, plunging deep inside and burying himself into her warm core.

Eleanor cried out, back arching as indescribable sensations rocked her body. This was not possible. It was not possible for anything to feel this good. But as Finn began to move inside her she realized this was real. This was happening. And it felt...perfect.

Eleanor clung to him, her hands sliding down his back, gliding over his tattoo, to where his buttocks bunched and released to the rhythm of his movements. Eleanor moved with him, her body instinctively shifting to meet his, their hips grinding together.

Finn's hair fell forward to brush her forehead and his breathing by her ear sounded more like a growl as their tempo increased. Eleanor heard the sounds coming from her own mouth, gasps and moans of pure ecstasy as the fire burning in her core began to spread, licking along her nerves like flames.

She couldn't hold on. She was burning. Burning. She let go. The fire roared, and she screamed Finn's name as her climax took her, consuming her in a raging inferno of unbearable sensation.

With a growl Finn gave one final thrust and then held himself deep inside her as he found his own release, his weight hard and delicious as it pinned her into the hay.

Eleanor wrapped her arms around him, holding him close as the ecstasy slowly ebbed, to be replaced by a sense of satisfaction, of completeness that Eleanor had never experienced before. Finn lifted his head to look at her and for a moment they just stared at each other, saying nothing. Then Finn kissed her gently, softly on the lips before rolling onto his back and pulling her against him.

"Eleanor," he said, his voice low and husky. "That was...that was..."

She lifted her head to look at him. God above, he was beautiful. She felt her heart swell. "Everything?" she offered.

"Aye, lass," he breathed, running his thumb across her cheek and staring into her eyes. "That was...everything."

FINLAY WOKE WITH A start, coming instantly alert, hand reaching for his dagger as he listened for the sound that had woken him. There it came again, a scratching outside the barn. He tensed, every muscle quivering. Then there came the unmistakable yip of a fox and he breathed out in a rush.

He looked down to where Eleanor lay sleeping with her head against his chest. The two of them were tangled together, naked, their limbs entwined, with only Finn's cloak thrown over them to keep out the chill. That hardly mattered. What they'd done last night had been plenty enough to keep them warm.

Heat rose in his loins as he remembered making love to Eleanor last night. It had not been only once, but over and over again, their bodies coming together in a rush of passion and need that had left them both exhausted and breathless but sated in a way he'd never experienced before. Finn had known women. Plenty of women. But he'd never felt the all-consuming desire or the sense of utter completeness he did when he'd taken Eleanor, made her his. It felt...right, like he'd finally found a piece of himself that he hadn't even known had been missing. Even now, as he looked at her, he felt his ardour rising, a fierce swell of desire that made his heart beat a little faster.

She is mine, he thought fiercely, reaching down and brushing a strand of hair away from her face. *I willnae let any man touch her. I will kill them if they try.*

Dawn light was beginning to seep through the gaps in the barn wall, weak and gray. Carefully, moving slowly so as not to wake Eleanor, he extricated himself from her embrace, edged over to where his clothing lay strewn about in the hay and quickly dressed. He looked back at Eleanor for a moment, then descended the ladder and padded outside into the dawn.

Dawn was his favorite time of day. The air felt clean and fresh and the dew clinging to the grass sparkled in the early morning light. The world was so quiet, so peaceful, and seemed full of endless possibility in the pre-dawn mist. As a boy Finn had often been up and out of the castle before first light, taking only his dog for company, and not reappearing until after breakfast, much to the annoyance of his father who always admonished him about the dangers of leaving the castle without a guard.

He scouted back along their trail and was relieved to find that the bindings on the horse's hooves had done their job. There was barely an imprint in the ground to reveal their trail and it would take the best of trackers a good long time to find where he and Eleanor had gone. If they made good time they should reach Brigid's Hollow today. Eleanor's way home. By tonight, she would be gone.

The thought made his insides contract as if he'd been kicked in the stomach.

I canna lose her, he thought. *I canna.*

How was he supposed to carry on his life once Eleanor wasn't in it?

It doesnae matter, he told himself savagely, gripping the hilt of his dagger hard enough to make his knuckles turn white. *She wishes to go home and ye made a vow to see her do that.*

And I'll keep it, he thought resolutely. *Even if it kills me.*

Chapter 15

Eleanor slept long and deeply, the heat from Finn's body keeping her warm through the night. But some time after dawn, a chill began to creep over her and she realized he was no longer by her side. She woke with a start. Light seeped through the gaps between the boards and the air was filled with the dawn chorus of birds.

She looked around, searching for Finn, and heard the rhythmic sound of a horse being groomed from below. A smile spread across her face and she breathed in deeply, savoring the moment, savoring this sense of utter contentment.

Her muscles ached but it was a delicious kind of ache, a reminder of all she and Finn had become to one another last night. Heat rushed through her as she remembered their night together. Holy crap, she'd never imagined she could feel like that, that anyone could take her to the heights of ecstasy that Finn had. He seemed to know instinctively what she wanted, what she needed, and took great delight in giving her exactly that.

Wrapping Finn's cloak around herself she crawled over to the hatch and peered over the edge. Sure enough, Finn stood in the space below, methodically grooming the horse. His shirt pulled tight over his back and shoulders every time he made a brush stroke and Eleanor couldn't help but watch, mesmerized as the contours of his body were revealed and then hidden again. His hands moved with strong, sure strokes, and she couldn't help remembering those hands on her last night.

"Good morning, Eleanor," he said without looking up. "I wondered whether ye were going to wake this side of midday."

Eleanor rolled her eyes. So much for sneaking up on him. Of course he'd known she was watching him.

"What can I say? I was tired. And whose fault is that?"

He looked up at her then, a flash of mischievousness in his emerald eyes, and Eleanor's breath caught. Did he even realize how handsome he was? How the sight of him lit an ache inside her that could only be quenched by his arms around her? By his lips on hers?

"Aye, I'll allow ye that one. There's breakfast waiting down here when ye are dressed. Can ye manage? Or should I come and help ye?"

There it was again, that mischievous glint, a hint of what would happen should she take him up on his offer. She almost said yes. She would love for Finn to climb up here with her and for them to pick up from where they'd left off last night. Lord, if she had her way, they'd stay in this barn forever, while the world outside could go to hell.

But the sudden barking of a dog in the distance made her jump in alarm, reminding her of the reality of their situation, the danger.

"What's that?"

"Dinna worry," Finn said. "It's many miles distant and is probably a farmer's sheepdog. If it were a pack of hounds on our trail ye would know about it. There would be a whole chorus of barking. Be that as it may, it's time we left. Get dressed. I'll ready the horse."

Eleanor nodded and crawled through the hay to where her clothes had been strewn. She dressed as quickly as she could, pulled her fingers through her hair to brush it, then climbed down the ladder and took a quick wash from a rain barrel in the corner. Finn handed her a meager breakfast of an apple and a couple of strips of dried meat and then they were mounting up, riding from the barn, and out into the Highland morning.

The early haze had yet to burn off and so they rode through a half-shrouded world of shifting curtains of mist that rolled along the valley bottom and poured along its edges like low-lying cloud. Dew on the grass sparkled like tear drops and a light breeze carried the scent of spring flowers. It was hauntingly beautiful and Eleanor suddenly found herself thinking of Irene MacAskill and the Fae. If any place spoke of those strange, otherworldly creatures it was this world of mist and shifting shadow.

"What's the plan?" Eleanor asked Finn. "Which direction are we heading?"

His arm, which circled her stomach, tightened momentarily, sending her heart fluttering. "East for a while," he said by her ear. "That way we can avoid the marshes then turn north when we reach the river and follow its course towards Brigid's Hollow. If all goes well we should be there by sundown."

Eleanor nodded, suddenly unable to speak. *There by sundown*. By tonight she would be home. Back to where she belonged, to where everything made sense and she wasn't in constant danger. So why did she suddenly feel sick? Why did dread weigh her down like a bowling ball sitting in her stomach?

You know why, she answered herself. *Because you'll be leaving him behind. Finlay MacAuley. The man whose presence makes the world seem bigger, brighter. The man whose touch makes you feel alive. The man you're falling in love with.*

She squeezed her eyes closed, laying her hand atop Finn's where it rested on her waist. His skin was warm, his presence behind her solid and reassuring.

How can I leave him? she thought to herself. Then, *how can I not? I don't belong here. This is not my time, my place. We are from different worlds and I need to return to mine.*

Don't I?

FINN STRUGGLED TO CONCENTRATE. He needed all his wits about him, needed all his trackers instincts honed to a razor's edge if he was to see them both safely to Brigid's Hollow. But despite his best efforts, as they rode through the mist, following the trail that meandered along the valley's base, his mind kept wandering. How was he supposed to concentrate with Eleanor sat in front of him like this? With her weight against his chest and her hair tickling his chin? How was he supposed to think straight with the sensation of dark dread that seeped through him with each step that brought them closer to Brigid's Hollow and the moment he had hoped would never come.

Several times he almost spoke the words aloud. They spilled onto his tongue, fighting for release. *Don't go. Don't leave me.* He bit down on them mercilessly. He had no right to ask that of her.

Finn didn't like riding through mist. It deadened sound and made it all but impossible to spot enemies approaching. Of course, it also blinded their enemies but this didn't make Finn feel any better. He was glad when the sun rose high enough to begin burning it off, revealing the morning landscape of the Highlands.

They'd climbed a rise and as the mist cleared it revealed a patchwork of wooded valleys and fields spreading out below, all glinting under the early morning sun. In the distance a wide river shone like a line of quicksilver.

"It's beautiful," Eleanor breathed.

"Aye," he replied gruffly. "It is."

Nudging the horse on, they set off, heading for the river. They would turn north along its banks, avoiding the marshes and, if fate smiled on them, avoiding any other travelers. This area was sparsely populated and little-traveled at the best of times and the rumors of the upcoming battle would mean any traveler with a dram of sense would take a different route, avoiding this area all together. Finn hoped this would mean they had the trails to themselves.

It was the kind of morning that came along only rarely in the Highlands. A golden morning, his mother would have called it. The kind of morning where the air smelled clean and fresh, a warm breeze stirring the leaves, the air full of the drone of bees as they bobbed along between the thick clumps of foxgloves that carpeted the valley bottoms. Despite himself, Finn found himself relaxing.

Eleanor suddenly glanced over her shoulder at him. Her eyes shone and she was smiling. "That was lovely."

"What was?"

"That song. You were singing."

Finn hadn't even noticed himself doing it. It had been a habit of his when he lived at Dun Ringill and his tutors had constantly admonished him for singing or humming when he should have been reading or studying his letters, but the habit was thoroughly broken when he'd become Stewart's creature. What reason did he have for such jollity in that man's household?

"Don't stop," Eleanor said. "I was enjoying it."

Finn raised an eyebrow then gave her a little mock-bow in the saddle. "As my lady commands." He looked around quickly but the only other creatures in sight were a hawk riding the thermals high above and a squirrel chirping at them angrily from a tree branch. He cleared his throat dramatically then threw one arm out and burst into song, loud enough to send a flock of grouse winging into the air.

It was a drinking song, rowdy and extremely rude, and had been one of his brother Camdan's favorites. Eleanor burst into laughter, the sound as delicate as the ringing of silver bells.

"That would go down a treat in my local pub!" she exclaimed. "Although they might be a bit shocked to hear me sing it. Teach it to me."

"Ah, tis not a song fit for a lady's tongue," Finn replied.

She twisted to look at him and raised an eyebrow. "And do I strike you as a lady?"

He studied her. "Now that ye come to mention it, I'm none too sure. Maybe a little too uncouth for a lady."

She punched his arm. "Oaf!"

"Oaf is it? And here's me thinking ye liked me."

Eleanor didn't reply, just looked at him.

Finn cleared his throat. "Very well. The first verse goes like this."

He spent the next half an hour teaching her the drinking song. She picked it up quickly and then they were both singing as they rode, her light, melodious voice a counterpoint to his own deeper one. Birds took off as they passed, a startled deer bounded away into the woods, and Finn was pretty sure they were making enough racket to wake the dead. He didn't care. For this moment, this one, joyous moment he let all his worries evaporate as he sang with the woman he loved. A fierce joy blew through him and he wanted to shout to the heavens for the pure, unadulterated happiness of it.

The song ended and Eleanor laughed, breathless. "That was fun! Let's go again!"

But Finn shook his head and pointed. "Nay, lass. We're almost at the river."

He pointed at an outcrop of rock ahead, a jumble of black boulders that stood out against the horizon. "Beyond that we will descend into the river valley and turn north towards Brigid's Hollow."

She nodded, sobering abruptly. "Oh. Right."

They soon reached the outcrop and began descending a steep, switch-back trail through gorse bushes and clumps of heather into the valley where the river meandered, wide and sluggish on its way to the sea. Once they reached the bottom Finlay pulled the horse to a halt and dismounted. He spent several minutes scouting the area, senses alert, searching for any sign of enemies nearby. He found nothing. Remounting behind Eleanor, he turned the horse north, following a narrow trail that followed the contours of the river along its northern bank.

The sky began to cloud over and it began spitting with rain. Finlay drew his cloak around the two of them and Eleanor clasped it eagerly, holding it closed with one hand and squinting ahead.

Maybe the sound of the rain made him miss it at first. He was so intent on their trail that he paid little attention to the sluggish river moving alongside them. But when the horse suddenly snorted and swivelled his ears forward, Finn came instantly alert, yanking the horse to a halt and going very still.

"What is it?" Eleanor asked.

He held up a hand for silence. Aye. There it was again. Voices off to the left, in the direction of the river and the unmistakable sound of oars cutting through water.

He swore under his breath, yanked the horse around, and quickly rode into the concealment of a bramble bush, still thick with last year's brown leaves. He dismounted and tied up the horse.

"Wait here," he instructed Eleanor. "I'm going to go take a look."

"Like hell," she replied. "I'm coming with you."

He nodded, helped her dismount, and together the two of them crept towards the river bank, keeping low to avoid being seen. They hunkered down at the water's edge and peered through the branches of lush vegetation.

The sound was clearer now, the crack of shouted orders and the slap of oars on water. Finn stared at the bend in the river ahead. The minutes ticked by, Finn's sense of unease growing moment by moment, until finally he spotted a flotilla of boats rounding the bend. They were wide, flat-bottomed, more like barges, and were being rowed against the current by crews of six men, three to either side. Finn counted eight boats in total.

He scanned the scene with a tracker's eyes, assessing the boat's size, their crew, their cargo. When his eyes settled on what filled the boats' decks, his eyes widened and his heart began to thump in his chest. Each boat carried three wheeled machines about the size of a small handcart that supported a long metal cylinder.

Cannons. And stacked at the back of the boat, barrels that could only contain gunpowder and cannon shot.

Then his eyes sprang to the man standing at the prow of the lead boat. His stomach dropped into his boots.

Eleanor hiss suddenly. "Oh my god," she breathed. "That's Balloch."

EVEN FROM THIS DISTANCE Eleanor could see Balloch's arrogant swagger. What was he doing here? Had he tracked them? Why was he riding ships loaded with cannon?

She glanced at Finn. He'd gone very pale, a vein in his temple throbbing as he glared at Balloch with murder in his eyes.

"Finn," she breathed. "What's going on?"

He didn't answer for a long moment. His gaze was fixed on the flotilla.

"Holy mother of God," he breathed at last. "This is it. How could I have been so stupid?"

"What?" she asked, laying a hand on his arm. "What is it?"

He shook his head, a look of disbelief on his face. "I should have seen it. Should have guessed. I knew something was wrong. I knew Stewart was up to something."

He wiped a hand across his face and then looked at Eleanor. "This explains it all. Why Stewart didn't move from his manor, despite being slowly encircled by MacAuley forces. Why he seemed too confident even though he's outnumbered and outgunned. Why Balloch kept dropping hints of a 'secret mission' he'd been sent on. North of here the river splits and a tributary goes west, through the Vale of Morwen and right behind the MacAuley lines. Sitting there all this time at his manor was a ruse to draw the MacAuley lines south. He's flanking them, moving cannon upriver to attack them from behind." His face paled even further and his voice became a hoarse whisper. "He's going to hit the MacAuley forces with cannon fire. They'll be torn to shreds."

Something cold slid down Eleanor's spine. Turning to look at the flotilla, her eyes were drawn to the cannons filling the decks. In the rain the black iron gleamed slickly, making them seem ominous and forbidding.

An image formed in her mind of those cannons belching out fire and death, ripping through the MacAuley and MacConnell forces. Ripping through Finn's people. His clan. His family. And she knew with a certainty that she could not let this happen. If she didn't act, if men like Alasdair and Balloch Stewart were allowed to triumph, then thousands of innocents would die. The Highlands would become a bloodbath.

"No," she found herself saying. And then again, stronger this time. "No. This will not happen." She looked at Finn. "We can't let those cannon reach their destination. We have to sink those boats."

FINN LOOKED AT ELEANOR. Her eyes blazed, her cheeks were flushed and her chest was rising and falling rapidly. But she didn't look afraid. She looked angry.

The boats were almost level with where Finn and Eleanor were hiding. A few more moments and they would be gone, the chance to act lost.

Still he hesitated. Every fibre in his being wanted to stop those ships, to stop Balloch and his guns from reaching the battlefield. But he'd made a vow. A vow to protect Eleanor and see her safely home. How could he ask her to become involved in this?

But she took the decision out of his hands. She grabbed his arm and almost snarled, "We have to do something! I know what you're thinking and Brigid's Hollow can wait! It will still be there when this is over. Do you really think I'm going to run away and let that bastard destroy your clan?"

Her eyes were alight with fury and fervour. Lord, but she was fierce. As fierce and brave as a hunting hawk.

He nodded. "Let's go."

They scrambled to their feet and pelted back to where the horse was tethered.

"I need cloth soaked in alcohol," he called to her. "And my flint and tinder."

She nodded, pulled the items he asked for from the saddlebags whilst he fetched his bow. They hurried back to the spot on the river bank and Eleanor tore strips from the hem of her dress and quickly poured whisky all over them. Finn risked a glance at the river. The first of the boats was passing, Balloch standing in the prow like some grotesque figurehead. They were moving slowly, against the current, for which Finn was profoundly grateful, otherwise they would have been moving too fast for him to hit.

He took the alcohol soaked rag Eleanor offered him and wrapped it around the bronze tip of his arrow. Seeing what he intended, Eleanor took his flint and tinder and carefully began striking it. The sparks flew into the soaked cloth and it began to burn with a fierce blue fire.

Rising to his knees, Finn slotted the burning arrow into place, pulled the string back to his cheek and sighted along the shaft, picking his target. In his head he calculated the distance, the angle, the breeze, just as his father had taught him. It was a difficult shot, almost out of his range. He cleared his mind. There was just him and his target. Him and his target. He let everything else fade away until he could see the trajectory of the arrow in his mind's eye, knew exactly where it would fly and what it would hit.

Then he released the string.

The burning arrow sped straight and true, plunging into one of the barrels of gunpowder with an audible 'thunk'. For a moment there was silence. Then, as the flame burned through the barrel, the gunpowder ignited with an explosion that tore the air and echoed down the valley like thunder. The boat disappeared behind a curtain of smoke.

Eleanor handed Finn another flaming arrow and he took aim again, swearing as the smoke from the first boat obscured his shot, sending the arrow hissing into the river instead. He fired a third, this one hitting a barrel on the trailing ship and sending another explosion ripping through the air. A fourth arrow, another hit, another explosion.

On the river all was confusion. The gray curtains of smoke obscured the view but Finlay heard the panicked shouting of the crew and the groan of timbers. He pulled Eleanor back from their hiding place in case the soldiers located their position and began firing, but no counter attack came.

He and Eleanor crouched in tense silence behind a large boulder, peering around the edges, trying to see through the murk. Finally, the wind shredded the smoke and Finn swore under his breath. Four of the boats were little more than splintered bits of wood, their crews swimming for shore, their cannons sinking into the depths of the river. But it was only four. The two leading boats, undamaged, were rounding a bend in the river. He could see Balloch striding up and down, bellowing orders.

"Damn it!" he growled.

They climbed to their feet and they hurried back to the horse. The men in the river would reach the bank soon and it would be wise not to be here when they did.

"What now?" Eleanor asked. "Balloch got away. Maybe we should chase the boats down?"

Finn shook his head. "Nay. They're warned and will be on the watch for any attack. We'd never get close enough for a shot before they loosed their muskets on us."

Eleanor's expression hardened. "Then we have to ride to the MacAuley camp. Balloch still has six cannons. How many do the MacAuleys have? None?" She could see from Finn's expression that she was right. "We have to warn them!"

Ride to the MacAuley camp? Find his brothers? Even a few days ago such a thing would have been impossible. His curse would never have allowed it. But now? His eyes strayed to the velvet bag containing his brand. Now anything was possible. Because of this woman. This woman who'd exploded into his life and changed everything.

He smiled, reached out a hand and ran his thumb across her cheek. "Ah, my brave warrior maiden. Aye, I reckon we need to even those odds."

She smiled. "Then what are we waiting for?"

Finn lifted Eleanor into the saddle then swung up behind her. Pulling the horse around in a tight circle he set his heels to the beast's flanks and sent him galloping away from the river, heading north. Towards his brothers.

Chapter 16

The going was slow and tedious. The only path left for them if they wanted to reach the MacAuley camp before the boats did was to cross the marshes—a path that Finn had hoped to avoid. As they came to yet another dead end and had to backtrack, Eleanor could see why. It was only Finn's tracking skills that had kept them from getting hopelessly lost in this labyrinth of soggy ground, stagnant pools and thick tufts of marsh grass.

They'd left the river behind and had seen not another soul since they'd entered the marshes. The river lay somewhere to the northeast, circling the marshes to come round behind the site where battle would be joined tomorrow.

Eleanor stared in that direction. Where was Balloch now? Had she and Finn managed to stay ahead of him by cutting through the marshes? The thought of that man sent a tingle of fury through her veins. She *would* stop him, if it was the last thing she ever did.

She glanced over her shoulder at Finn. He didn't notice, engrossed as he was in picking them a safe path through the teeming ponds and brackish water. Tension was written in every line of his body, from the hunch of his shoulders, the set of his jaw, the vein that throbbed in his temple.

Eleanor longed to say something, anything, to ease his foreboding but knew there was nothing she could say. He was riding towards the family he'd not seen since his curse turned him into a traitor. The family he'd betrayed. How would they react to seeing him again after all this time?

A waterfowl winged into the air ahead of them, squawking raucously and the horse shied suddenly, forcing Eleanor to grab the pommel to keep her seat.

"Easy, boy," Finn said in a soothing voice. "Easy."

He got the horse under control and then bade him to stand whilst he rose in the stirrups, looking around with a troubled expression on his face.

"What is it?" Eleanor asked. "What's wrong?"

"These waterways," he replied. "They're swollen. Some of them are wider and deeper than I remember. Maybe navigable for a boat."

Eleanor's eyes widened. "You mean Balloch? You think he'll come this way?"

Finn shook his head. "I dinna know. But it would make sense. If he knows a route through the marshes, it would be much quicker than the river and still bring him out behind the MacAuley lines."

Eleanor looked around, suddenly nervous, but all that met her eyes were the glistening pools and narrow trails they'd been traveling through for the last few hours, their only company the waterfowl that made the place their home.

"Then we'd best make sure we get there before he does."

"Aye."

They continued on their way along a high bank between a row of huge weeping willow trees. The rain had abated and the sun was beginning to cut through the clouds making the pools and waterways shimmer like mirrors. On another day Eleanor would have taken the time to appreciate its beauty but not today. Today she had no time for such niceties. An urgency was beginning to burn through her, an inexplicable sense that they had to hurry.

Finally the ground began to dry out, the waterways to narrow, and the marsh grass to be replaced by scraggly hawthorn. Finn pulled the horse to a halt then leant down to examine the ground for tracks.

"Damn it," he breathed. "There are fresh tracks here. They're further south than I expected. We have to get out before—"

"Dinna move," a voice suddenly said from the trees. "There are five arrows pointed right at ye. Make any sudden moves and we'll turn ye into pincushions."

Eleanor gasped as shapes materialized out of the trees, five men in long gray cloaks and hoods drawn over their faces. They held bows trained on her and Finn. Finn dropped the horse's reins and held his arms wide to either side, showing he held no weapons.

"We aren't a threat," Finn said calmly. "We bring urgent news for Laird MacAuley."

A sixth man ducked under a branch and into the clearing. He was tall, as tall as Finn, with broad shoulders and blond hair that fell onto his shoulders in waves. Ice-blue eyes the color of a winter pond raked over them.

As his eyes settled on Finn, the man suddenly paled, one hand going to the hilt of the sword hanging at his waist. "Nay," he breathed. "This canna be. It isnae possible."

Finn stared back at him, unblinking, that vein in his temple throbbing double-time. Then he spoke into the thick, heavy silence.

"Hello, Camdan."

FINN STARED, UNABLE to take his eyes off the man before him. It was like seeing a ghost. Or a memory come to life. The blond hair, so unlike his own, was the same as Finn remembered. The icy blue eyes were the same. The confident stance and penetrating gaze hadn't changed.

But his middle brother, always the most hot-headed of the three of them, looked at Finlay with a steadiness in his gaze that had not been there the last time they'd met. He studied Finn, his look calm and assessing, his hand on his sword-hilt, a slight flare of the nostrils the only thing that gave away his unease.

Camdan hadn't called his men off and five arrows were still trained on Finn's heart. The silence held for a long, heavy moment, the air between him and his brother thick with tension. Then slowly Camdan raised his hand and gave the signal for his men to stand down. Finn heard the rustle of clothing as the men put away their bows.

Without taking his eyes from Finn, Camdan said to one of his men, "Go and fetch the laird. Tell him to get his arse here right now."

The man nodded and melted silently into the trees.

"Dismount," Camdan barked. "Slowly." He pointed a finger at Eleanor. "Ye first."

Eleanor glanced at Finn and he nodded. She clambered down from the horse ungracefully and stood facing Camdan.

"Step away from him," Camdan instructed.

"Who do you think you're ordering around—"

"Do as he says," Finn cut in.

Eleanor glanced up, gave Finn a scowl, but then stepped away. One of Camdan's men darted forward and seized her, quickly checking her for weapons.

"She's unarmed," the man confirmed.

Camdan nodded. "Hold her." The man grabbed Eleanor's shoulder in a firm grip and Camdan turned his attention back to Finn. "Now ye. Get down slowly."

Finn gritted his teeth. He glanced at Eleanor then slowly swung his leg over the horse's back and jumped to the ground.

"Take off yer cloak and turn around."

Finn unclasped his cloak, slung it over the saddle, and then turned in a slow circle. "Should I dance as well?" he growled.

There was the sudden thud of running footsteps and more men burst into the clearing. This time they were led by a bear of a man with the same jet black hair as Finn's and deep, serious eyes. The man skidded to a halt by Camdan's side, his men spreading out in a circle around them.

The man's commanding gaze fell on Finlay and Finn's breath caught. It had been a long time since he'd seen his eldest brother, Logan, laird of Clan MacAuley, but he was still as serious and imposing a figure as he remembered. His eyes widened at the sight of Finn and for a moment his composure slipped and a rush of emotions crossed his face. Then the cool mask of the laird returned and he looked Finn up and down, his deep eyes appraising.

Finn couldn't tell what Logan was thinking. Did he know about Finn's allegiance to Alasdair Stewart? Did he know about all the ways in which Finn had betrayed him?

Logan and Camdan moved closer, halting less than three steps away. Finn lifted his chin, meeting their gazes. If they despised him so be it, but he'd face his elder brothers like a man, not some chastened child.

"Finlay?" Logan said at last. "It canna be. Is this another Fae trick? I willnae be fooled again! Take off yer shirt."

Finn held his brother's gaze for a moment, then yanked his shirt over his head and tossed it atop the saddle with his cloak. "Is that enough for ye?" he snapped. "Or would ye like me to remove my plaid as well so ye can see my bare arse?"

"Turn around," Logan commanded.

Gritting his teeth, Finn did as he was bid. As he turned, exposing his back, he heard an intake of breath. He glanced over his shoulder to see his brothers staring at his tattoo.

"Finlay?" Camdan whispered. "Is that really ye? After all these years?"

Then all the breath was knocked from his lungs as Camdan cannoned into him, folding him into a bone-crunching embrace.

"Little brother," Camdan whispered by Finn's ear, his voice thick with emotion. "The Lord has answered my prayers."

Finn went rigid, unsure how to respond to his brother's unexpected show of emotion. Then something inside him cracked and tears sprang into his eyes. With a sob, he threw his arms around his brother and buried his face in his shoulder as Camdan held him tight, like he'd done when they were children.

Finally Camdan released Finn and Logan took his place. There were tears shining in Laird MacAuley's eyes, a rare show of emotion. He laid his hands on Finn's shoulders and stared at him long and hard.

"I canna believe it," he breathed. "I never thought this day would come. Oh, my brother, I canna tell ye how it lifts my heart to see ye."

Finn nodded. He pulled his shirt back on while he gathered his thoughts. "And I ye. But I havenae come for a reunion. I've come to warn ye of danger. A portion of Alasdair Stewart's men are coming upriver on barges."

"Ha!" Camdan cried. "Ye think we havenae thought of that? Dinna worry, little brother, we have a rear-guard in place in case the sneaky bastard did such a thing."

"Ye dinna understand, Cam," Finn said, shaking his head. "He has cannon."

"Cannon?" Logan said, his eyebrows rising in alarm. "Alasdair Stewart is naught but a renegade lord, little better than an outlaw. Where would he have gotten cannon?"

"From a deal with the border barons at a guess," Finn replied. "They willnae be pleased if ye roust Stewart from his position in case ye turn yer attentions to them next."

Logan rubbed his chin, assessing. "How many cannon?"

"Six remaining. We managed to sink the rest of them."

"Six cannon," Logan breathed. "He could tear through our lines with those."

"Aye," Finn replied. "That's why ye must pull back yer lines, stop those boats from landing."

Camdan and Logan shared a long look. Then Camdan fixed his piercing eyes on Finn. "What I am wondering, little brother, is how ye know all this? How would ye have access to Stewart's battle plans?"

Here it was then. How would they react when they discovered the truth? He glanced at Eleanor who was standing next to her guard, watching with interest. She nodded slightly.

Finn drew in a deep breath. "Because I'm an officer in Alasdair Stewart's army. I lead his tracking units and have been privy to his councils."

The words dropped like stones into a well of silence. Logan and Camdan stared at him.

"Ye work for Stewart?" Camdan growled. "For the enemy?"

Finn opened his mouth to respond but before he could utter a word, Eleanor stormed over.

"Oh for God's sake!" she cried, planting her hands on her hips and glaring at the three of them. "Are you all just going to dance around it? Why don't you ask the questions that really matter? Why don't you ask him where he's been all these years? Why don't you ask him what your curse did to him?"

"Eleanor," Finn murmured, holding out a hand. "That's enough."

"Enough?" she growled. "Not even close! We haven't risked our lives just to stand around whilst these two decide if they can trust you!" She turned her glare on his brothers. "Yes he works for Alasdair Stewart. But do you know why?

Because he has no choice! That's what your damned curse did to him! Made him a slave to a man he hates!"

Logan watched Eleanor steadily. His eyes narrowed as if assessing her words.

"Is this true?" he asked Finn. "Is that how the curse took ye?"

Finn ground his teeth. He hated the pity in his brother's eyes almost as much as he'd hated the suspicion.

"Aye," he ground out.

"That bastard," Camdan growled. "I'll carve his heart out."

"Not if I find him first," Eleanor muttered.

Logan's eyes narrowed as he looked at Eleanor. "Wait one moment. Yer accent sounds mighty familiar. Where have I heard it before?"

"This is Lady Eleanor Stevenson," Finn said, laying a hand on Eleanor's arm. "An outlander from across the sea. I couldnae have made it this far without her help."

Eleanor nodded. "Pleased to meet you. Although I wish it was under better circumstances."

"Tell me," Logan replied, his eyes shrewd and penetrating as they fixed on her. "This place ye are from across the sea. It isnae called America is it?"

Eleanor's eyes widened. "Yes!" she gasped. "How did you know that?"

"Yer accent," Logan replied. "Both Cam and I have heard it before." He glanced at Camdan who nodded. "From our wives. My wife Thea and Cam's wife, Bethany, are both from America."

"What?" Finlay asked incredulously. "Ye are both *married?*"

"Aye," Logan replied with a smile. "And the only reason we managed to convince Thea and Beth not to march with the army is because Thea is nursing our infant sons." A broad smile split his face. "She gave me twins. Two healthy boys."

Finn opened his mouth to speak but no words came out. It seemed there was much he had to catch up on.

Camdan's eyes flicked around the clearing. "Come," he said. "We can talk about all this later. Right now we have to get out of here. If ye are right about Stewart's forces we have to move quickly." He turned to his men. "Alec, Graham, ye will escort Finn and Eleanor back to the camp."

"Nay, Camdan," Finn said. "I canna return with ye. I came only to warn ye of Stewart's cannons. Now I must leave."

"Leave?" Camdan replied incredulously. "Dinna talk horseshit! We willnae lose ye again, little brother!"

Logan laid a restraining hand on Cam's shoulder. "What is it?" he asked Finn softly.

Finn's eyes strayed to the velvet bag that hung from the saddle of his horse. "My curse isnae broken," he said. "The Fae still have a hold on me. Only death can break my curse. I'm here only because Eleanor found a way to give me temporary reprieve. Now I must see her safely back to her homeland before the curse takes me once more."

Silence fell in the clearing. Logan and Camdan looked at him, Camdan fingering the hilt of his sword as though he wanted to hack at something.

"Then we'll help ye," Logan said. "A score of guards, good men, to escort ye and Lady Eleanor to where ye need to go—"

"Nay," Finn cut him off. "We must travel quickly and without being detected. Send yer forces to McKinley Crag. That is the likeliest landing—"

He cut off suddenly as a horn sounded in the distance, calling three short blasts.

"Attack!" Camdan cried, drawing his sword with a whoosh of steel.

He spun, bellowing orders to the men, and suddenly everything exploded into chaos. Finn heard the clash of weapons in the distance, the shouting of men. He pushed Eleanor behind him as he drew his dagger and turned, eyes scanning the trees.

Shapes were flitting through the undergrowth, shapes that materialized into men wearing the colors of Alasdair Stewart. The MacAuley warriors stepped to meet them and close-quarter fighting erupted throughout the clearing, the clash of steel on steel and grunts of exertion.

Finn shoved Eleanor roughly aside as a stocky man with a scar down his face charged, swinging a sword. Finn dropped to one knee, swept the man's legs out from under him then followed as he fell, burying his dagger in the man's stomach.

He pulled his bow from the saddle and the horse, spooked by the sudden commotion, went charging off into the trees. Finn cursed under his breath but didn't have time to follow. Instead, he nocked an arrow and fired at two men converging on Camdan. One of them fell with an arrow through his eye and Camdan dispatched the other with a slice across the man's throat. Camdan gave Finn a quick nod of thanks before spinning to face another attacker.

Finlay fired in quick succession, taking down one, two, three men in Stewart's colors but more came pouring through the trees. It was difficult to gauge numbers through the shifting shadows but Finlay guessed there were at least thirty men—roughly the same number as the MacAuley party.

It was a lightning raid. Somebody in Stewart's command had realized that Laird MacAuley had gone out scouting with only a small guard and seized their chance.

But how would they have known Logan was here? he thought. *There's no Stewart force this far north. Unless...*

His blood turned to ice. *Unless I was followed.*

Even as the thought formed, a voice bellowed from behind. "I want them alive!"

Stewart's forces disengaged and retreated, melting into the trees but Finn knew they would not have gone far, waiting for the order to attack again.

"To me!" Logan bellowed. "Protect Lady Eleanor!"

The MacAuley forces formed a circle with Eleanor in the middle. They stared into the gloom of the woods, awaiting the enemy's next move.

"Ye know yer problem, Hound?" The voice shouted again. "Ye are forever underestimating me. Mayhap it's time ye learned yer mistake!"

Finn's neck prickled. He knew that voice. His fingers tightened on his bow as a grinning man stepped into the light.

Balloch Stewart. And he was carrying Finn's brand.

Chapter 17

"Bastard!" Eleanor yelled as Balloch emerged into the clearing.

Before she realized what she was doing, she was sprinting at him, no thought in her head other than she'd make him pay for everything he'd done. But Finn caught her, dragged her to a halt.

"Easy, lass," he breathed, holding her close. "Easy."

She glared at Balloch and if a gaze could kill, Balloch would have been lying on the ground, bleeding. How the hell had he gotten here so fast? Had he gone through the marshes as Finn had feared? Had he known all along what she and Finn had planned?

He was wearing that cocky grin, as always, and, as she realized what he gripped in one meaty fist, her fury turned to cold fear. *No. It cannot be.*

The copper of Finn's brand glinted dully in the dappled sunlight, seeming full of menace as Balloch tapped it nonchalantly against his palm. Eleanor's eyes flew to where Finn's horse had gone galloping off into the trees—and straight towards Balloch's men.

No! How could she have been so stupid? How could she have left the brand hanging on the saddle where anyone could take it?

With a growl, Finn walked towards Balloch.

"Stop right there," Balloch snapped. "Right now my archers have arrows trained on Lady Eleanor's heart. Come any closer, any of ye, and she dies. Understood?"

Finn ground his teeth and halted. He dropped his bow to the ground and held out his hands.

"It's me ye want, Balloch. There isnae need for further bloodshed. Our forces are evenly matched. Ye canna prevail. Leave now and I will come with ye quietly."

Balloch raised an eyebrow. "*Our forces?* So ye've thrown yer lot in with my uncle's enemies after all, and after the kindness he's shown ye. I always knew ye were a black-hearted traitor, Hound. Ye are quite incorrect though. Aye, our forces are evenly matched but ye are forgetting that I have a secret weapon: ye. I keep telling ye not to underestimate me. Did ye really think I didnae know it was ye that attacked us on the river bank? Or that I didnae guess ye would head through the marshes to warn the MacAuley? It wasnae difficult to follow yer trail. In fact, I must thank ye on behalf of my uncle for leading us to Laird MacAuley. In one fell swoop I will cut the head from the MacAuley clan and bring victory to the Stewarts!"

"Do ye think so?" Logan growled, fixing Balloch with a baleful stare. "Then step forward and let's see if ye are right."

"Me?" Balloch said. "Oh, no, I willnae be the one that takes yer head, Laird MacAuley. Nay, that honor I leave to yer brother. Has he told ye how many times he's betrayed ye? Has he told ye how many times he's helped my uncle to thwart ye? How many MacAuley warriors have died because of him? Too many to count. Well, one more willnae make any difference will it? How does it feel to know that your own brother is going to kill ye?"

"Shut yer mouth," Finn snarled at Balloch. "Ye are a fool if ye think I will harm my kin."

"Oh, ye willnae have a choice," Balloch replied. He lifted the brand. "Ye aren't the only one to underestimate me. My uncle did the same. He thinks I'm ignorant of what this thing is. He thinks I dinna know of the curse that binds ye to him. But I am nay such thing. I watched and learned, biding my time until I was ready. Now ye will all see the folly of underestimating me."

He raised the brand over his head and began chanting words in a strange language. It sounded otherworldly, as though it had been dredged up from the bowels of the earth.

In response, the tattoo on Finn's back flared to life, burning white hot. His lips pulled back in a rictus snarl.

"Ye are mine now," Balloch said, grinning. "And ye will do as I command. Here is my first order, Hound: kill Laird MacAuley."

With a howl of anguish Finn's head snapped back and Eleanor saw that his eyes blazed with a strange light. Then, with a cry, he grabbed a fallen sword, blisters erupting on his palm as the iron touched his skin, and threw himself at his eldest brother. Logan staggered back, parrying the wild swing of Finn's blade.

For one long, frozen instant, Eleanor stood rooted to the spot in horror. Balloch was right: they'd all underestimated him, thinking him a thug with little ambition or intelligence. It turned out that he was way more than that.

Then the rest of Balloch's men surged out of the trees with a ringing battle cry. Fighting erupted. Most of Balloch's men converged on Camdan and suddenly the second MacAuley brother was fighting for his life, pushed inexorably away from Logan and Finn, stopping him from intervening in their fight.

Eleanor grabbed a fallen branch. It was a poor weapon but better than nothing. She took a step in Finn's direction but one of Logan's men grabbed her, yanking her out of harm's way. The man pushed her behind him as a screen of attackers spilled across the clearing, blocking her view. She craned her head, desperately trying to see what was happening. Logan and Finn were circling each other, looking for an opening.

"Hold!" Logan bellowed at Finn. "Stop this madness!"

But Finn's expression didn't change. He pivoted, bringing the blade around and driving Logan back a step. His lips were pulled back and the veins in his neck stood out like ropes.

Balloch watched with a grin on his face.

At the sight, fury consumed Eleanor. She scrambled away from her guard, ducked under a swinging blade that would have taken her head off, and darted across the clearing.

She caught Balloch by surprise. With all her strength she swung the branch and brought it smashing down onto the arm that held the brand. With a grunt of pain Balloch's fingers opened and the brand went tumbling into the dirt.

She made a grab for it but Balloch was quicker. He punched her in the stomach hard enough to double her over then grabbed her hair, yanking her head back. A knife suddenly rested against her throat.

"Bitch!" he growled by her ear. "That's two I owe ye. Time for payback. Starting with watching yer precious Finlay murder his own family."

With the blade just millimeters from her jugular, Eleanor froze. Her ragged breathing sounded loud in her ears. She didn't want to look but she felt her gaze dragged relentlessly towards Finn and Logan and her heart quailed at the sight of them locked in battle.

Fight the curse, Finn, she thought desperately. *Fight it!*

FINN DESPERATELY TRIED to fight Balloch's control. With every ounce of strength in his body, he tried to resist the cold, alien will that drove him on. His lips peeled back from his teeth, his veins bulged with the effort, his muscles trembled as he strained, strained to thwart the command that thrummed through his veins like molten metal.

But it did no good.

He watched, almost a bystander, as he hacked and slashed at Logan, howling inside as his brother blocked every stroke, never counter-attacking, trying only to keep Finn at bay.

Finn's heart quailed, hating himself, knowing he had no choice. Balloch's will flowed like poison through his blood, sweeping away his own volition and leaving nothing in its wake but a command he must obey.

Kill Laird MacAuley.

His tattoo was blazing, his back a throbbing, beating hub of pain, pulsing to the rhythm of his hammering heart. His lungs burned, his arms ached and the palm of his hand was burned and blistered from the touch of the iron sword-hilt. But still he moved, lunging and spinning and hacking, using all of his MacAuley-trained skill to fulfill his master's command.

From the corner of his eye he saw Balloch grab Eleanor and press a knife against her throat. A jolt of pure terror went through him, enough to break Balloch's grip for an instant. In that moment his grip wavered and Logan's sword broke through his defences and scored a gash along his cheek. It burned like wildfire, sending him almost senseless with pain.

Logan was beginning to tire. His eldest brother was the most skilful warrior in Clan MacAuley, except for Camdan, but even he could not defend himself indefinitely against such a furious onslaught. His movements became a fraction slower, his breathing heavier.

Any second now one of Finn's attacks would find its way through Logan's defences, find its target and end Logan's life. And Finn would be a murderer and kinslayer.

Nay, he snarled to himself. *I. Will. Not. Do. It.*

The cut on his cheek was still burning, the touch of Logan's iron sword causing pain far beyond what it should.

Iron, he thought suddenly. *Anathema to the magic of the Fae.*

Only death could end his curse.

And suddenly Finlay knew what he had to do.

He glanced over at Eleanor and once again, the terror of seeing her in Balloch's grip was enough to shatter the curse's hold for the merest instant. He took that time to lift his chin, turn to meet the thrust of Logan's blade—

—then throw his own stroke wide, allowing Logan's blade to sink into his stomach half-way to the hilt.

Pain ripped through Finlay, so blinding that he staggered, blood erupting from his mouth. With a strangled cry, Logan snatched back his blade and Finn tottered a few steps.

He heard people calling his name—Eleanor? Camdan?—but they were distant, muffled, as if heard from underwater.

Agony turned his body into a burning torch. A growing crimson flower spread across his shirt.

"What have ye done?" Balloch cried. He released Eleanor and stepped forward. "On yer feet! I command it! On yer feet, Hound!"

Finlay's curse flared in response to the command but it was weak, no longer strong enough to compel him. He felt the magic inside him dying, severed by the iron that had claimed his life.

"Listen to me..." he whispered, raising his eyes to look at Balloch. "I have to tell ye..."

Balloch stepped closer. "What? What did ye say?"

Then, as Balloch stepped within range, Finn marshalled the last reserves of his strength. He swung his borrowed blade, a wild, poorly timed swing, but it did its job.

Balloch's eyes bulged as the blade whipped across his jugular. His hands flew to his throat where blood spurted and he staggered, gurgling and gasping. Then he toppled backward onto the damp earth and lay still.

With a cry Eleanor threw herself at Finn and caught him as his legs buckled, bearing them both to their knees. He tried to lift his arms to touch her one last time, but his arms would no longer respond. His breath was coming in short, ragged gasps, barely enough to form words.

"Forgive me," he said in a wet whisper filled with blood. "I failed ye."

"Don't talk like that!" she cried. "You'll be fine. I'll patch you up."

Finn shook his head. He had to make her understand. "Too...too...late for that." His vision was going dark, her face fading until all he could see were her eyes, so deep he could drown in them. "She...she was right. Irene. She said I could be free, despite my curse. And I was. Loving ye. That's what set me free."

He didn't hear her reply. The darkness rose up and smothered him.

Chapter 18

Eleanor blinked. Surely this was a nightmare. It had to be. There was no other explanation for Finn collapsing in her arms, his breath rattling out of his chest in a long, final exhalation.

"Finn!" she screamed, shaking him roughly. "Finn!"

He didn't respond. His eyes had drifted closed and he wasn't breathing. Blind panic punched her in the stomach like an electric shock and for an instant her world exploded into fragments.

No! she thought. *He needs you! Get a grip!*

She forced away the panic, forced herself to think. *Remember your training. Get on with the job.*

Check his pulse.

It was faint.

Check his heartbeat.

Nothing.

Ignoring the fighting that still raged around her, Eleanor clicked into the cool detachment she always did when treating a patient, reducing the panic to a wild, seething thing that battered on the protective shell of her calm. She refused to let it in. She rolled Finn onto his back and began CPR.

Thirty compressions of the chest. Breathe. Thirty more. Breathe.

"You're not leaving me," she muttered. "Don't you even think about it!"

But he remained unresponsive. She continued. Thirty compressions. Breathe. Eleanor put her ear to his chest. Still nothing.

"Damn you! Breathe!"

Panic was starting to break through her composure and her compressions of Finn's chest were becoming erratic, her hands slippery with his blood.

Logan and Camdan knelt by her side. She didn't glance at them. All her attention was fixed on Finn.

Time was slipping away. She guessed he'd not breathed for two minutes now. She was losing him. She desperately felt for a pulse, felt it weak and fluttering as though it might stop any second. The panic suddenly reached up and pulled her under.

She couldn't save him. Oh god. It was happening all over again.

And suddenly she was standing in that shopping mall again. She watched as her mother staggered, her face going bone white. She watched as her mom collapsed to the floor, her eyes rolling back in her head. She watched as others ran to her aid, store keepers, shoppers, a security guard. She watched as one of them called 911 and the security guard began CPR. All of this she watched in horror, frozen, unable to move, paralyzed by fear. She was a medical student, the one person who might have been able to save her mom. And yet she did nothing.

No! No! No! she cried inside. *Mom! I'm sorry! I panicked. I froze. Please forgive me!*

The terrible guilt she'd carried around ever since suddenly rose up like a dark wave, threatening to sweep her away. It didn't matter that it was later revealed her mom had ventricular fibrillation and there was nothing anybody could have done. She, Eleanor, should have *tried*. She should have found a way, instead of freezing like a deer caught in the headlights of a speeding truck. What kind of doctor did that make her? Hell, what kind of *person* did it make her? Weak. Useless.

And now she was going to lose Finn because of that same weakness.

A hand settled on her shoulder and she looked up to find Logan watching her. His eyes, as dark as Finn's own, were haunted.

"Dinna give up, lass," he breathed, his fingers digging into her flesh. "Finn had faith in ye. Dinna give up on him."

You don't understand! she wanted to shout. *I can't do this! I'm not strong enough! I've never been strong enough!*

But she had to be. The only other choice was to lose him and that was no choice at all.

I. Will. Not. Let. This. Happen!

Anger surged through her. Never again. Never again would she allow someone she loved to be taken from her. Never, ever again.

The CPR wasn't working. What she needed was a defibrillator but the nearest one lay hundreds of years into the future. Gritting her teeth, she curled her hands together into a double fist, raised it high over her head and then brought it cannoning down onto Finn's chest with all her strength. His body flopped like a landed fish.

"No!" she growled. "You aren't going anywhere! You will come back to me! You will!"

She thumped him again. And then a third time.

His body twitched. Then his mouth opened and he drew a great, heaving breath. Eleanor pressed her ear against his chest and almost fainted with relief when she heard a heartbeat. Pressing her fingers against his neck, she timed his pulse and let out a long, slow breath when she realized it had steadied. But he wasn't out of the woods yet. She turned her attention to the stab wound in his stomach.

Logan's sword had pierced him just below the rib cage. A neat slice oozing blood marked the entry point but Eleanor had no way of knowing how deep the blade had gone or if it had pierced any internal organs. She needed an MRI scanner and a team of surgeons for that. All she had were Logan and Camdan and the basic supplies she had in her medical bag.

She bit her lip, despair welling up inside her again. Only twenty-first century medicine could save Finn's life.

Or Fae magic, a voice whispered in her head.

Only death can end my curse.

Finn had once told her he was protected by Fae magic and that's why he'd healed so quickly after his beating by Balloch. The iron of Logan's blade had severed the Fae magic, as Finn had known it would when he'd allowed Logan to stab him.

But the iron was no longer in his body. Logan's bloodied blade lay in the grass several feet away where he'd dropped it. If Eleanor could somehow revive the Fae magic in Finn's blood...

Her eyes fell on the branding iron. It lay next to Balloch's body, his fingers reaching out as if he tried to grab it in his last moments.

"Quickly!" she cried. "Pass me the brand!"

Camdan grabbed it and quickly handed it to Eleanor. "What are ye going to do?"

"I don't have the equipment or the drugs I need to save him," she replied. "I think he's bleeding internally. The only thing that can save him is the Fae magic that cursed you all."

Camdan and Logan paled. Then Logan's expression hardened. "Do it."

Eleanor grabbed the handle of the brand, rolled him onto his side, and pressed the end against Finn's tattoo, resting it lightly against his skin. She had no idea if this would work but she was out of options. At first nothing happened. Then there was a flare of light so bright that Eleanor had to shade her eyes. When it faded she saw that Finn's tattoo was glowing again but only faintly.

She dropped the brand into the dirt and leaned over him. "Finn? Finn can ye hear me?"

Nothing. Finn lay lifeless and unresponsive. His skin was waxy, pale, already taking on the pallor of death.

Despair engulfed Eleanor. She dropped her head into her hands, pressing her forehead against the heels of her hands as she felt herself falling, falling...

"Eleanor?" a voice rasped.

With a cry, her eyes flew open. Finn was watching her, a slightly glazed expression on his face.

"Finn?" she gasped. "Oh my god, Finn? You came back to me!"

He raised his hand and ran his thumb across her cheek. "Aye, lass. Didnae I give ye my word? I'll never leave ye."

She threw her arms around him and buried her face in his shoulder. Tears ran down her face. Finn was alive. After that, nothing else mattered.

"I was so scared," she mumbled into his shoulder. "Don't you ever do anything like that to me again, you hear?"

A wry smile twisted his lips. "I'll try."

He pushed himself into a sitting position, his hand going to the wound in his abdomen. It had stopped bleeding and Eleanor could see there was already a scab forming where the flesh was beginning to knit together.

Finn glanced at the brand lying in the dirt and then Balloch's body sprawled on its back. A spasm of grief crossed his face and he wiped the back of his hand across his brow.

"It's really over then." He looked at Logan. "Forgive me."

"There is naught to forgive," Logan replied. "It's the Fae who are to blame for this, all of it."

Finn held his brother's gaze for a moment and then nodded.

Finn allowed Logan to pull him to his feet then reached for Eleanor. She went to him, pressing herself against his side. He leaned on her slightly, still weak despite the Fae magic.

"We must return to the army," Logan said. "Ye are sure ye willnae return with us?"

Finn shook his head. "I must get Eleanor home."

Logan looked long and hard at Finn and then clapped him on the shoulder. "God speed to ye then, little brother. I'll pray that we meet on the other side."

Camdan folded Finn into a tight embrace. "Stay alive," he said gruffly. "Just stay alive."

As Finn gathered the horse and they mounted up, Eleanor watched him closely for any sign of pain but the Fae magic appeared to be doing its job. He barely even winced as he climbed into the saddle behind her.

With a last wave to Logan and Camdan, Finlay set his heels to the flanks of the horse and sent him cantering into the woods, towards Brigid's Hollow and her way home.

THEY RODE AS SWIFTLY as Finn dared, keeping to the thickest part of the scrubby woodland that bordered the marshes until the trees finally peeled back and they started climbing towards the uplands.

He held tight to Eleanor, trying not to think of what lay ahead. His mind swirled with everything that had happened today. Meeting his brothers again after all this time. The confrontation with Balloch. The fight with Logan...

He could barely make sense of any of it. Inside he felt empty. Hollow and brittle, like a dry reed that might snap any minute. But he still had a job to do, a promise to keep.

Their flight to find his brothers had brought them closer to Brigid's Hollow than he'd realized. It lay only one valley away from the place where the battle between MacAuley and Stewart forces would be joined. Was it coincidence that had brought him and his brothers so close to a place of the Fae?

Of course not. There were no coincidences where the Fae were concerned.

Eleanor said nothing but she clung tight to his arm and he could feel her tension. Was she eager to go home? Or was she dreading it as much as he was?

Ask her, that voice whispered in his head. *Ask her to stay.*

I canna, he answered himself. *I willnae condemn her to my life.*

They climbed steadily, the wind increasing until it tugged at Finn's hair and sent it swirling out behind him, icy fingers caressing the back of his neck. Then, on the brow of the hill something came into view: a grove of oak trees silhouetted against the sky. Finn balked at the sight and the horse shied, picking up on his master's unease. Eleanor stiffened, her lips parting in a hiss.

"There it is," she whispered. "Brigid's Hollow."

Finn licked his lips. "Aye. There it is."

He brought the horse under control and they climbed up towards the copse. The oaks were huge things with tangled limbs that seemed to grasp at the sky like greedy fingers. As they drew closer Finn saw that the trunk of the largest had split down the middle and now formed a kind of living archway through which he could see the sky.

The hairs prickled on the back of his neck. *We are the Fae,* the place seemed to whisper. *This place is ours. Ye are not welcome here.*

He pulled the horse to a halt and sat motionless, listening and watching. All was still. Even the wind had fallen silent.

Finn dismounted then helped Eleanor down. When they were both on the ground he held out his hand and she curled her fingers through his. She glanced at him, her eyes round and huge and he forced himself to smile, even though he felt sick to his stomach. Together they approached the archway.

Suddenly, from the corner of his eye he saw movement and he whirled as a group of armed men rose from their hiding places in the long grass. They wore Stewart colors and carried swords.

With a snarled curse Finn drew his dagger.

"Put away yer letter opener," said a sardonic voice. "It willnae do ye any good here."

Alasdair Stewart stepped out from behind the split trunk, his hands tucked demurely behind his back as though he was out for an evening stroll.

Finn's hackles rose at the sight of him. He stepped closer to Eleanor, ready to defend her with his life.

"What are ye doing here?" he growled at Stewart. "Yer army is about to engage in battle. Should ye not be leading them?"

Stewart cocked his head, regarding Finn. "Ye know, I really am disappointed. Even the most stubborn, stupid of beasts learns its place with enough training. Except ye. Some might say that my bargain with the Fae turned out to be more trouble than it was worth. I would disagree. True, ye have become a right royal pain in my arse, but ye have brought me something much more valuable—the victory I've been seeking all these years."

"Victory?" Finn snarled, his hands curling into fists and aching for violence. "I dinna think so *Lord* Stewart. Balloch is dead. Yer plan with the cannon is revealed to the MacAuleys. Ye will have no victory this day."

A flicker of emotion passed across Stewart's face at mention of Balloch's demise but it was gone in an instant. He waved a dismissive hand. "I always said that boy's lack of brains would get him killed. He should have listened to me. As ye should have listened. Do ye not know by now that ye canna best me? Do ye not realize that ye have already brought me victory?" A cruel smile twisted his lips. "I can see that ye dinna. Ye think that battle with the MacAuleys is the victory I speak of? Oh, small-minded, foolish Hound! Nay, my victory is something much, much bigger than that."

He took his hands from behind his back and Finn saw an odd-looking device like a small flat box on a strap dangling from his hand. A look of triumph flashed across Stewart's face.

By Finn's side, Eleanor gasped.

ELEANOR STARED AT THE thing hanging from Alasdair Stewart's hand. It was her digital watch which she'd lost when she first came through the arch. It looked so out of place, so alien, that she could hardly take her eyes off it. The display glowed in the gloom beneath the trees, seeming to announce for all to see that it was not of this time.

She ripped her eyes from it, forced herself to look at Stewart. "Where did you get that?"

He raised an eyebrow, gave her a sardonic smile. "From this very spot. My men brought it to me after following yer trail all the way back here to Brigid's Hollow." His gaze sharpened. "To the portal where ye came through time."

Eleanor's mouth dropped open, a soft hiss escaping her.

Stewart barked a laugh. "Did ye really think I didnae suspect? Do ye really think me such a fool? My faithful Hound brings me an outland woman, one who behaves and dresses like no decent woman should, a woman with healing skills far beyond what even the great Italian universities can teach. A woman with more holes in her story than a weevil-ridden biscuit. Did ye really think I didnae know of time-travel? My bargain with the Fae has taught me many things. Oh, aye, I recognized straight away that no device like this exists in this time. What other conclusion could there be other than ye are a time-traveler, Lady Eleanor Stevenson?"

Suddenly, from far away, came a noise. It took Eleanor a moment to realise it was the call of horns braying in the distance. And then the unmistakable cough and roar of cannon fire.

"Ah!" Stewart said. "Do ye hear that? The sweet sound of my army's victory. Even now my troops are cutting down the MacAuley and MacConnell forces, mopping up those that my cannons didnae get first. By tonight there will be naught left of those once-mighty clans."

He looked at Finn, his hawk-like face alight with glee. "And I will have achieved everything I set out to do: fulfil my bargain with the Fae by bringing war to the Highlands, take revenge on yer family, and gain a power greater than any in this rotten little world." His eyes glittered. "The power of time."

"You're one crazy asshole," Eleanor growled. "You really think this tree is a portal through time? Then you're more stupid than I thought!"

Stewart gave a soft, low laugh. "Good try."

The wind suddenly picked up, howling around the hill with enough force to make Eleanor stagger. She threw her arm in front of her face to protect her eyes from the dust that swirled into her face. A strange sound carried on the wind. It sounded like...like... laughter. Stewart's men shifted uneasily, glancing around with wide eyes.

Then the wind died as suddenly as it came.

"Ye mortals are such fools," said a voice that sounded like the cracking of stones. "Ye think ye can cheat the Fae? Not so. We play the long game and we always win in the end."

Eleanor's gaze flew to Stewart. The voice came from his mouth but it wasn't Stewart's voice. It sounded ancient, as if dredged from the very bowels of the earth. Stewart was sweating and his eyes were so round that she could see the whites all around them.

Eleanor's neck prickled. Slowly, she began to back away.

"Where are ye going?" Stewart said with a cruel laugh. "I thought ye wished to pass through the arch?"

"Who are ye?" Finn demanded.

"Dinna ye recognize me?" Stewart replied, turning his gaze on Finn. "Look closer!"

For a moment Stewart's form seemed to waver and Eleanor saw another image superimposed over his. She saw a wizened old man with leathery skin and a bald head. Black eyes like chunks of flint stared out at them, filled with malevolence.

"It's him!" Finn breathed. "I dinna believe it!"

"I see ye recognize me after all, Finlay MacAuley. How long has it been? How many years since we stood together at the Stones of Druach and ye sold yer soul to me?"

Finn swallowed then lifted his chin. "Let Eleanor go. I'm the one ye want."

Stewart raised an eyebrow. "Such an overblown opinion of yerself. Aye, ye were useful to me for a time. A play-thing for my amusement. But I no longer want ye at all. I want something far more important. And Lady Eleanor Stevenson can give it me." Stewart's gaze flicked to her and the malice in those eyes hit her almost like a physical blow. "Ye will take me to yer time. Now."

"Never!" she snapped. "I'll never go anywhere with you!"

An amused smile crossed Stewart's face. "Oh come now. What use is this pretense? We both know ye will. It is yer only way to get home. And I will go with ye."

"Like hell you will!"

Irritation flashed across Stewart's face. "I begin to lose my patience, woman. Come over here, right now. Take this chance to go home. It is the only one ye will get."

"I don't care," Eleanor said, shaking her head. "I don't care if I never walk through that arch. You know why? Because I'm already home, you asshole!"

From the corner of her eye she saw Finn look at her in surprise but all her attention was fixed on Stewart. His face contorted into a snarl.

"Ye will do as I say! Ye will take me through the arch!"

Sudden understanding dawned on Eleanor. Irene had told her that everything was a choice and she'd learned from Finn that the Fae were governed by rules and bargains. It suddenly made sense.

"You can't go through on your own, can you?" she asked. "You need a time-traveler to take you. And that time-traveler has to do so willingly. It's all about choice. Right from the moment Finn made his choice to make a bargain with you, to right now when I have to choose between going home or staying here. Well, I've made it! I'm staying right here! I'll never take you through that arch!"

Stewart howled, a horrible sound full of fury and frustration. "Ye will or ye will watch yer precious Finlay die!"

"He speaks empty threats," Finn said. His eyes blazed as he stared at Stewart. "Dinna listen to him, love. He willnae hurt anyone. This ends here. One way or another."

FINLAY LAID A HAND on Eleanor's arm. She looked up at him and he held her gaze for a second before gently pushing her behind him. He'd meant what he said. He would stop Alasdair Stewart and the Fae who possessed him. He would end this. One way or another.

A strange sense of acceptance filled him. He felt as if all the events of his life had been leading to this point, a trail of crumbs stretching back all the way to the night when he'd stood by the Stones of Druach with his brothers.

"Our bargain is over," he said to Stewart. "Ye willnae hurt Eleanor. Ye willnae hurt anyone ever again."

Stewart's hands twitched, his fingers clawing into fingers as though he longed to throw himself at Finn. But he didn't move.

In that moment Finn realized Eleanor had worked something out before he had. Rules. The Fae were bound to them just as tightly as the mortals they snared. The Fae could not use any magic against Finn except what had been agreed by the terms of a bargain. Nor could he attack Finn with anything other than what he had to hand: Alasdair Stewart and the men under his command.

Finn glanced at Stewart's guards. In an instant he took in their formation, their weaponry, their mood. In the space of a heartbeat he'd deduced that three of them were nervous, frightened by what they'd witnessed and wanting to be somewhere else, two were angry, looking for bloodshed, and one was eyeing Eleanor with the raw lust of a man given to violence against women.

"I challenge ye," he said to Stewart, or the Fae, or both. "Fight me. Just us. As it should always have been."

For a moment something like fury blazed in Stewart's eyes. The man tensed, his hand going to his sword hilt. Then he relaxed. "I dinna think so, Hound," he said in an odd voice, a mix of his own and the Fae that possessed him. "Why would I accept such a challenge? A master would hardly lower himself to fight his own dog." He waved a hand at his men. "Kill the MacAuley."

Stewart's men surged forward. Finn had been waiting for this. With a strange sense of clarity he saw one man's body tense as he prepared to move, and in that instant Finn spun, drew a dagger and threw it. It shot through the air, a flicker of copper brilliance, and buried itself in the man's eye socket. The man dropped without a sound. It was the one who'd been leering at Eleanor.

A second man moved and Finn nocked an arrow to his bow and let fly before the man had taken more than a single step. At this close range the arrow tore through the man's throat in a shower of blood. He staggered back and hit the ground with a thud.

The others stopped, wary now.

A strangled scream made him turn. One of the men had grabbed for Eleanor and now they were grappling with the velvet bag that held Finlay's brand. The man ripped it from her grip and tossed it to Stewart whose hand shot up and snatched it out of the air.

A smile spread across Stewart's face. "Our bargain is over, is it? I think not. Not until ye are dead."

Finlay balked. A sliver of fear worked its way down his spine. Stewart pulled the brand triumphantly from the velvet bag and held it out as if it were a weapon. The metal glinted dully in the light. Such a simple thing. A piece of copper, twisted into a swirling design. Nothing more than that. And yet, this thing had bound him as tightly as an iron chain.

Stewart grinned. "Oh, Hound. Ye belong to me. When will ye realize this?"

A wave of black hatred flared inside Finn. "Do yer worst."

He marched towards Stewart, pulling his remaining dagger.

"Ye forget yer place, Hound!" Stewart growled. "Ye are mine to command! Have ye forgotten what I can make ye do? I will make ye kill Eleanor Stevenson!"

Stewart held the brand high and yelled some words in the language of the Fae, words Finlay knew only too well.

In response, the brand in Stewart's hand began to glow white-hot and the tattoo on Finn's back flared to life, burning with an agony that took his breath away. He gritted his teeth as pain forced him to his knees.

Nay, he thought. *Please! Not again!*

The pain was unbearable. For a second it robbed him of his senses, wiping away all thought but the consuming agony. He braced himself for the bite of his curse, for that sharp coldness as the will of another took hold of him. He was a fool to think he could defeat Alasdair Stewart. He was a fool to think he could escape the Fae. Any second now that terrible cold would descend on him and he would become a monster, one that would kill the woman he loved.

No! he howled inside. *Please!*

But the cold never came.

Instead, the pain in his back began to fade, moving from fiery agony to a dull ache. And he remained Finlay MacAuley. No compulsion seized his mind, no will overrode his.

I dinna understand. My curse...

Only death can free ye.

And then suddenly, like the sun coming out from behind a cloud, Finlay understood.

He surged to his feet, gripped his dagger, and strode towards Alasdair Stewart. The man looked panicked now.

"Stop!" he shouted. "I order ye to stop!"

But the command had no effect. Not anymore. Stewart drew his sword and swung it at Finlay. He caught the blade on his hand, feeling a burning pain as the steel cut into his palm. He ignored it.

"Men!" Stewart screamed. "Kill him! Kill him!"

Stewart's remaining guards started forward but stopped as a sound suddenly tore through the air. It was the sound of horns, ringing clear and urgently in the valley below. Three short blasts, over and over, the command imperative and desperate.

"Hear that?" Finn said to Stewart. "Those are yer horns calling. And they are sounding a retreat."

Stewart paled, took another step back. "I order ye to kill him!" he shouted at his men.

But they were no longer listening. They'd turned to the west where the sound of cannon had fallen silent, the call for retreat telling them exactly what had happened on the battle field. They glanced at one another, and then looked at Finlay with blood dripping from his hand and a grim expression on his face. He could see them putting together all the strange events they'd seen today and weighing it against their loyalty to Alasdair Stewart. Then they ran. In moments they'd disappeared over the brow of the hill.

"Inspiring loyalty isnae one of yer strong points, is it, my lord?" Finn said.

Stewart drew himself up, raising his sword. "I will kill ye myself."

He lunged at Finn. The man was an expert swordsman, moving with the grace and poise of a predator. In a flash, his blade was arcing towards Finn's throat, ready to tear out his jugular.

But he missed. Stewart might be an expert swordsman but Finn was better. Years spent as a tracker had honed his instincts to a fine point. So he pivoted away, as light on his feet as a dancer, and hammered his fist into the back of Stewart's head. The man staggered, and his blade tip touched the ground.

"I will kill ye," Stewart growled in a voice not his own. His face flickered and once more Finn saw the wizened features of the Fae glaring at him. "I will kill ye and leave yer body for the crows to fight over! Nobody escapes my bargains!"

He grabbed a handful of dirt and threw it into Finn's face. Finn staggered, rubbing his eyes and Stewart surged up, aiming a thrust at Finn's midriff.

"Watch out!" Eleanor cried.

Finn stepped to the side, allowed Stewart's momentum to carry him past and turned, shaking his head to clear the last of the dirt from his eyes.

"Give it up," Finn said. "Canna ye not hear the horns? Yer army is defeated, yer plan in ruins. Surrender and my brother might show ye leniency."

Stewart gave a high, shrill laugh with more than a little madness in it. "Surrender?" he asked, and this time the voice was his own. "Ye think my bargain will allow me to surrender? The terms were clear. I would destroy the strength of the Highland clans and receive the life of the youngest MacAuley in payment—vengeance for what yer family did to me. When I won the battle my reward would be greater still: the power of time. But if I failed? Oh, if I failed! What do ye think I would be required to give?"

"What a bargain with the Fae always requires," Finn replied. "Yer life."

Stewart nodded. "And my soul. So ye see, Hound. I will never surrender."

For a moment Finn felt a flicker of understanding for this man. Perhaps they weren't so very different after all. Both had sold themselves to the Fae, both had been trapped by the bargains they'd made. But there the similarities ended. Finn had made his bargain in order to save his clan, Alasdair Stewart had made his from a thirst for power and revenge. He and the Fae were welcome to each other.

Finn looked at the man. His image flickered, the eyes alight with a terrible light, his lips pulled back in a chilling smile. Finn could no longer tell where Stewart ended and the Fae began. He raised his dagger.

"Let us end this then."

Stewart's maniacal grin grew wider. "Aye. Let's do that."

He charged suddenly—but not at Finn.

Instead he sprinted towards Eleanor.

A jolt of terror punched Finn in the stomach. He saw Eleanor's eyes widen, saw her rooted to the spot. He saw Alasdair Stewart closing the distance, saw the blade flashing in the sunlight. And he saw one chance. He grabbed the brand from where it lay in the grass and tossed it at Eleanor.

With a strangled cry she caught the brand and swung it, knocking aside Stewart's sword and sending the heavy metal crashing into the man's temple. He staggered back, sword-tip drooping, and in that space of time, Finn threw himself at Stewart, grabbed the man's sword-arm, yanked him close, then punched his dagger hilt-deep into Stewart's heart.

Stewart's knees buckled and he clung to Finn, a red stain spreading across his expensive shirt. His fingers plucked at Finn's arms but there was no strength left in the grip.

"Nay," he whispered. "This isnae the way it's supposed to be. This isnae what we agreed. Curse ye! Curse the MacAuleys and the Fae both!"

His strength gave out and Finn allowed him to slump to the floor where he lay still, his sightless eyes staring at the sky. A sudden howl of rage rose all around Brigid's Hollow. It filled the air and Finn sensed malevolent black eyes glaring at him before the wind tore the scream to shreds and carried it away.

Silence fell. It was over. It was finally over. Exhaustion washed over Finn and he collapsed to his knees beside the man who'd been his tormentor.

Eleanor gave out a strangled sob and suddenly skidded to her knees in front of him. She threw her arms around him and pulled him close, burying her head in his shoulder. She was weeping. Finn hugged her close, gently stroking her hair. He could feel her heart beating next to his, could smell the scent of her hair, hear the in-out of her breathing. She was alive. They were both alive. And free.

"It's done," he breathed. "It's over, love. Ye are safe now."

She lifted her head and nodded. Her cheeks were tear-stained, her eyes red-rimmed, yet in that moment Finn knew he'd never seen anything so beautiful. He cupped her face in his hands and pressed his forehead to hers.

"How did you do it?" she asked.

Finn looked down at her. "Do it? Do what?"

"When Stewart grabbed the brand and ordered you to kill me. How come the curse didn't work anymore?"

"Because of ye, love," he replied softly. "Only death could break my curse, remember? And I died in that clearing when Logan's blade pierced me. Ye brought me back. Ye wouldnae give up on me. Ye started my heart with that twenty-first century knowledge of yers and then healed me with the Fae magic in my brand." He looked deep into her eyes and held her gaze. "When ye did that the power of the brand passed to ye. I belonged to Stewart no more. I belonged to ye instead."

Eleanor gasped. "You mean..."

"Aye, lass," he replied with a smile. "Although ye dinna need any Fae magic to hold power over me. I've belonged to ye since the first time I saw ye. Dinna ye understand that yet?"

She reached up and slowly traced the line of his jaw with her fingers. "Maybe I do. Just as I've belonged to you from that moment when I first saw you in the woods. Don't you understand that by now, Finlay MacAuley? You're a slave to nobody any more, you hear? And that damned brand will be melted down and destroyed."

He cocked his head to look at her. "Did ye mean what ye said to Stewart? About not caring if you walked through the arch? About already being home?"

"Of course I did. It took me a while to realize it but I don't think I could have walked through that arch, even if Stewart hadn't been here waiting for us. I couldn't go anywhere where you aren't. I'm home, Finn, because you're here." Her gaze locked with his. "Because I love you."

Something exploded inside him. Something he'd kept buried deep, never thinking it would be his. Joy. He suddenly felt as light as a feather, as strong and invincible as a mountain. An idiotic grin spread across his face.

"Then stay," he said breathlessly. "Marry me. Let me spend the rest of our lives showing ye how much I love ye. Eleanor Stevenson, will ye be my wife?"

She grinned in response, her eyes sparkling. "Jeez, I thought you were never going to ask! Of course I will!"

A shiver of pure elation went through Finn. He bent his head, pressed his lips against those of the woman he loved, the woman who would be his wife, and forgot the world for a while.

Chapter 19

"You're being very brave," Eleanor said to the boy seated on the bench in front of her.

Archie, the eight-year-old son of Dun Ringill's cook, nodded.

Eleanor carefully finished sawing through the plaster cast on the boy's arm and gently levered it off. The cast had worked surprisingly well. Nobody in Dun Ringill had ever heard of this technique for treating broken bones and they were generally treated by splinting and strapping—a wholly unsatisfactory treatment in Eleanor's view. Determined to find something better, she'd experimented with draping the bandages in the same wet plaster the workmen used on the interior of the castle's walls. Much to her delight, it set just like plaster of Paris. She was well pleased with the result.

With gentle fingers Eleanor probed Archie's arm then instructed him to open and close his fingers a few times. "Does that hurt?"

Archie's mother looked on anxiously. They were seated by the fire in the kitchen, Archie's legs dangling from the bench, whilst the rest of Dun Ringill's army of cooks bustled about the kitchen, busy with preparations for today's feast.

Eleanor ignored them and concentrated on her patient. Archie shook his head.

The lad had broken his arm when he'd fallen from the curtain wall after climbing it as a dare. Eleanor was sure the tongue-lashing from his mother had hurt more than the injury and she doubted he'd be doing it again in a hurry.

Eleanor ruffled his hair and smiled. "Good. It's all better now. You don't need your cast on anymore."

Archie broke into a beaming smile. "I dinna?"

"No, but don't go climbing again and be careful not to bash your arm. If it starts hurting you're to come straight to me, right?"

"Aye. Thank ye, mistress." Archie hopped off the bench and threw his arms around Eleanor's waist.

She laughed and returned the little boy's hug before he raced over to his mother, brandishing his arm as though it was a trophy.

Cook Alice gave him a big kiss then looked up at Eleanor. "My thanks, my lady. He had me right worried for a while there."

"Boys will be boys. As long as he's careful it should be fine."

"Well, I'm grateful for ye taking a look at him, today of all days especially."

"Today? Why, is something special happening?" She couldn't help grinning.

"Oh, get away with ye!" Alice said. "Now, ye best be on yer way. If ye are late, I reckon Lord Finlay would have my head!"

Eleanor laughed, gave Alice a kiss on the cheek, ruffled Archie's hair one last time, then walked out of the kitchen and made her way outside. It was a warm early summer morning and Dun Ringill was alive with activity. As Eleanor crossed the courtyard, her medical bag slung over one shoulder, she looked around her new home. She and Finlay had been here for several weeks now and she could still hardly believe that she was living in a castle. Dun Ringill was a striking place. Perched on a rocky coastline, it had the crashing waves of the sea on one side, the rolling uplands of the Highlands on the other. A large village spilled out around the castle, home to Laird MacAuley's people.

My people, she thought. *Or at least they will be, after today.*

"There you are!" said a voice. "Jeez, I've traipsed round half the castle looking for you!"

A woman of around Eleanor's own age was walking towards her. Eleanor stopped and waited for her to approach.

Bethany MacAuley, wife to Camdan and legal advisor to Laird Logan, marched up to Eleanor and put her hands on her hips. "Where've you been? I thought I might have to send the guard out looking for you!"

"I was doing my rounds," Eleanor said. "Old Marjorie's bunions needed seeing to and Archie's cast had to come off."

"Doing your rounds?" Beth said incredulously. "Elle, you do realize today is your *wedding day?*"

Eleanor pursed her lips and frowned, scratching her chin. "It is? I'd completely forgotten."

Beth burst out laughing. "Oh, come on. Thea's just about ready to pull her hair out. We've only got an hour before the ceremony starts."

"An hour? Oh dear. It will probably take that long to get me into the dress."

Beth took her arm and the two women crossed the courtyard and entered the castle, moving through corridors and rooms festooned with garlands and flowers ready for today's events, and made their way up a spiraling staircase to the set of chambers Eleanor shared with Finlay.

They found a dark-haired woman pacing around inside. She spun as the door opened.

"You found her!" Thea MacAuley cried. Then she winced, glancing at the crib where her infant sons were sleeping. "Oops. Shouldn't shout like that. I've only just got the little beasts off." She folded Eleanor into a tight hug then pushed her to arm's length and looked her over. "You ready for this?"

Thea was Logan's wife and, like Bethany, had been brought to this time by Irene MacAskill to help Logan and Camdan break their curses. Both had chosen to stay. Eleanor couldn't believe her luck in finding two friends from her own time. It had helped her to settle in, to find her place in this new world, and she was immensely grateful to them both.

"Ready?" Eleanor asked with a smile. "To walk down those stairs and marry the love of my life? You bet I'm ready. In fact, why don't we go now? I'm sure my work dress will do the job just fine."

Thea looked scandalized. "It will do no such thing! Do you have any idea how long it took to sew this dress of yours? The seamstresses have been working on it for weeks!"

Eleanor laughed. "Relax. I'm kidding."

Thea and Beth helped her to change into the beautiful sky-blue gown that had been made especially for today. It had a tight bodice and bell-sleeves with a long train. Early summer flowers were sown into the head dress. Once dressed, Eleanor held out her arms to either side.

"How do I look?"

Beth sighed and Eleanor saw a tear sparkling in the corner of Thea's eye.

"You look amazing," she breathed. "Finn is a lucky man."

There was a knock on the door and Beth answered it to find one of the pages waiting outside. Eleanor grinned as she recognized Donald. Freshly scrubbed and wearing his best outfit, Finn's tracker was barely recognizable. After the victory over Stewart's forces, Finlay had ridden out in search of his old squad and offered them places in the Dun Ringill garrison. They'd all accepted and now they worked as trackers for the MacAuley clan, under Finn's command.

Donald cleared his throat. "If it please ye, my ladies, I've come to tell ye that Laird MacAuley awaits yer presence in the Great Hall."

Despite herself, nerves began to flutter in Eleanor's belly. She gathered herself with an effort. "Thanks, Donald. We'll be there presently."

Donald nodded, gave them all a bow, and made his escape. Eleanor glanced at Thea and Beth and both women gave her warm smiles. They were her matrons of honor. In the absence of any family members of Eleanor's own, Thea, as the lady of the castle, would give her away. It was a little unconventional but the MacAuley clan had gotten used to unconventional since Thea and Bethany arrived. A pang went through Eleanor as she thought of her mother and the father she could barely remember. They would have been so happy for her. Proud. She wished with all her heart that they could have been present today. To her surprise that familiar pang of guilt when she thought about her mother didn't come. Just like Irene MacAskill had predicted, with Finlay she'd found what she'd been looking for all along. Peace. Acceptance. And forgiveness for herself.

"What is it?" Thea asked. "What's wrong?"

"Nothing," she replied with a smile. "Just thinking of home."

Thea and Beth gave her a sympathetic smile. Thea squeezed her shoulder then lifted the carry-cradle in which her twin sons slept. "Come on. Let's get down there before Finlay comes looking for us." She glanced down at the sleeping infants. "And before these two wake up!"

The three of them laughed and swept out of the room. Her two friends walked tight by her side as they approached the Great Hall. At the huge arched doorway that led inside, Eleanor hesitated, the butterflies doing somersaults in her stomach. She was terrified and exhilarated at the same time. If she stepped through this door, there was no going back. She would be choosing a future that lay hundreds of years away from everything she knew.

Not everything, she thought. *Some things are no different no matter where or when you live. People. Friendships. Love.*

Finn's face flickered into her mind and the nerves evaporated to be replaced by eager excitement.

They stepped into the room and the rows of guests turned to look at her. Beth had seen to the arrangements for the Great Hall and it looked beautiful. The high-ceilinged, cavernous room was decked out with ribbons and flowers and a group of minstrels were playing up on the balcony. Eleanor took in these details superficially as her eyes flew to the end of the aisle and the man who waited for her there.

Finlay MacAuley stood with his brother, Camdan. The two men, one dark-haired, one blond, turned as the door swung open and even from this distance, Finn's eyes found hers. Her breath caught. His hair shone as shiny as a raven's wing as it fell onto his shoulders and he looked resplendent in his MacAuley plaid. A ceremonial dagger hung at his side. He no longer needed to avoid the touch of iron but he still wore the bronze weaponry in deference to the path that had led them both to this point.

At the sight of her, Finn's eyes sparkled and the smile he gave her almost stopped her heart. Holy shit, he was gorgeous. He was strong and kind and more...everything... than she had ever dreamed. And he loved her. She could still hardly believe it.

With Thea and Beth on either side, Eleanor walked down the isle. She barely registered the greetings or words of encouragement from the guests, she barely noticed the smiles and the warm nods of approval. She had eyes only for Finlay MacAuley, her love, the man who would soon be her husband.

As they reached the end of the aisle, Thea and Beth took seats on the front row and Camdan gave her a mischievous wink, his grin wide and welcoming. Eleanor couldn't help but smile at his enthusiasm as she turned to his younger brother.

Finn stared down at her. He said not a word but the depth of feeling in his eyes was enough. They shone with all that he felt for her. He took her hands in both of his and together they turned to face Laird MacAuley.

Logan looked every inch the stern leader in his MacAuley plaid, ceremonial sword and ermine-trimmed cloak. His expression was firm as he looked them over, resting his strong gaze first on Finlay and then on her as though assessing them both. But a moment later he grinned and the stern expression evaporated to be replaced by one of joy.

"Ye all know why we are here," Logan said, raising his voice so that it carried through the hall. "Just over a year ago we stood here to witness the marriage of my brother Camdan to his wife, Bethany. That day I didnae think I could have felt any prouder. I was wrong. Nor did I ever think I would see the day when Finlay, my youngest brother, would return triumphant to his clan. Again, I was wrong. The good Lord has seen fit to grant the dearest wish of my heart —indeed of all our hearts—and return Finlay to us. And not only that, but to lead him to his own love in the process. I canna describe the pride it gives me to have the honor of joining my brother, Finlay MacAuley, and Eleanor Stevenson in marriage and to welcome them both home."

Home. The word echoed in Eleanor's head. As Logan began the words of the ceremony she gazed up at Finlay and realized that Logan was right. She *was* home. Home didn't lie in some empty house in the twenty-first century. It didn't lie in working 9-5 then blowing her wages in a bar at the weekend. It lay here, with this man who loved her and these people who'd accepted her as easily as if she'd lived among them her whole life.

Finn spoke his words first, shining eyes fixed on her, hands clasped tightly to her own, as he made promises that would bind him to her forever. Then it was her turn. There was no stumbling, no hesitation. The words fell from her lips, eager to escape, eager to be heard and bind her to Finn.

And then it was over. Logan was pronouncing them husband and wife and Finlay was scooping her up, kissing her hard and deep enough to make her head spin. An explosion of cheering and clapping threatened to take the roof off the Great Hall.

Finn broke the kiss but pressed his forehead to hers so he could look deep into her eyes. "We made it," he breathed. "Lord, I can hardly believe it."

"Believe it," she replied. "This is real, husband."

He smiled. "Husband. I like the sound of that." He straightened and took her hand. "Come then, wife. It's time to show ye why the MacAuley clan has such a reputation for our hospitality."

AS IT TURNED OUT, THE MacAuley clan's reputation was wholly justified. Hundreds of people turned up for the festivities, all of the inhabitants of the castle and pretty much the whole of the village as well. The Great Hall wasn't big enough to hold them all and so the gathering spilled out onto the training ground, a wide open area to the side of the castle. The summer weather was kind and the light lingered until well into the evening, meaning the festivities could go on all day and well into the night.

Tables had been set up in rows spanning the training ground and when the tables ran out bales of straw were used instead. Eleanor, Finlay and their family, were seated in pride of place at the main table and from here Eleanor could look out and see the castle to her left, the village spilling down the hill in front, and the landscape of the Highlands stretching out into the distance. A warm breeze carried the scent of summer flowers and the sound of the ocean crashing against the shore. Eleanor took a sip from her goblet and sighed, feeling utterly content.

Finlay squeezed her hand. He'd not let it go since the ceremony and Eleanor hadn't wanted him to. But now, as the first course was served he picked up their shared trencher and began piling food onto her plate as though she were a great lady and he a servant.

Alice and her cooks had outdone themselves and the roasted grouse served with glazed and crispy vegetables was every bit as delicious as a meal you would buy in an expensive restaurant in the twenty-first century. The wine too was excellent, and Logan informed her he'd struck a trading deal with some Italian wine merchants that meant they would have a regular supply. More and more Eleanor was beginning to reassess her ideas about life in this time.

After the meal there were Highland games. Eleanor hiked up her dress and joined in the tug-of-war, much to

Thea's horror, and Finlay took on Camdan in the final of the archery contest and won, much to his elder brother's annoyance.

Then, as it began to grow dark, candles were lit, and sleepy children were taken off to bed by their parents, the minstrels gathered in the open space between the tables and began to play. It wasn't long before many of the guests were up and dancing, some of them none too steady on their feet by this time.

Logan leaned over to Finn. "How about it, little brother?" he said. "Ye used to be clan bard. Reckon ye've still got what it takes?" His eyes sparkled with mischief and challenge.

"Got what it takes?" Finn replied. "I could outplay any of those so-called musicians ye've hired, brother!"

"Care to prove it?"

Finn accepted the challenge. He stood and, with Cam at his side, they strode down to where the minstrels were playing. As the guests saw what was happening, they began cheering and calling Finn's name. The minstrels bowed and moved aside, handing their instruments over to the two brothers. Cam took up the fiddle, Finn took up the lute and together, they began to play. It became obvious immediately that they'd played together many times before and despite the gap of empty years since they'd last done so, they slotted into it as if they'd never been away.

Cam, it turned out, was skilled with the fiddle but he had nothing on Finn. Eleanor leaned forward, knowing she was watching a master at work. Finn's fingers moved over the strings of the lute in a graceful dance, coaxing a haunting melody from the instrument.

Then he began to sing.

Everyone fell silent. To Eleanor, it seemed as if the very world itself held its breath to listen. His voice rose and fell like the waves of the sea, hauntingly beautiful. He sang the same song she'd first heard him sing in Stewart's hall, a song of the Fae, and he held his audience spell-bound as he wove a tale of ancient, shadow filled groves, of meandering streams under moonlight, of rings of standing stones high on lonely hillsides. Eleanor felt goose bumps ride up her arms and tears pricked the corners of her eyes. If she'd thought Finlay could sing before, it was as nothing to the performance he put on now.

Finally his song ended, his last note piercing the air for one, two, three heartbeats before falling into silence. For a second nobody moved, there was utter silence over the gathering. Then there was a chorus of yelling and cheering and banging of tankards on tables. The crowd shouted for more. But Finlay handed the lute back to the minstrel, gave a bow to the audience, and then strode off without a word, disappearing into the darkness.

A look of concern flashed across Logan's face and he made to rise but Eleanor caught his arm. "No. I'll go."

Logan nodded and Eleanor hurried off in the direction her husband had gone.

She found him sitting by the stream that marked the northern boundary of the training ground. Finlay was sitting on the bank with his knees drawn up. He held his bronze dagger and was slowly turning it over in his hand, the moonlight glinting off the blade.

Eleanor sat down beside him and he glanced in her direction.

"Return to the feast, love," he said. "I'm sorry to have dragged ye from it."

She raised an eyebrow. "Nah, there's only so much cake a girl can eat before she's sick. You did me a favor."

He smiled, but it didn't reach his eyes.

"I dinna know why I chose that song," he said. "It felt right at the time. After all, the Fae are responsible for all of this, for everything that's happened to bring us together." He took her hand and the moonlight was reflected in his eyes. "And for that I'm grateful. I wouldnae change a thing. But it also brought back unpleasant memories."

Eleanor reached out and gently stroked his cheek. "I know. But that's all they are now. Memories." She smiled at him mischievously. "And this is our wedding night. How about we start making some new memories?"

He grinned in response. "I am, as ever, yers to command, my lady," he said with a little mock-bow. "Come. I have something to show ye."

He stood then pulled her to her feet. He led her down to the stream's edge and across a bridge. On the other side Finn took her hand and she hiked up her dress, allowing him to lead her deeper into the woods that lay on the northern side of Dun Ringill.

The moon was so bright that even Eleanor could see the way and besides, even if it had been pitch black she would have trusted Finn to lead her safely. This was his element, where he belonged, and as they wove through the silver-dappled darkness she could see him relaxing in a way he rarely did when surrounded by the bustle and busyness of Dun Ringill.

They walked for around half an hour, neither speaking, enjoying the night and each other's company, but eventually they began to climb, the ground sloping up gently to a large clearing. On the far side of this sat a house. Its lower story was constructed of large gray stones, its upper story made of timber and the roof of wooden shingles. Candlelight shone from the large windows.

Eleanor stopped and stared. Turning, she saw that the elevated position of the house gave a fabulous view of Dun Ringill below and beyond that, the rolling, thrashing sea.

"Do ye like it?" Finn asked.

"Like it?" Eleanor replied. "Finn, this place is beautiful! What is it? Why have you brought me here?"

"This was once my father's favorite hunting lodge," Finn replied. "And now it's ours. Our home. A wedding gift from Laird MacAuley."

"Our...our home?" she said, turning to look at the little house. It was perfect, from the veranda that would allow her to sit outside, even on wet days, and enjoy the view, to the grassy clearing that would make the perfect kitchen garden for her herbs and remedies, to the stone-built outbuilding that could be used for drying and storing said herbs and remedies. Close enough to Dun Ringill to give easy access to her patients and yet far enough away that she and her new husband would have some privacy and Finlay would be able to enjoy the freedom he so longed for.

She sent a silent thanks to Logan. The laird of the MacAuley, it seemed, understood his little brother far more than she'd given him credit for.

Finlay was watching her intently, gaging her reaction. She turned and put her arms around his neck.

"It's perfect," she said. "Just perfect."

The smile that broke over his face nearly took her breath away. He lowered his forehead to hers. "I'm mighty glad to hear ye say so, my love."

Then he scooped her up in his arms, kicked the door open, and carried her over the threshold. Somebody—she suspected Bethany and an army of helpers—had been in before them. The place fairly sparkled and was filled with flowers and garlands. Candles burned in all the windows and a roaring fire crackled in the hearth.

There was a large, canopied bed in one corner of the room but Finn ignored it, instead carrying Eleanor over to the thick rug that sat in front of the fire, and lowering her gently onto it. He knelt in front of her. The firelight played over the lines of his face and reflected in his eyes. There was no sound except the crackle of the flames.

"My wife," Finn breathed, as though testing out the word. "My wife." He ran a thumb over her cheek and Eleanor leaned into the touch. His hand, as rough and calloused as always, felt warm and wonderful against her cheek.

She rose onto her knees facing him and placed her arms around his neck. "You know, you're gonna have to get used to that word. You're stuck with me now."

His strong arms went around her waist. "Ah well, I suppose I'll just have to grin and bear it. We all have our cross to bear."

Eleanor grinned. "Don't we just?"

Finn's answering grin was mischievous. "I'm sure I can find a way to make it bearable. Mayhap like this?"

He bent his head and gently kissed Eleanor's lips. His touch was light, the barest brush of his skin against hers, but it was enough. A tingle walked all the way down her spine.

"Well, that's a start," she murmured.

Finn kissed her again, more deeply this time, his lips moving insistently, forcefully. Eleanor moaned, her eyes sliding closed. His tongue forced her lips apart, forcing his way inside and she was happy to let him, their tongues each caressing the other. After a moment, his hands swept down her back to her buttocks, pushing her body tight against his. In response, Eleanor tangled her fingers in his luscious hair, pulling him into her kiss.

He began pulling at the laces of her dress and in seconds he had it untied and was pushing it off her shoulders, pulling it down and exposing her breasts to the warm air. Finn rocked back, his eyes roving over her, his gaze dark with lust. Then he bent his head and took one nipple in his mouth, caressing the delicate skin until it hardened with arousal.

Eleanor gasped and flung her head back, her fingers digging into the hard muscles of his shoulders. Finn's hand cupped her other breast and Eleanor gasped a breath. Finn knew exactly what to do, knew her body as intimately as if it was his own, touching her in just the right way, in just the right places to bring all her senses painfully alive.

Arousal sent a flush to her cheeks and quickened her breathing. She tugged at the knot on his plaid, almost tearing the fabric in her haste. Finlay grabbed the knot and yanked, tearing the garment from his body and tossing it away. The linen undershirt went next then Finn grabbed her dress and jerked it down to allow Eleanor to wriggle out of it. This too was tossed into a corner.

Eleanor's eyes fell greedily on her new husband's body. His tanned, muscled chest, his strong arms, his hard thighs—and his manhood standing straight out, attesting to how much he wanted her. She ran her fingers over the lines of his chest, down his sides and then gently along the length of his erection. Finn groaned and then his mouth caught hers again, kissing her roughly, fiercely.

He pushed her onto her back on the thick rug and she pulled him down with her, his weight pressing her into the rug's soft embrace. He ran a hand along the length of her body, all the way to her thigh and then pushed her legs apart. His kiss became hard, desperate, and Eleanor answered in kind, her tongue cavorting with his in a savage dance. Her hands grasped his shoulders, feeling the hardness of his muscles as his hips pinned against hers, allowing his manhood to bump against the spot between her legs. The sensation almost drove her wild. She needed him to take her.

Finn broke the kiss, raised his head and looked down at her. "I love ye," he whispered.

"And I you," Eleanor responded, her voice rough and husky. "Always."

His eyes slid closed and for a moment he trembled with emotion. Then, with a hard thrust, he drove himself inside her. Eleanor gasped, crying out as his body joined with hers. She gripped his back, tracing the line of his tattoo, as he began to move, his muscles bunching and contracting as he drove into her over and over. Each thrust sent spears of burning ecstasy through her body and she moved to meet him, matching his rhythm, her hips grinding against his, his hot skin gliding over hers.

Something began to burn deep inside Eleanor. It sent tingles out from her abdomen, along her arms, down her legs, right to the crown of her head. Her breathing began to come in ragged moans as she writhed beneath him, lifting her legs to wrap them around his waist. Finn growled deep in his throat, sounding more animal than human, and his thrusts became harder, faster, more urgent.

The firelight was hot against Eleanor's skin, adding to the heat that was building inside her. She felt her nails scoring gashes down the length of Finn's tattoo, leaving marks in his flesh that claimed him as her own. Finn barely seemed to feel it. His breath was as ragged and wild as her own, a thin sheen of sweat covering his muscled torso.

The inferno inside Eleanor began to build and now it sent licking flames up from her core and through her body. She screwed her eyes closed, arched her back beneath him, and dug her fingers into his shoulders as the fire caught, sizzling along her nerves and tearing gasps and moans from her lips. She began to come apart, losing herself in the hot, blinding ecstasy. She teetered on the edge for one long, delicious heartbeat and then the inferno engulfed her, ripping through her body with enough force to obliterate all thought.

Eleanor bucked and cried out Finn's name as she reached her climax, screaming it into the rafters, not caring if the whole world heard her cry. Finn grunted and shuddered as he reached his own release and then collapsed on top of her.

For an eternal moment they lay tangled and sweaty, bodies joined, as the fire burned, burned, burned, all through Eleanor's body. Only gradually did it begin to die away. Finally she returned to her senses enough to open her eyes.

Finn's weight pinned her against the rug. His chest was heaving in great gasping breaths and their bodies were slick with sweat. She ran her fingers through his soft hair. Not in her wildest dreams had she thought she could feel this way. But this was no dream.

Finn raised his head, looked at her and smiled. "A good thing we came up here, love. Otherwise I think the whole castle might have heard that."

Eleanor laughed, joy blowing through her like a summer wind. "Imagine the embarrassment at breakfast!"

He lifted himself up onto his elbows and looked down at her. "Aye. But up here we can make as much noise as we like."

She pulled him down to kiss her again, already feeling desire stir inside her once more. "Then let's see if we can bring the roof down."

MUCH, MUCH LATER ELEANOR woke with a start. She wasn't sure what had awoken her but she could have sworn she heard somebody calling her name. She looked around, rubbing at her bleary eyes. The fire had died down to embers, casting the room in a warm, ruddy glow. Finlay

lay on his side, curled protectively around her, one arm flung across her hips. Looking at him, Eleanor smiled. He looked so peaceful in sleep. Her heart swelled. God, how she loved him.

She almost settled back down to sleep but she suddenly heard that voice again. It wasn't a sound but more like a summons ringing in her head.

She wriggled out of Finn's embrace, careful not to wake him, and wrapped herself in his plaid. Silently she padded to the door and stepped outside onto the veranda. It was a warm night and the Highlands stretched away ahead of her, a dark cloak spread across the face of the world.

Eleanor pulled in a deep breath of the still night air, feeling it settle into her lungs, sweet and fresh.

"Ye look well, lass. The Highland air obviously agrees with ye."

Eleanor spun. A figure was sitting in one of the chairs on the veranda. She spotted the silhouette of a tiny woman, a bun curled around the back of the head and a wide smile sparkling in the darkness.

"Irene?" Eleanor asked incredulously. "What are you doing here?"

Irene MacAskill's smile widened. "Speaking to ye by the looks of it, my dear." She patted the seat next to her.

Warily, Eleanor edged over to it and sat. "Let me put it another way. *Why* are you here?"

"Ah, now that's a better question," Irene replied jovially. "Ye are getting better at this, my dear. Why am I here? To complete the circle, of course. It's all about choice, as I think ye've figured out. Ye were given a choice when ye came here.

Ye chose to walk a dangerous path and in so doing help restore the balance of the world. Now ye must make another choice. Will ye remain here? Or do ye still wish to go home?"

"You would send me home?" Eleanor asked, startled.

Irene nodded. "If that is yer choice."

Eleanor stared at the woman. Irene stared back, her eyes dark and unreadable. "Did you know what would happen?" Eleanor asked. "When I came back in time? Did you know I'd meet Finn? And everything that followed?"

Irene reached out and patted Eleanor's hand. Her skin felt as dry as old parchment. "Didnae I tell ye that sometimes we are born many miles and many years apart from those whose lives we are meant to share? This was the case with ye and young Finlay. Aye, I knew ye'd meet. But beyond that? I knew naught for certain. It's all about choice, remember? Everything ye've done, all the steps that led ye here have been made of yer own volition. I canna act to influence ye. Such a thing would destroy the balance."

"And you have rules you can't break," Eleanor said. "Rules and bargains govern the Fae just as much as they govern us."

"Aye," Irene said nodding. "And that's why I'm here. A second choice, Eleanor Stevenson. Will ye go home? Or choose to stay here?"

Eleanor sighed and looked out into the Highland night. Just a few short months ago she would have jumped at Irene's offer. She'd wanted nothing more than to return to everything she knew. But now? It was no choice at all.

"I've already made my decision," she said. "I made it that day by Brigid's Hollow." She turned to look at Irene. "You were right. I was walking the wrong path. Now I've found the right one at last."

Irene's face broke into a wide, cherubic smile. "Ah, it gladdens my heart to hear ye say such a thing, lass. It makes it all worthwhile."

"Is it over now?" she asked. "The Fae that cursed the MacAuley brothers is defeated?"

"For now," Irene replied and she suddenly looked old and tired. "But the struggle to keep the balance is a never-ending one. Light and dark. Day and night. Winter and Summer. Always pulling against each other."

"Just as the Fae do?" Eleanor replied.

Irene watched her steadily for a moment. "Aye, like the Fae," she breathed at last. "A never ending struggle between the Seelie and Unseelie. Those who would guard yer kind and those who would harm them." Then she brightened, her eyes sparkling and a smile spreading across her face. "But tonight, all is well with the world. Tonight is a good night to be alive. Go on, my dear. Return to yer husband. If he wakes and finds ye gone he is likely to tear the house down."

Eleanor smiled and climbed to her feet. Then, on impulse, she bent down and gave Irene a hug. "Thank you," she breathed. "For everything."

The woman's thin arms came around Eleanor, returning the embrace with a delighted laugh. "Ye are most welcome, my dear."

Eleanor stepped back, gave Irene a nod of farewell, then walked back to the house. With each step she took she felt her future settling around her. Her feet were finally on the right path. Finally.

Once inside she leaned on the closed door for a moment, watching Finn sleep. Then she lay down next to him, threw the plaid over them both and burrowed into his embrace. His warmth began seeping into her skin and contentment washed over her.

Yes, she was finally on the right path. And tomorrow she would begin taking the first steps into her new future. And Finlay MacAuley would be by her side every step of the way.

THE END

Want some more Highland adventure? Then why not try the other books in the series? www.katybakerbooks.com

Would you like to know more of Irene MacAskill's story? *Guardian of a Highlander*, a free short story is available as a free gift to all my newsletter subscribers. Sign up below to grab your copy and receive a fortnightly email containing news, chat and more. www.katybakerbooks.com

WHAT DO YOU DO WHEN destiny comes knocking?

Irene Buchanan is running from hers. Gifted with fae blood, she is fated to become the Guardian of the Highlands.

But Irene wants none of it. Soon to be married to her childhood sweetheart, she has everything she ever dreamed of. Why would she risk that for a bargain with the fae?

But Irene can't run forever. When a terrifying act of violence rips all she loves from her, she realizes she must confront her destiny. If she doesn't, she risks the destruction of all she holds dear.

The fate of the Highlands lies in her hands.

Printed in Great Britain
by Amazon